D0991773

TO SAIL THE BARREN SEAS

Enjoy the Read

K. Adrian [illegible]

Books by K. Adrian Zonneville:

Novels;

American Stories

Carrie Come To Me Smiling

Great Things, A Novel

To Dance Among The Stars

Biographies/Memoirs:

Z; One Family's Journey from Immigration

through Poverty to the Fulfillment

of the Promise of America

A Life in The Wings; My Sixty Year

Love Affair with Rock and Roll: A Memoir

Children's Books:

Lost Dog Found

To Sail The Barren Seas

Mankind is Destroying the Planet

K. Adrian Zonneville

Mumford House Publishing

ISBN 978-1-7344332-5-8
ISBN 13-978-1-7344332-5-8

First Printing, 2020
Second Printing 2022

Dedication

This book is dedicated to those who believe there is a little magic in all life, a deep spirit throughout the world. That belief makes all things possible. To my children for allowing me the life I have led. To my parents for gifting me the love of the written word. To David Spero for believing in me. To those who have supported my meager efforts in writing. But mostly to my wife who has supported my dreams, my en-deavors, my love of writing, performing, and the road. Mostly she has been my inspiration and one true love.

Acknowledgments

It is with great love that I thank those who inspire, correct, challenge, and force me to be better than who I see in the mirror. To my dear Friend Bob 'Bear' Marks, the true Bear of this book, I miss you every single day. To those who work tirelessly to save the planet and all who reside here, you are the true heroes of this blue marble. To my children, Kathryn and Adrienne, their significant others, Rich and Michael, and my brand-new eleven-year-old granddaughter, my Lexi, this book is for you and your future. To my wife who allows an old man to live his perfect life with his perfect dogs and perfect mate; Perfect!

Cover art, design, and brilliance Janet Sipl

Edited by Linda Calkin

Foreword

A brief synopsis.

Peace reigned for more than a decade once the laceration in the fabric of the universe had been healed. Bear unknowingly had torn it asunder when his heart shattered at the death of his mortal wife. He had known intellectually that She would pass before he, after all he was immortal and She was not. And She had not been his first mate, but She was his match, his equal and beyond in so many different ways. What the humans called a soul mate.

Once healed the universal energies rewarded him. An unexpected benefit had been the return of Her, She who filled him, completed him. He had no idea why She had been permitted to return from the dead, but She had. The Mother conjectured it was because he was willing to sacrifice himself for the good of his family, of all, of her, the Mother of all. It was as good an explanation as any he could come up. The weird aspect was She came back as an immortal and his true mate. Not just his mate but another Spirit Animal to the bears, his spiritual and eternal partner.

Though none of this could explain the discovery of Alexandra, their beloved granddaughter, also an immortal. No pairing of immortal and human had ever produced any kind of scion, let alone a skipped generational immortal. The world spins and all you can do is ride.

The People had come together to lend their strength to the healing and it had brought all the Spirit animals, the true first people, closer than they had been since the dawn of time. It was good. Suzette, she of the otter clan, had become a regular visitor at the Beach household. The two houses bookending the comfortable craftsman were usually occupied by her, Doe, the deer, and Willow of the Rabbit people, Coyote, would stop by to share a bottle and a toke; even Oscar, of the owls became a regular guest. For someone who had been so intent on remaining neutral upon their first meeting, he had become a friend. Tatanka, the bison, and Lawrence, the Elk, would stroll by as they migrated from north to south and south to north. The pipe would come out, the bottle would be passed and relationships renewed. Evan believed that, as much as Suzette swore she came to spend time with Her—She would always be Her or She to him out of utmost respect and love, especially with Her return—he suspected she had a thing for the good sheriff. Sheriff John was the one mortal who stood by them throughout their efforts to restore balance to the universe. Evan could say nothing, he had no ground to stand on when it came to immortal/human relationships.

As Bear considered all, it was family and it was good. Hell, he'd even got used to Coyote, Mika by human name, showing up when he was in need of a toke and a meal. He laughed to hisself, the great Bear had become kind of a father figure to all the People. Now if only he could do something about humans.

The main job of a spirit guide was just that, to guide their children, try to keep them out of harm's way, and that meant mankind. Oh, there was good humans but they was in the minority. They was the ones who still believed and held to the old ways. They would still talk to the spirits, those that could lend them strength or wisdom, show them where some lost item could be found. Immortals with a thousand, thousand lifetimes of experience and learnin' to share would always be there for those who asked. The People could advise on war, peace, when to move from one place to another, how to talk to the girl who made you stutter and blush. They were not magic, per se, but they could influence the elements. Push a little energy here, bring a breeze to cool down the oppressive heat of summer. They could run in the dreams of humans to send messages to loved ones, reassurance, or guidance, to those in need. Humans thought only the nightmares rode their dreams but it was any of the spirit animals. All could ride the Dream Road while the believer slept.

The hardest job was to guide their actual children, the nations of fauna throughout the world, out of harms' way. Try to keep them away from mankind's need to destroy one and other. That was something humans never considered, how their warring affected the innocent, those who only wished to graze, breed, live. Human bombs killed, maimed, and left orphans too young to care for themselves. They destroyed habitat, grazing land, forests, polluted rivers, lakes, and oceans. Death does not care, it comes for all, it needs no help from man. And man remained oblivious.

There's Something in the Water

Bear loved rivers.

He loved streams, creeks, every form of moving, running water. He could stand on the bank for hours and listen to the burbling, playful eddies, the cascading flow over rocks and debris as if the water sang to him. It promised sustenance, a cessation of thirst, and, most of all, life. The flow reminded him of the passing of time, the constant moving forward of life, even for an immortal. It also reminded him of those who flowed through his own existence.

That was the worst part of immortality, mortals. It is not that he didn't enjoy them, they just didn't last long enough. About the time he got to like one or feel close, the damn thing would die. No matter how you hardened yourself to the inevitable, it still hurt deep inside if you let yourself get too close.

He'd had this conversation the other year with Dog. It helped Dog to understand how people felt when one of his passed too soon; and it was always too soon. Though he could now understand the grief, the sad down in the soul, that humans felt when they lost one of his, a dog. He could see how they wouldn't understand the necessity of the shortness of life. There were so many dogs who would never know the love, the immersion into the life of, someone who held them most dear. It was why he could not understand the cruelty that some humans showed, not just to his children, but also to those of all the kingdoms of fauna.

The sound of the rushing water roared in Bear's ears until the sound and thoughts of man faded into the background. Man made more noise than any other creature on the Mother. It was as if Man was terrified the Mother would forget he was here. How anyone could think such a thing when they were as grand an irritant as had ever existed, made Bear smile.

He'd flown into Anchorage and then strolled down the edge of the Cook Inlet until he came to the Iliuk Arm of Naknek Lake. He'd crossed glaciers, what was left of them, forests, what was left of them after fires and over-logging, and now he relaxed in the waters that would take him to Brooks Falls. It was late August; it had taken him a month of travel from Anchorage, though he had been in no hurry.

Now, deep in the woods, surrounded by life, pure and elemental, the trip had been worth every step. His children would soon be hibernating. Well, if it cooled down, they would. It had hit the upper nineties not long back and no one was in the mood for sleep. Too hot. And they were grumpy.

Bears did not like interruptions to routine. They ate, they mated, they ate, they slept. Simple and set in stone. Or had been for thousands of years until you know who showed up and decided the Mother provided a wonderful place to leave all their shit. Now the weather was fucked up and the natural inhabitants were the ones to pay the price. What man never seemed to understand with all his brilliance and ingenuity was that he might be able to invent and tweak his way out of discomfort—air-conditioned homes and cities in the oppressive heat of climate changed summers and coal fired electric to heat same in winter, create foodstuffs from chemicals and genetic technology—but the original inhabitants of this world were left to live with the consequences.

Bear had come to consult, to deliberate with his people. All the animal spirits were doing the same. They had seen what happened when they all joined together during the last emergency. How strong they had been when they worked as one. They would need every ounce of that strength if they were to set the Mother right.

He had explained all of this to Her before he left, hoping it would convince Her to come along, but She preferred the homelands and the company of the Grandchild, The Little Bear. The first immortal born of human and immortal genes, something not even the Mother had thought possible. He didn't think he would ever think of Her as anything but She or Her, it was respect and love. She understood him and his wants and needs. While he might be here to save the world, first he would do some fishing and cavorting with the extended family.

You could not change the essential element of the soul of Bear. He could live among man, coexist with the noise, the disruptions, and the violence, but this was where he belonged. This was his joy. This was his dance. This was where he wished all could return, but man was man, and he would not change any more than those he sought to dominate.

Oh, there had been some humans of good heart and soul, many really, who through strength of will, education about how the pollution and violation of the Mother would affect all, and, through pure stubbornness, thought they could reverse the damage. They were not near enough when compared to the billions who swarmed over the Mother now. That was a main difference between man and the natural organisms. No species had attempted to cover the planet with their presence until humans had evolved. They desecrated the natural world, excreting where they lived and slept. Dumping poisons into the rivers, streams, and lakes which carried those same toxins to the great oceans. It should have been obvious from the introduction of humanity, as it was their stench that allowed them to survive in the first place. They had stunk so horribly no one wanted to eat them. Survival of the raunchiest.

That was the reason Bear had come to the Brooks River attempting to get away from Man if only briefly. He wanted to bathe in the cool waters and eat his fill of salmon, fresh salmon, as fresh as it could be, right from the river. He wanted to breathe the fresh, sweet mountain air, away from the stench of civilization. At the Brooks Falls bears had sat in the cold water while Salmon took turns jumping from the river into their awaiting open mouths. It had been this way almost forever, he knew.

And now he found himself sitting in the lukewarm water while his belly growled, the salmon too tired and weak to make the journey from river to open Bear mouth. It was depressing on a level only a bear could understand.

Where were the salmon? It was time for the run. He was in the right river, at the right place. The few salmon he saw looked like they'd been rode hard and put away wet. Well, they were salmon so that explained the wet, but who had been riding them? He was bored, hungry, and this was a waste of time.

Shit! Come to think of it there weren't many bears gathered for the occasion either. At first, he had thought he had timed this just right and arrived before the feast began. This was good, as he would be first to feast. Or maybe the other bears had given him a wide path as they knew him for who he was. Respect can be a decent motivator. Especially when you were more than a few feet taller and several hundred pounds heavier, they tended to move out of the way. Maybe he should talk to the few who had made the trek and were wading aimlessly in the falls hoping to find a fish worth eating.

"Hey fellas," he growled and did a quick couple steps of the Bear dance in greeting. "What's going on here? Where's all the others and where are the salmon?" It seemed as good a place to jump in as any.

Several of the healthier specimens looked his way, huffed, splashed the water with a forepaw and sat in the warm water. The others too wore out to care. And that was when he realized what he had failed to note before. Most of these kin were thin, almost emaciated. Brown bears should be eight foot tall and twelve hundred pounds of sleepy bear right now. Hell, the females should be five hundred and almost as big, but these folks looked like they had just come from a forced march of a thousand miles without stopping for vittles. Something was horribly wrong. And what made it wronger in Bear's head was he hadn't known about it until now.

Looked like he was going to have to find a restaurant nearby if he was going to fill the empty place in his gut that he had created just for this occasion.

This had obviously been going on for a long time, he should've felt the wrongness no matter where he was. Yeah, there was a lot more off kilter here than a few dozen scrawny bears. He needed to find out what, AND NOW!

"Ya hey," he ambled up beside the largest of the healthier looking folks. "Fishing not too good?" Keep it friendly.

"No, not for a long time. See any humans around here?" the brown gestured with his head towards where humans usually congregated to snap their pictures of the dozens of bears catching fish and gulping them down.

'Now that you mention it, no. And when I think about it, they were pretty scarce on the trip up here." Bear scratched his head with his right paw in thought, "actually was pretty nice, now that I consider. Usually, they are like ants crawling all over every inch of the Mother they can find." He sat back into the warm water. "And why in hell is the water so warm up here? It's supposed to be cold! It refreshes, cools down a bear through his winter coat, and the salmon seem to prefer it as well." The warm water didn't cool a bear down like it should. His hide was beginning to itch.

The large brown he had been talking to didn't say a thing but stared at Bear as if he were the dumbest creature walking the road. He waited. "When the living ain't worth a human showing up the living ain't worth much. Them things screw up the habitat then move on to fuck it up somewhere's else." What energy the bear had left went into the saying.

Evan's brain kicked in with almost an audible snap. Salmon wanted cold water to swim upstream in, they needed it to spawn. Warm water meant they would stay in the colder waters of the ocean. Only the hardest headed ones would chance swimming upstream and they would look like the ones here, almost white, and sickly, rather than silver or red with humps and thick. No meat on these bones translated to no meat on bear bones.

Looked as though Bear, as protector, would need to see if he could find out the why's and wherefores of another mystery threatening his people. But where to begin? He should check in with the Mother and see how she fared. She had to be aware of these great changes. Why hadn't she called out to him? This was his purpose in the pantheon of life, he was to safeguard the people, their habitat and how those changes might be affecting her.

But, as long as he was in the neighborhood, and couldn't fill the empty place in his gut, why not see if he could talk to Salmon and get the lay of the ocean and rivers from her. Good a place to begin as any.

Shit, he just wanted a nice few weeks of stuffing himself and lounging with the kin.

The Red Dog Inn in King Salmon was Evan's kind of place. He sat at the bar with a cold beer in front of him while a guy with a guitar droned on in the background. It was a dive and reminded him of his favorite place back home. The place where he'd first met Glen/Dog, and the mountain who caused such a major disturbance in the fabric of the Universe and then disappeared. Ah, memories. Here he was just a big guy having a beer, he was large but so were most of those in attendance.

The Red Dog was a typical Alaskan joint, filled with folks who weren't necessarily harsh or uncharitable, they just didn't go out of their way to be friendly. He liked them, they left you alone when you wanted to be there.

There were maybe a dozen other bar denizens either sitting quietly conversing with a bottle and a glass, and sometimes another human, or playing some game and exploding in expletives followed by laughter. Or just ignoring the guy with the plaintive voice and slightly out of tune guitar.

She walked through the door allowing the late sunlight to illuminate the dust before the wood door could block it out again. She had been pretty a long time ago but wasn't used up yet. Dressed in mismatched shades of pink, orange, white and silver, a stripper's bola clipped in her hair like a rainbow fishing lure. She was tawdry in a granny sort of way and as she passed, he caught the scent of the ocean.

She walked down the bar, ignoring all the open stools before turning about in a smooth motion and coming to a stop next to Evan. "This seat taken?" She sat without waiting an answer. Well!

"Beer?" Evan asked, might as well be amiable.

"And a grilled shrimp salad without the grill," she looked straight ahead at the emptiness between bottles. "I'm so hungry I could eat bear."

Her eyes were tired, the skin droopy beneath them, she slouched on the stool as if it took all her strength to sit erect; or it wasn't natural. Her skin was pale, almost transparent, Bear thought he could see her heart beat.

"What brings you up here," she asked finally turning towards him. "ain't much for you or your kind to dine on." There was indignation and annoyance coating her words though it was as tired as her eyes.

"I didn't make the circle of life, the Mother did. We all serve our purpose. I'm sorry some of yours has to die so mine can live but we only take what we need to survive. You know that." His tone defensive though he didn't know why, he hadn't made the universe just walked through it. He took a hard swallow off the almost empty bottle before holding it up and signaling the barkeep for two more. He wasn't here to create a ruckus, just to find out what was going on in this part of creation.

"I know," she sighed, "just been a long, hard lifecycle."

Bear ordered her salad, with the instruction of raw shrimp, and a four-cheese bacon burger, him thinking he shouldn't order seafood, especially salmon, might be considered boorish, and they settled into conversation and waiting for the grub.

"How long this been goin on?" He dug a claw in the dirt. He didn't have to say what, it was obvious.

"In human or spirit time?" She knew it didn't matter but sometimes it's hard to talk about the death of your children. "Dunno, maybe a half century as the human flies. Started slow, hardly noticed it, but now we're dying off faster than we can procreate. I ain't much longer for this eternity." Her head drooped almost to the bar and the singer began a heartbreakingly slow tune, almost like her melancholy was contagious.

"Cheeses," she whipped around so she could glare good and proper at the guy, "Don't you know nothing happy or at least not suicidal?" She didn't shout, didn't scream, it was a harsh whisper, which was far more frightening.

"You drink bourbon?" It was simple offer.

Yet she whipped around on Evan, "I live in the ocean, I drink whatever kind of shit they throw in it, got no choice, pesticides, herbicides, fertilizers, detergents, oil, industrial chemicals, sewage; bourbon sounds better."

Bear didn't know if bourbon went with shrimp but he knew it always made him feel better and warmed a cold night. And this was a cold, cold night and showed signs of getting colder.

"Look, I came up here to relax and get away from all the insanity of mankind, instead I find my people looking like skeletons, your people in no better shape and I want to know why. Your folks should be running like crazy to spawn, mine should be fat and getting fatter while they ready themselves for the coming winter. I look around and see a lot of people who are not going to make it to next year or make it upstream to keep the bloodlines going." He ran out of gas just as the bourbons showed their pretty little selves.

She stared at the glass for a split-seconds before shrugging and taking it all with one gulp. She didn't choke or cough, so either she had drunk enough crap in her life or she was one cool character.

"Nice," she said though a bit breathy, "smooth."

Evan saw the bottle and smiled, Buffalo Trace, he would have to thank his friend for lending his name to such a high-quality drink.

"This shit's been going on for years," she said gesturing what was happening to the people, his and hers, thirty miles from here and all over the world, "How is it you don't know nothing about the people dying?"

"Well," Bear began defensively, "I was kind of tied up for a short minute and then life kind of took an unexpected turn for a decade or so."

"Yeah, I heard you died." She snorted and motioned to the barkeep for two more of the small drinks. "Guess you didn't much care for dead, you look pretty alive to me."

"It was nice for a while, restful, quiet, though not much to do when you're dead. Got boring in a quick heartbeat. 'Sides I found out my family wasn't exactly what I thought so I came back to spend a few centuries with those I loved." Succinct and all that was needed.

"Now that you're back you got some work ahead of you if you want to avoid extinction." The food arrived and they both dug in with the hunger of their emaciated people. "And the rest of us might like a little help as well." She spoke around a large shrimp and tipped her glass to him in hope.

Evan turned to her to comment on his burger and ask about her raw shrimp but was stopped by her appearance. Where she had been wan, she now had a glow of health, from one meal, one decent meal. She smiled, "Yeah, it really doesn't take a banquet to change the course of my people just some clean water, zoo plankton, fly larvae, shrimp, whatever, but they are becoming as scarce as clean water."

Evan thought of his own people and their condition and felt the guilt creep up his back. He had been so wrapped up in his family, the discovery of his granddaughter's nature, the return of Her—which he still didn't grok how that happened, neither did anyone else, even the Mother. That had been the greatest life changer in, literally, forever. Shoulda been impossible, but such are the ways of the Great Spirit—he missed all the signs of his people's deterioration. He had failed his people as completely as the years he'd forgotten who and what he was.

He felt a great need to find the cause of the depredation, though he was purty sure where the source of the problem was. It was up to him to push them off the road to extinction and plant anew to fill the belly of the future so all the people would survive and thrive. But where to begin?

He knew if he held a council the People would immediately blame humans. He wanted to blame them, too, but was that completely true? Shouldn't human's survival instinct kick in just as surely as the rest of the inhabitants of the Mother? Was it all humans? No, he knew there was good ones working to stop this. Why didn't mankind see what they was doing?

He had a niggling feel at the base of his neck, a feeling of wrong, an itch that couldn't be scratched, that more was afoot here, and he didn't like the implications. They had never discovered who, in fact, had led the troubles from a decade or so ago. He believed when he had healed the break he had created, all should have gone back to normal. Instead, the deterioration of the Mother had snowballed. The question was why and who, or what, was behind the destruction. And whatever happened to that mountain who had fallen into Evan's lap at the bar? Shit, he hadn't thought about the guy once since coming back from the dead. He would have to question those who'd been at the house and see if they knew anything. Could he still be the thorn in Ev's backside? And why? He was only one man and one man didn't have that kind of power. Somebody or something was behind all this. Too many unanswered questions. Looked like he was about to become the traveling Bear, he required more information and the only place he would find it was with the People!

Wolf had been through this destruction in the past, hell, he had been damn near exterminated until some decent humans stood up and halted the killing. He required a meet. He and Wolf had gotten on to pretty good terms back when they served in the Mother's army, he needed to rekindle that relationship. He'd have to stop off home, grab the pipe, the rolling papers, the good stash, and head up to Montana. He was pretty certain that was where Wolf was running these days.

No Place Like Home, For a Minute

Evan abandoned the leisurely forms of travel that had brought him to Alaska. Speed was needed and he could, in his natural spirit form, be back home in seconds. She was pleasantly shocked when he strolled through the door.

"You're home early," She smiled as he folded Her in his arms.

"Something came up and I felt it needed my attention," he kissed her on the forehead and on each eye, the embodiment of calm.

Alexandra raced into the room and threw herself into his arms as he let go of Her. Alex may be in her twenties, chronologically, but her love for him was still filled with all the innocence and exuberance of a small child. She loved her grandfather and he returned that love. This was family.

After the welcome, filled with a hundred questions asked in rapid fire succession, all answered with, 'in due time', they enjoyed a family meal, joined by Suzette, who happened to be visiting and staying next door. If the excitement of a decade and a half ago had done nothing, it had brought together the family of the People. The animal Spirits had been solitary creatures throughout time but they had discovered a need and a joy in working together and the familial connection. Many of the People had become frequent visitors at the bear den.

Now, fat, and happy Evan explained, in as much detail as he could, his meeting with Salmon and the condition of Bear and Salmon's people. He kept his manner relaxed as if this were the most natural thing in the world. He was not going to win an Academy Award. They could tell he was deeply concerned and worried as to the cause and how to correct this imbalance without starting a war with humans. After the last upheaval they could hardly blame him. But Bear was the Healer and Protector of the people, this would be his responsibility.

"What are you going to do?" She asked, as bad an actor as Her mate.

"I need to talk to others of the People to find out how their children fare. The health of all is an indication of the health of Mother. Once I collect all the facts, I will go find the Mother and confer with her," he spoke cautiously as if reciting lines, but his mind had already left and was traveling north.

"Evan, Evan, " She prodded to his distracted countenance, "What do you need us to do?" All three women leaned in.

"I need you to stay here, safe, out of harm's way, but keeping an ear out for any inconsistencies among our children. I want to know every change in weather patterns and how they are affecting each species. Looks like I am going to school to learn the science of the environment on more than an instinctual level." He grimaced, spirit guides did not usually need scientific knowledge, but it was a changing world. "And while I'm thinking of it," he rubbed his chin in thought, though his concern was more concrete, "I want you to sniff around and see if there are any signs of that big mountain of mischief from before. I don't remember anyone mentioning him since before the little war out front. Does anyone remember seeing him? Was he injured? Killed? Though I don't think anyone was, but still, it bothers me that he seems to have just disappeared from the planet, just as things were really heating up. Last thing we need is for him to just pop up at the wrong time."

"I'll talk to John," Suzette replied thoughtfully, " see if he's heard anything or remembers hearing any word since."

"How is our Sheriff?" though Evan knew, fifteen years older, slower, more cantankerous than ever, but still John. He just wanted to give a little tug on Suzette's chain. He knew she was still sweet, in her way, on the good man.

"I haven't seen him in a while," she fibbed, " but will rectify that today."

"And I need to make my way to Montana and see if our dear Wolf, Sung, has any thoughts on the changing climate," Evan rummaged through his tired brain compiling a list of things he might want to take.

"I think I'll take the truck, give myself some time to think, really haven't slowed down long enough to grasp the implications."

"When do you leave again," She asked, a longing concern in Her voice. She worried for Her mate as he worried for all the people. He might be immortal; She now knew the truth of that and his stories—though She had always found truth in them—but She also knew he could be hurt. He might bear the pain but She would not. She would lose her sweet disposition and go she-bear on those who caused him damage.

"I guess it can wait a couple days," he wanted time with Her as much as She wanted time with him. Yes, they had all the time in the world, but that didn't negate their need to be together for the majority of it. The intensity of their love had not lessened just because they had forever.

Sheriff John hadn't wasted any time coming by for a visit once he found out that Evan had returned to the warm embrace. The big man had been gone for a month or so and John wanted to catch up, or as She would say, share a glass with Her husband. Evan was taken slightly aback by the appearance of the Sheriff. Mortals aged so quickly. The paunch betraying where once the sheriff had been solid as granite around the middle, his hair thinning and almost completely white. Geez, how old was the man now? Maybe early sixties, if Bear calculated right. He shouldn't be showing his age yet, should he? He had jowls coming in at cheek and neck, bags under his eyes and didn't stand quite so military erect as he had when Bear first met him. He would die before a blink of their immortal eyes and that saddened Bear more than he would've thought possible.

"Suzette told me you were back," the sheriff said patting her hand laying gentle on his arm. "How was Alaska?"

"Worrisome," answered Evan as he shook the Sheriff's hand. "Have a seat, my doting granddaughter, here, will fetch us some libations."

Alexandra's smirk and mocking bow bought her a gentle smack on her bottom to hurry her mission.

"How are things in town?" Evan began, "Any strange occurrences?"

"Nope, we are back to our happy boring normal," the sheriff smiled as Alex handed him a glass and then poured just a dram or two before repeating for her grandfather and setting the bottle on the table. "Why?" His sheriff sense tingling at the question.

"Whatever happened to that big fella who wanted me to know such discomfort?" Evan sipped as he locked eyes with his old friend.

"Damn, in all the commotion I completely lost track of the sonofabitch!" John stopped the glass just as it came to his lips. "Don't remember seeing him once the deputies took them four fellas off to jail and the hospital. Guess them turncoats must have set them other boys free when they took off for the mountains. Must've made themselves scarce after their run in with you. You did take a good measure from them, more'an they gave you, if recollection serves." He rubbed his chin in thought and then scratched his head to see if that would bring back any detail me might be missing. "Damn! How in all hell did I miss keeping track of a problem that huge?" Now, he was hip deep in blame and feeling stupid.

"Well, you were all pretty busy trying to stop the town from being overrun by herds of crazed animals and even more crazed people, if memory serves. Easy to have some loose ends when you're attempting to save a few hundred lives." Evan knew the threat that all the Spirit Guides had faced that day and what it had taken to save the townsfolk warped by whoever—and they still had no idea who had been behind that insanity—had taken advantage of the rent in the fabric. Another fact that had been niggling at the base of his skull for the past few years.

"I guess," the sheriff accepted the bone grudgingly, "and I guess since we ain't seen hide nor hair since that day he must've high tailed it well out of here."

"Probably, but I sure hate having him out there, somewhere, just waiting for another chance to disrupt the flow of life. Shit, he probably don't remember even being part of it. If one of the Spirit Animals was using him, he wouldn't have no memory of it, might not remember ever living around here."

"You know, come to think of it, I don't remember ever seeing the guy up 'til his run in with you," the sheriff scratched at the itch inside his head that wouldn't be satisfied.

"Meg, talked as if she knew the guy, if only from coming in the bar, maybe you could ask her. She's still tending last I knew," Bear now took his sip along with the sheriff who nodded his agreement. "Until then I'm going to be here for a day or two then I got some business up Montana way I got to see to."

"Anything you might be needing me for?" as much as the sheriff enjoyed not having the world stomping in his lap, he couldn't deny the boredom.

"Not yet, but you know how that can go. Keep yer shitkickin' boots on just in case," and Evan finished his drink.

The two days passed far too quickly. Evan wanted time with Her and Alex. He wanted to visit with Suzette, sit around the fire and swap some friendly nonsense. Instead, he was in his 1952 Chevy pick-up driving north on I-25 towards Montana and a, hoped, meeting with Sung. He feared what the Wolf would tell him. Evan knew what his people had looked like, how would the mighty wolves fare?

Sung sat atop the rocky outcropping, the wind whistled and eddied around the butte as if challenging. He stared at nothing, no, he thought, correct that, he stared at oblivion. The prairie east, and far below, vast, and open; and barren. The Beartooth Mountains mocked his despair. Head hung low, pale, and drawn, his leather jacket and jeans hung on him like an impoverished scarecrow. He had the bearing of a man contemplating the end. A lone tear crawled down his right cheek before ending its existence on the hard rock below.

He was once proud and fierce, one of the most powerful creatures to roam the western mountains and prairies of North America. Now, he was shrunken, like a very old man on his death bed. The sound of horse hooves pounding the hard earth echoed in his ears, yelps of the hunter as they closed in on the hunted caused him to shiver and jerk with fear. This was not how his people should be treated. And he would feel every single one of their deaths. Their terror, their gallant attempt to fight back, he would hear their snarls and last whimpers.

He had done his very best to keep them within the confines of the protected area, though wolves did not know, nor respect, boundaries. They roamed the wide open, they followed the scent of survival. They did not kill for sport. They didn't destroy out of pure malice. They were not cruel creatures. They killed to feed the pack, to keep the cubs fed and themselves strong. They were not man, they only wished to be left alone.

But man would not be denied. Sung had been through this before. His children had been hunted almost to extinction a hundred turns of the Mother in the past. The men had their guns and their blood lust. Who could overcome such? Man feared the wolf, said wolves killed their cattle and their profits. Sung choked off a sob. Yes, they sometimes killed ranchers' cattle. Not a great amount, one of thousands, and only to survive. When the hunting was scarce and bellies were empty you took only what you needed. Man thought he needed everything. That was what terrified him of wolf, wolves were strong, fierce, they had honor, morals, they protected the pack, and never killed just to kill.

And now Sung faced extinction once again. He thought of Bear, Bear who had come back from his own death a few years ago. Sung had witnessed the resurrection. You can be resurrected from your own death as an immortal, but you could not be resurrected from extinction. He wished he could see Bear one more time. He wished he could converse and share a bottle and a smoke; it would be good. He wished the Mother would come and save his children, but she could not, would not, it was how life worked for all. Even the Mother.

This time he allowed the sob to find its brothers and sisters and he wept. He wept shamelessly in torrents. He wept for his children and all the children of the world. The wind kicked up dust on the prairie below, the clouds skitted across the darkening sky. Rain would come and then the snow and his people would not survive another winter cold, hungry, and hunted. He jerked upright at the report of a long gun. Were they successful? Did they thin the pack a little more? He could do nothing but wait the inevitable.

Evan bounced along the gravel road which had once been paved. Apparently, the state of Wyoming didn't shut roads down when they tore them up, they just tore them up and rebuilt while you drove them. He had been bouncing inside the cab of the ancient Chevy for the past half hour and was just about to park it and walk when he was once again blessed with blacktop. Maybe he should've stayed on the highway. No, he was in search of a Spirit animal who did not run the highways and crowded roads, he was a creature of solitude, the actual Lone Wolf. Bear would search for him in the back country.

It was almost Montana when the wolf ran across the road right in front of him. Evan tried to see the rest of the pack but there was none, just a cloud of dust coming toward him in a din of yelling, jangling of tack, and the pounding of hooves. Evan stopped the truck, though trying to keep an eye on where the wolf went in the hopes of talking to it. Once he rid himself of the brave calvary needing thirty men to chase down one wolf. He wanted to spit.

They rode up to him stopping just short of the paved road. He might have been slightly overexaggerating how many it took, but not by much. He stepped out of the truck just to be friendly, and possibly block any of these brave, brave men from spotting where the she-wolf had got to.

"Hey fellas, out running the wide open on a lovely chill Tuesday?" Evan wasn't sure what day it was but liked the sound of Tuesday as it made this seem even more ridiculous than it was.

"You seen a wolf lope by here?" asked the apparent leader of this posse. He chewed tobacco while he rode and spit as he stopped, Evan wished the guy would choke on the chaw.

"That scrawny looking thing was a wolf?" Evan barked the laugh before pointing to the southeast. "Went hightailing it out thataway hell bent for freedom. Though, don't think it's going to git very far, looked 'bout half dead and running on fumes. Even you fellas ought to be able to catch it." He knew he shouldn't poke these fellas, they looked about ready to chew iron, but he couldn't help himself. Idiots and hate were a bad combo anywhere but when they were just bent on killing something that couldn't harm a rabbit, well, fuck 'em.

Bear had to find Sung and he had to find him now. That wolf looked to have three paws in the grave and its ribs were poking through her fur. This was not a good sign. Things were worse than he had thought. As he made to get into the truck he saw that poor, emaciated creature stick its head around the rocks where it had hunkered down. Its eyes were almost vacant, death was being patient, but wouldn't wait forever. Evan slowly reached into the cab where the remnants of his sandwich lay on the bench seat. He pulled it out and tore off a piece of roast beef—not his usual fare, but when in Wyoming—and tossed it to the ravaged animal. It took it down without chewing, so Evan threw another piece and another.

When the sandwich had served its purpose, he opened the passenger door and waited. He thought about showing the critter who he was but then reconsidered. If it saw him for who he was it might take off and not stop until the reaper cuddled it. Let's just see if a little trust could get this girl in the cab. They could talk while he drove.

Sometimes life just beats you so hard you get to the point you don't care anymore, if it is death that holds the door, walk through. Tired is tired, and enough is enough, the wolf seemed to be saying. It had run everything it had out of it and maybe it would be better to ride comfortable to death rather than scared. It hopped in the truck. Evan walked easy around to the other side and slid in, nodded to the wolf, and turned the key.

They rode in silence for a bit while building a little trust and tearing down the wall that separated. The wolf lay on the seat, tongue lolling out of the left side of its mouth, Evan would have to see if he could find a stream or a place to buy water.

"You know Sung?" what the hell, there was nothing to lose.

The wolf cocked its head.

"You know who I mean? Sung, Wolf, he sings your people and watches over," could she really understand.

Now, she perked up, her head bobbing almost as if saying 'yes'. She yipped and pointed her nose straight ahead.

"You'll show me where?" Evan pointed where she was looking.

Again, that turn of the head as if in question and then a nod. Almost as if she was sayin, 'you want to tussle with Sung, yeah, I'll take you.'

Evan wasn't sure where this might lead or if he was just hoping this wolf understood, but he had nothing else to go on. Chances are for taking, not passing by.

They stopped by a roadside pull off that sat next to a nice little creek and Evan let the wolf out so she could drink. Then cupped a handful or two in his own mouth. The evening was approaching and he hoped he wasn't just driving 'round in circles.

Another half hour passed, by the position of the sun, before the wolf yipped loud and seemed to nod with her head at an outcropping atop a small butte on the eastern edge of a mountain. Evan pulled the truck off the side of a side road and shut it down. The quiet was nice. He liked driving the old truck but he loved the sound of the Mother breathing, though there was an incongruity to the sound.

He began to climb the butte, the she-wolf at his side. Apparently, she wanted to see what happened when this human came face to face with the great Sung. Evan smiled, he wanted to run to wherever Sung was. He hadn't realized how much he missed the Wolf.

Evan stopped in his tracks as he came around the slight bend in the path atop the butte. He held his breath. Shock reverberated through his soul. If he hadn't detected the almost negligible movement of Sung's chest he would've thought him dead or a statue. Emaciated and wan, the lone wolf sat on the edge of oblivion.

"Sung," Bear whispered so none but the intended would hear.

Sung turned, ever so slowly as if it pained him to do so. He rubbed his eyes, not believing the visage that presented itself. Bear standing mouth agape and a very thin she-wolf next to him. She must have brought him here. He stood, slow, like the rising of the mountains themselves, and turned to greet his friend.

"Bear!" How one word could contain so much hope, love, desperation, longing, and grief, Evan couldn't figure, but it had.

"Wolf, I came to see how things go with you, but it would appear I can see for myself." The sadness so thick in his words they had trouble leaving his mouth. "Come, sit back down and let us talk. I brought something to drink and smoke, let's see if we can't find some joy and solutions."

Bear set himself cross-legged on the outcropping as Sung sat across from him, the she-wolf laying next to him, her head in his lap. The sun had almost disappeared in a blaze of glorious reds, purple, golden rays, and deep blue to black behind the Beartooth. It felt appropriate.

"I'm afraid I don't have anything to reciprocate the kindness," Wolf hung his head in shame at his poverty.

"You have yourself and that is all I need. I know this will bring no joy, no solace, but you are not the only one suffering this devastation. I came here to find if that was true and to see if between us, and the others, if we can find the reasons and a way to stop our destruction." Bear lit the joint took a deep hit and passed it to Wolf.

Sung laughed a joyless bark, "You want to know where and why? I'll tell you, Man! There is the culprit behind my demise. And I do not overstate my position, I am two breaths away from extinction. And, as if the changes to the Mother aren't horrid enough, now these yahoos have put a price on the heads of my children. All because they hunger and wish to feed their pack." It had taken every of the ounce of energy he possessed to make his statement; now, wolf sat quiet. Evan feared he would fall over into the abyss as they sat.

"That would explain the cowboys I saw chasing this one," he reached over to rub the head and chin of the she-wolf. "I sent them elsewhere."

"Thank you," Sung gave a shallow, sitting bow, "but it will only keep her alive for a while. They do not give up trying to kill every one of my few children."

"Why, for what purpose do they kill?" Bear was shocked that this cruelty had not been bred out of humans.

"Do they need a reason? I have traveled the long road and their cruelty ceased to surprise me centuries ago. They claim my children kill their cows. Their cows! I do not belittle the animal but there are millions of cows, there are but few of us. And we only kill out of need, hunger." He took the proffered bottle and drank deep before wiping his dry, caked lips and handing the bottle back to Evan. "Shit, they are going to kill the damn things anyway. Won't even use all of them, just the choice parts. Wasteful and stupid. They are all fat, satisfied, they do not starve, my people starve. Many will not survive the winter. I will not survive the winter." He howled forlorn and grief into the vast empty world.

"Can you get your people to move to a place where they can rest and replenish their energy? Would they leave to come south?" While driving and bouncing through the back country Bear had come up with a plan if he found what he feared and had found. It wasn't perfect and he couldn't guarantee shit but he thought it was worth a try. They needed to buy some time and strengthen Wolf, and that meant saving as many packs as they could. And that meant feeding and caring for as many wolves as they could save. And that meant one helluva a lot more work for somebody, Bear most like, though maybe he wrangle some-body else into it!

"I can try. What do you have in mind?" for the first time in years Sung felt a brief spark of hope in his chest. He knew Bear, and Bear would do everything in his power to help, but how much power did he have?

A Conspiracy of Convenience

Suzette eased out of bed, her joints aching and she could hear creaking like something rubbing on something it shouldn't be rubbing on. She was tired, as if she had been swimming in circles the entire night. She gazed at the dark circles under her eyes, deep pools that showed the distress she felt inside. Pushing back her hair, strands clung to her nails and floated to the top of the dresser. What the hell?

Dressed and ready for another uneventful day she hobbled out to the backyard to see if any of the others had made their way here and if anyone had made coffee. Bear's mate and the cub, Alexandra, came out the back door with a plate of fruit and a carafe of coffee, the day was improving by the minute. She realized, as they brought the goodies, she had no idea what the woman's name was. Everyone referred to her by Bear's demarcation of Her or She, but the woman must have a name, right?

Coffee poured and bowls of deliciousness placed before her, she delicately munched in silence breaking her fast for a few moments before breaking the silence. "I'm sorry, quite rude of me, actually, but I have never asked your name, certainly you have one?"

The, now, middle-aged woman leaned back in her lawn chair and smiled, "Evan never told anyone my name? What did he call me?"

Suzette's laugh was the tinkling of fairy bells, "Well, he, and then the rest of us always referred to you as 'She' or 'Her' and all knew to whom that signified. There was no other who earned that honorific."

"He is the sweetest man," She wiped a bit of love from her eye, "Of course he would. I guess he was taken aback by my death."

Alexandra gasped, "It damn near killed him and the rest of the people on this planet, as well. I don't know how all this magic, resurrection, all of y'all coming back from the dead, or whatever, came about, but I thank the Great Spirit it did. He was a mess, just as sad as any creature ever." And she wiped a lot of love from her own eyes at the memory.

"He was that bad?" She was taken aback by the depth of feeling Alex was describing.

"He was just lonely, even with me coming over as often as I could, you could feel the lonely, the grief coming off him like heat radiating from an open oven. He'd walk down to some watering hole in town to have a couple beers and say he had been immersed in humanity. But I went with him one-time years back, and it was just a few guys, almost as bad as him, sitting in silence and sippin' on despondency. Like a hermit's club. Bet they didn't utter more'n a dozen words the whole time I sat with him.

"When we left, I felt like I'd been swimming in a pool of sorrow. We walked out into bright sunshine and even that couldn't help none. I asked him why he went there it was so depressing. He just said it was a place where he could be by people without having to actually be with them. Nobody bothered nobody, nobody intruded on your lonely. They just drank a bitter drink and went home. It was melancholy with a doleful chaser." She shivered at the memory and put her forkful of berries down, staring at the empty place where Evan usually sat.

Silence wrapped the morning and threatened to drag them to the depths when a cheery 'hello' brought their attention to the corner of the house. A beautiful woman with tan and white hair had entered the back stronghold.

"Doe! My deer!" Cried Suzette, the relief released in that one syllable was a rush of air the Mother didn't know she had been holding. The Earth breathed deep; bliss washed the despondency from the assembled.

"Well, there is a welcome, welcome. Nice to know I am not an intruder but a timely distraction," she scrubbed her short hair as she took an empty seat, taking the proffered cup of coffee and a handful of berries.

"You look good," gushed Alex and Suzette in unison, "maybe a little too thin, but good."

"We all could use to pack on a few," Doe responded taking in the other three.

They all took stock of each other with an honest eye. And honestly, she was right, they all had a gaunt mien, not emaciated but the roundness now had sharp edges. Why no one had noticed they couldn't say, maybe because all had been around each other and the weight loss had been gradual, but they definitely needed a sandwich.

"Well, what brings you back to our loving embrace?"

"I need to council with Bear. What are you three up to?" Doe attempted to bring the subject into some focus.

"I am attempting to discover what Her name is," Suzette pointed directly at Alex's grandmother and laughed.

"It's not a secret," She said defensively, though not knowing why, "it's Rebecca. It's an old family name." She smiled at the sound of her own name, this being the first time anyone had mentioned it since she came back. Though, she hadn't noticed that fact 'til now.

"It fits you," said her granddaughter, the other two nodding in agreement.

"So, where's the Bear?" Doe didn't want to seem rude, but she had questions and a need of advice.

"He went in search of Wolf. There are things afoot he finds quite discomfiting and he wanted to confer with Sung. I'm guessing you are here on the same errand." Rebecca spoke her words drenched in concern.

"I think it best we remain together and wait for his return, see what he has discovered. And in the meantime, see what we can find out about this hunger, this imbalance in the Mother. We need to know if this is happening in a limited area or all across the Mother's garden. We have got to find a way to check in with all the People, those of the land, air, and water." Rebecca looked to the others for confirmation, it was slow in coming but absolute in union.

"I will take the water as it is as natural to me as land," Suzette said thinking of her visage in the mirror that morning.

Doe chimed in, "I will try to contact as many of the land, Tatanka, Elk, the Cat families, Willow and the others," she clicked them off on her fingers.

"I have a little history with Iktomi and her children, maybe they can help me, once again, with those who crawl and weave." Alexandra remembering, they had saved her life; she would have no qualms about dealing with those who creeped and crawled along the Mother.

"Guess that leaves me with figuring a way to speak to those who live on the winds," Rebecca said thoughtfully, "I think I know who, just have to figure out the how."

"I could stay and help you," Alex wanted to be with her grandmother, to help her, this was all so new to her and Alex, maybe they should help each other.

"No, you have enough to deal with Iktomi and the others. We need to concentrate on gathering all the information we can so when Evan returns, we can have an informed council, not one based on conspiracies, conjecture or lies."

They made their plans, said their farewells, and steeled themselves for the tasks ahead.

Chain, Chain, Chain, Chain of Fools

The young woman wrapped the chain around the huge Maple-Leaf Oak. She knew in her heart it was a gloriously asinine gesture, but she was wedded to it and she would see it through. There were only about six-hundred or so of these trees left in the world, she would not allow this one to be cut down.

Her current boyfriend, Brian Harper, was tied to the only other Maple-Leaf Oak they could find. They would make their stand and show the world someone cared for the trees. They were officially tree huggers. Now, if only the news people would show up. She knew the extinction of a tree that only grew in a small part of Arkansas would not change the course of the world, but it was symbolic of all the destruction around the world. Their defense of such a grand, yet doomed, species would shame the country, the habitat destroyers, the leaders of the corporate money-grubbing political elites into doing the right thing. She also knew they were being cultivated but these were close to home and her finances were limited. She could save the world from itself, if only she had the cash.

It was almost impossible to bring the reality of deforestation to the mind of the public. The masses didn't care about trees, pollution, or climate change, a catastrophe that could happen within their life span. It was in the future, their children could deal with it, not up to them. They were too busy zoning out, mindless in front of the tube watching reality shows and political pundits who played to their fears and biases of who was trying to take what from whom. And they were the whom. And the others were the 'them'. There was always a 'them', the others, the ones who just wanted to take, the entitled who didn't have to work for what they wanted, they just wanted what you had worked so hard to get and wanted the government to then give it to them.

Every time you tried to bring the destruction of the Earth, their home—the only one they would ever have and if she died so would they—to their attention, the great unwashed masses turned a blind ear. They knew you wanted to take away something they had worked hard for, the talking TV heads told them so. Like their own death, she snickered in her head, they'd worked themselves into standing on the brink of their own destruction by worrying that the 'other' was coming to take away their trailer and fifteen-year-old car. They were on a path to self-destruction and couldn't see the light of the train racing towards them. Well, she would make them listen.

Except there was no one to witness her sacrifice. She and Brian would stay chained to the trees until they died, then maybe people would listen! But to whom would they listen if she and Brian died in this ridiculous, pathetic gesture? Their dry, white bones? There was no sign that anyone from the media cared, no television trucks driving madly through the desolate forest to interview the two loonies chained to trees to save the world.

What the fuck was she doing? There had to be a better way to bring the destruction of the world to the attention of the troglodytes slowly dying of weight, inaction, and slovenliness while the other half starved. All controlled by the wealthy powerbrokers who demanded governments dance to their chorus of more, more, more. She was giving her life for the life of the planet and all those who lived on it. She clicked the lock, the chains remain, and waited her death.

The little man with spikey hair and Pince nez perched on his nose strolled out of the forest, hands in front pockets, as if being this far from civilization and coming upon a couple crazed tree huggers was the most natural thing in the world.

"Afternoon," he chimed, doffing his hat which he had, apparently neglected to don.

"I don't suppose you happen to be with any of the media, do you?" hope found its way into her words though she instinctively knew it was not a welcome guest.

"No, no," he shook his head while taking off and cleaning the pince nez with the tail of his shirt. He was squat, no more than five and half foot on a good day, with a round belly, vest, over shirt and under top-coat, and pants too small around the waist so had found a home under that belly. But it was the ears that seemed off kilter, one lower than the other by a good inch or more. Or was the other higher, she couldn't tell, it was just off-balance. "Just out for a breath of mountain air and happened to hear the chains rattling." He grinned though it was not an uncharitable gesture. "Out to change the world?"

"Out to save the world before humans destroy it," she shifted her body slightly to take the weight of the chains off her midriff.

"A virtuous endeavor. Is this tree something special to the cause?" he gestured to the object to which she was attached.

"This is a Maple-leaf Oak, of which, there are only about six hundred in the world," she began her prepared statement just in case the portly man actually was a representative of the media, "and on the cusp of extinction. They represent what we have done to this Garden of Eden we were gifted. I don't know if you are aware but there are hundreds of animals, insects, birds, that are in danger of becoming extinct. All because the greedy overlords of this and every other country don't give a shit about this planet, only profit. Each piece of the puzzle, when lost to avarice by money-grubbing whores of the capitalist elite, and which cannot ever be replaced, might be the proverbial straw that breaks Mother Earth's back and we will all die!" the intensity of her statement became more animated as the volume rose. She emphatically wanted this man to know he was standing on the precipice of the end of life on this planet. That was what this one tree represented.

"Interesting," he spoke the word as if observing the mating of jelly fish. "Have you alerted the media?" he continued, again wiping the non-existent grime from perfectly clear spectacles.

"I texted every single one of them." She said, though the righteous indignation had been lost.

"And they responded positively?"

"I texted them and the text had been delivered," she said as if technology would accomplish the end.

"And they responded positively?" He asked once more.

"It said all had been delivered!" she said as if that settled the case.

"I am not entirely conversant with the mode of communication you refer, but shouldn't they have responded either positively or negatively to the request?" He tucked his shirt tail just inside the breeches.

"The text had been delivered! I put a message on Instagram!"

"I see," though he didn't, but he also did not want to aggravate the young woman any further. "Then I will leave you to your task." He turned to walk away.

She wanted to scream at this uncaring, horrid little man, but she was spent. The ludicrous nature of her impotent attempt to publicize what, she felt, was man's inhumanity to tree, had fallen flat in a forest of trees and no one had heard.

"Brian, unchain me, if you would, our work is meaningless," it was time to go home and lick wounds.

"I thought you had the keys," came the feeble response from the effeminate, weedy boyfriend chained to the other specimen of dying Oak.

"Shit! Excuse me, sir, but could you see if there is a set of keys laying on the ground near me," defeat filled each syllable. If she'd had the strength she would've wept, but she no longer cared.

He turned and took the few steps to where she was secured and began kicking around in the dead leaves covering the forest floor. After several minutes and expanding the scope of the field a single jingle of metal on metal caught his ear and he bent to pick up the ring with several keys on it. Within a few breaths he had both young lady and boyfriend extricated from their self-effected imprisonment.

"I don't mean to intrude on your meaningful endeavor, but do you suppose there might be a slightly more productive course of action," if his tone had been a bit less jovial, she might have thought he was mocking her. Instead, he seemed to be almost suggesting that he had a better idea.

Which, of course, he was. He had only that morning communicated with Rebecca, the She of Evan's life, and had come out to the forests to clear his brain and try to jump start a few advantageous concepts. His running across the human hostages to a dying world had been serendipitous. Mayhap he could enlist them, they certainly had the energy and desire. And Rebecca, the She of Evan's desire and life, had mentioned they might have need of a few more volunteers of the human species. These two would seem to fit the bill, though how they would help was beyond him. Though, there was that energy and desire on which all revolutions rely.

"What did you have in mind?" the young woman was suspicious, yet interest could not be veiled. If there was a better way to save the planet, then who was she to stand it the way.

"My name is Oscar," he extended his hand in the human way, she took it, shook it once, "Anna Marie." It was immediately obvious she was not a fan of the moniker. "Oh, and, Brian Harper," she pointed at the aforementioned male of interest, though the tone conveyed limited interest.

"Do you live nearby?" He required information of their roots to determine the probability of travel.

"No, we're from NY but the trees were here. It was easier to bring us to them than them to us," ah, sarcasm, a human trait he found particularly endearing. Oscar smiled at the attempt. "Yes, we live about an hour from here, over by Hot Springs."

"Would you be interested in one of the greatest adventures of all time, " and he knew of all time. He had decided to ignore the young woman's obvious penchant toward sarcasm, "and have an actual opportunity to save the planet?" Test the waters.

"OK, what do you have in mind? Really!" Her tone said it all, she'd had enough bullshit from those who thought they knew better, she wanted truth.

If the young woman wanted it straight, and her humor had run its course, then he would tell her. All of it.

"We have a group that is intimately interested in the preservation of the Mother and inhabitants thereon. We are not your normal, run of the mill human types, as a matter of fact we are not human at all, we are the Animal Spirit guides of Native legend and lore. We are immortal, well, at least on paper and initial concept, but if our children become extinct, then so do we. There is no need for a spirit animal representation of an extinct species. The loneliness alone would kill it. We are attempting to convene and find a way to stop your species from eliminating all of ours. Interested? It does involve some travel, great desire, purity of heart and soul. Oh, and grave danger, I should mention." He smiled, satisfied with his concise explanation.

"You're shitting me, right?" Anna Marie stared hard through the pince nez to read this guy.

"I assure you I am not," he appeared insulted she would not take what he had given as absolute truth.

"You're nuts," she made to pick up her chain and go home.

Brian hesitated.

"What?" She said glaring at him.

"What if he's not?" He had a strange expression on his face, as if something he believed in as a child, or wanted to, at the very least, had become real right in front of his face. "What if he is telling us something really cool? You might be walking away from finding out there is real magic in this world. That myth is fact and lore is true? What if we are allowing our preconceived and learned bullshit to stop us from going off on a great adventure?" He was pleading with her, but he didn't care. In fact, he had already made up his mind, he just would prefer not to make it up alone.

"You're kidding, right?" But she could see he wasn't. The question now was, was she going to let him go off on this thing without her. "What if he's bullshitting us?" Not yet, she told herself, I'm not giving in yet.

"Then we're off on some wild goose chase that's stupid and a huge waste of time. Like chaining yourself to a tree in the middle of a forest where no one gives a shit. I'm going!" He didn't have great reserves of moxie but he was all in. He stood his ground for the first time in his life. "Look, no I don't believe he is some 'spirit creature', but if he is working with others who want to change the world, that's what we signed up for." He did his best to sound reasonable.

Well, Anna Marie was not going to let him do this alone. It would not be told forever how she had allowed this twig of a man, this willow bending to every breeze, to leave her in the dust. "OK."

As The World Turns

Snow had begun to fall in the highest elevations of the Rockies, Bear could see from where he and Sung sat in the rest/viewpoint atop Craig Pass, somewhere down below was Shoshone Lake, but they couldn't quite make it out due to thick free growth. Sung had needed a break from the few hours of travel, he didn't look well. His skin pale, his breathing labored, Evan worried they wouldn't accomplish what he hoped would save the species.

"Are you alright? You don't look very well," Bear was concerned, Sung had taken on a pallor the last few days. He feared for the Spirit's existence.

"More, more deaths all the time. A half dozen poisoned to the northwest of here." He spit and tried to take a deep breath coughing and spitting once again, "For what? What did they want? To live, that was all. Yes, they killed a couple cows, they didn't hurt one human, just cows, cows that are used for food." He coughed a weak bark of laughter, "food for humans, but not for my children. How selfish can one species be? And the humans used the hunger of my people to kill them, how depraved is that?" His anger spent he stared for a minute at eternity and shook his head hoping to cleanse it of what he'd experienced.

"Can you feel any of your people close to here?" Bear asked the Wolf eager to force Sung's attention elsewhere.

"Not many like in days long past, but there are a few packs roaming nearby." Sung's grin carried little joy. "They are weak, hunting, eating whatever others leave behind, like scavengers!" the disgust in his voice cut through the air like a bolt of lightning, though wan and dim.

"Can you call to them? Bring them here?" It was time to see if his plan had any chance at all. Now, when Sung had the strength, soon it might be too late to even try this insane idea.

"I will try," with great effort he transformed back to his natural state. The noble beast was still grand in size though thin, his skin barely containing the ribs beneath. He took a deep breath and howled. A cough punctuating the sound. The call strong riding the breeze. They would come.

The first pack to arrive was lean, hungry, pacing close enough to scent but not near enough to be threat or threatened. Yes, they knew who Wolf was but they also could scent Bear, and the scent was stronger than the Wolf. They wanted no trouble with him, they were too weak. The second pack, also badly in need of a meal, kept clear of Evan, Sung and the first pack. And though they stayed well out of sight of all, a third pack had shown up and kept to the trees. All were intent on keeping their distance and assuring themselves of a quick, clean getaway if required.

"What do you want me to ask?" Sung had gained a modicum of his color back, his coat had a sheen that hadn't been there moments before.

"Will they come to the town, my town, well, the forest up range. Will they stay up in the mountains nearby. I can call the sheriff and explain my idea. I feel confident he will help us protect them. I think if we get them away from here for a while, let them hunt in the pristine forests up from town, we can improve their health. And yours." He was thoughtful, hopeful. Would the sheriff agree to having wolf packs roaming the hills and mountains around town? Could Sung control them so they would leave the ranchers cattle be? They had never taken a lot of cattle up north but the ranchers had decided one was too many and the hunting had gotten out of hand. Maybe Evan could convince the folks down around him to leave the wolves alone. And maybe Sung could convince the wolves to try to keep their hunting to the lush, plentiful forests of the southern Rockies. Hope springs. And, "I will use some of the money Alexandra has been raising to help those in need, to purchase cattle from the ranchers. We can keep them contained so the wolves will never be hungry, though they can still hunt for themselves. Yes," he almost shouted to the mountaintops, "this is the perfect solution. If your people will agree to leave the town and ranches nearby alone."

All Evan knew for certain was they would need to get all the People in the best shape possible if they had any chance of stopping the destruction of the Mother. If he had to find solutions one species at a time, he would, though he felt certain it would take too much time and the Mother would die before he could accomplish his purpose. But if he could do this, then the others could see a way to find their own short-term solutions. Yeah, hope is an addictive feeling.

There was the requisite snarling, snapping, and letting of blood as they discussed in their way, the proposal. They asked him questions of whether Bear could be trusted, if his word was good. Did he speak truth for all or only for himself? How could they be assured they were not being led to their deaths? Sung answered all their concerns. Sung allowed their voices and feelings to be heard and shared before he put his paw down. Even in his weakened state his voice was mighty, he would not be challenged, his word was law. "You are dying right now, by the tens and hundreds, you can starve year by year until your children die in borning and all the Luna wolves lay on the ground as meals for the coyotes or you can take a chance on living." He was done. They hung their heads accepting truth and reality.

"They'll come. It will take us about a week, that should give you time to smooth over the concerns at home." Sung knew he would have to travel with them if he had any hope of keeping them together.

"I would like you to travel with me but will understand if you would prefer to be with your children," Evan liked the company of the Wolf, but it was more than that, he wanted someone who knew, really knew to his bones, about survival. Wolves had been hunted since the beginning of man, almost to extinction several times over the centuries. He would know what that felt like, what to look for, how to react and how to fight. He might be their greatest living ally. The rest who knew what it was to be hunted to extinction were long gone to dust and memory.

"I would love to spend time with you, just the two of us, but deep in my heart I know my place is with my people. I need them as much as they need me. I can protect them best by guiding, standing watch, leading them, it is essential I travel with them. And maybe we can pick up the scent of more packs and strays. I want to save as many as I can." Sung looked so tired Evan wanted to reach out and hold him, instead he grabbed his forearm and clasped it tight, lending whatever strength he could. Wolf might have more wisdom than they knew, maybe Evan should take a little extra time and collect some of his people on the trip as well.

This was beginning to feel like the fable of Noah come to life. The Ark would be the mountains around their town, Evan, Alexandra, Suzette, and She would be the new family come to save the world. The flood, as always was humanity as it raged across the land. He would take a few days to make his way back home. He would talk to his children, tell them what he was doing and what they needed to do to survive. It would be up to them, he would force not one bear of any kind.

Taking his time to come through the mountains had been an excellent choice. He required quiet, solitary time. To visit with some his own people who were faring better than most he had seen on this journey. They were eating regular, berries and fish were plentiful throughout the Rockies, not as plentiful as years past—heat, drought, abnormally brutal winter storms take their toll—but all in all they were healthy. They would survive, his concerns were with those in the Canadian Rockies and those of Alaska and the Arctic. Those were the bears taking the brunt of the environmental devastation. Though he also knew he would need a few days in Europe, South America, and Asia. The days he spent here were well considered, but it was time to head in the direction of home. He would be traveling the Spirit roads a lot in the coming days and months.

He knew, soon or late, the destruction of the environment would come here, there, everywhere. How was it possible that humans could not see, feel, taste, or sense the coming ruin? Was their arrogance so great they felt they could withstand the destruction of their home? After all, they needed the Mother as much as any other, how could they not see that? Where did they think they were going to go in such a short time? There was no Stepmother to go to, some other planet they could run to when they had burnt this one to the ground. This was it. Stupid, just stupid. When would they learn?

And that was it, wasn't it? There wasn't that much time left, not in the grand scheme of things. Decades, at best, before it would be too late to turn back, then what would they do? So many questions, so few answers. He wanted to go to the capitals of every country of the human race and shake some sense into whoever was supposed to be running things, but what could one bear do?

It was imperative they, the original occupants of this beautiful garden, join together and force the hand of those in charge. The politicians, the greedy bastards who thought the resources of the Mother were infinite, and the 'every' man and woman who threw plastic in the oceans, streams, and rivers, who dumped their chemicals where they could do the most damage and allowed their fertilizers to pollute lakes and drinking water.

How could they not see how shitting where you slept and pissing in your own well would kill you, kill your sport, kill everything you claimed to love. It was maddening and the great Bear's good mood died a borning on the vine. He had to get home, to hold Her, to feel love and intelligence. He had to get as far from humans as he could.

Well, not all humans. When the time had come, and he had some reception on his cell phone, he had explained his plan to save the wolves, and maybe others, to Sheriff John. Bear was reticent and unsure of the reception he would receive. But John was a good man who had now witnessed more than he thought possible. He believed, if not viscerally at least intellectually, that Evan and his friends were who he said they were. And he had grown up on this prairie and in the mountains, he knew the necessity of the balance of nature. You lose one piece of the Jenga and the whole thing comes tumbling down. No, John knew the necessity. He had seen what he had seen, and while he might want to deny the reality of it, he was a man bathed in a life of law enforcement and could not deny his own witness, especially when that witness was him. He'd laughed when Bear had told him how nervous he was that John would think him nuts for this, but John assured Evan he had questioned Evan's sanity for a long time now, this would change nothing.

John explained he had been reading a lot lately in the newspapers and watching specials on PBS. He'd had to chastise himself for not being much of an egghead before meeting Evan and learning about the decimation of animals all over the planet. And learning to be hopeful, as due to the actions of environmentalists and the government habitat was coming back. It was because of the reintroduction of wolves that now thinned the elk herds, the land was allowed to heal. Because the great herds of elk had been reduced, they would not be over grazing. Birds, and rodents not seen in decades had retuned. Beaver, Aspen, ravens, eagles, coyote and, yes, Bear's people, had all benefitted from the reintroduction of wolves. Yet people were hunting and killing them because they took a few cattle, out of thousands, tens of thousands. How insatiable could one species be?

John knew, and he would be able to explain it to the townsfolk. The wolves and other species needed to survive, they were part of the ecological fabric, and so was man. They all had to work together; they'd see that. Besides, he was the sheriff and had been for decades, the townsfolk would trust him and his opinion would carry a lot of weight. The laughter they had shared as John shared his doubts carried Evan the rest of the way home.

He pulled into the drive and was mobbed by his loved ones, even Glen was there. Doe, Alex, and Her, by the Great spirit he couldn't see Her, yet, but he could sense Her from where he sat in the truck. She smelled of nature, the outdoors, the mountains and spring, early autumn and the cold of winter. She was the scent of life. She was life.

The questions machine gunned until he had to raise his voice for them to stop! "I will tell you all I have found and we can discuss alternatives once I am settled," he reassured, his voice, like the rest of him, was tired. "Where's Suzette?" He surprised himself by how much he relied on the diminutive woman's intelligent council.

"She had some kind of emergency, she didn't say what," his wife explained as she showed up next to him, holding his arm, and hugging him close, "she said she would return as soon as she had seen to whatever it was that required her attention." She shrugged her lack of concern; she also had come to trust and rely on the diminutive Otter. She also trusted the woman to take care of herself.

"She didn't tell anyone what it was that drew her away?" Evan was concerned and he was pretty sure he knew why. His concern was born of information the others didn't have.

"Thought I heard a ruckus coming from out this a 'ways, all the way in town," Sheriff John said as he walked up to the homecoming from his police car parked in the street. His eyes took in the assembled and registered some disappointment, Evan knew why. He'd felt a little of same on not finding her here.

"They can be a bit much." Now that the Sheriff knew about all the folks associated, they no longer needed to express themselves using the local idiom. At least, not around him. "Need a cold one?" asked Evan glancing at the tree across the street to check the time.

"Well, I shouldn't..." replied the sheriff glancing at another side of the same tree.

"Everybody out back," commanded the lord of the house.

On the way through they grabbed water, wine, beer, and a bottle of the good stuff. If they were going to have a meet, they needed to prepare, which, of course, included a pouch of something to smoke and a pipe. Sheriff John had come to accept the ritual as part and parcel of their ways. Shit, it was just pot. As they each found a place of comfort—chairs, stools, upright logs or on the ground—they were surprised by an unknown heavy-set man as he lumbered up from the small river a quarter mile back of the house.

He smiled a hello, taking off his hat and wiping his brow in the midafternoon warmth. It was not hot for most of them, but he carried a great amount of extra padding which intensified the heat. His face drooped in an expression of sorrow, even though he smiled. It was as if the jowls around his cheeks and chin pulled his face down with them.

"Hello," he said in a very effeminate voice, "I am Chastity, I don't believe any of us have met. Who is Bear?" She, they all corrected their misconception—some chastising themselves of assuming—took in the assembled, apparently seeking one who appeared to be what she thought was a bear. None knew of her or whom she represented, and that she was one of the People none doubted. They could feel her. Bear would act as liaison as he was whom she sought.

"I am Evan, Bear," he corrected himself, "and whom do you represent?" he held out a cordial hand.

"I am of the sea and often mistaken for human. From a distance," she smiled, "I am what they call a Manatee."

"And what do you prefer to be called?" Evan ever the polite host.

"Chastity," she grinned a humorous reply.

Evan pulled up a picnic table bench for her to sit on. "Where are my manners, this is my wife and grandchild, Rebecca and Alexandra," an intake of breath for the congregation as none, including Alex, had ever heard Evan actually speak Her name, he grinned his own humor, "of course I knew She had a name." He dismissed their shock, "this is our good Sheriff, John, Glen here is Dog, and this is Doe, a deer. I don't know where our dear Suzette is but you will certainly meet her." That was the gist of them, ", Please tell us why you came all this way."

"You know how word spreads among the People," she began to nods of assent, "I'd heard you were discovering something we have known about for quite some time. We are all being affected in a negative way by the encroachment of man, either by destroying habitat, hunting, or stupidity. We, the People of the Sea, thought maybe I could help by sharing our experiences and learning what you are attempting to do."

Evan was pleased that she only gave quick facts, not embellishing, so they could evaluate her usefulness to whatever they might be proposing. She sat back and waited as Evan considered her proposition.

He, of course, wanted any help anyone could bring. One way to best use that help was to consider what each brought to the table and how best to use all those available resources.

"It would appear I, especially, am late to the party. I had known of the troubles of my Polar cousins to the north but had hoped it was temporary and minor. I am as guilty of not heeding the signs as the humans, it would seem." His shame and embarrassment couldn't, or wouldn't, be hidden from the others. He was the protector of the People and their children. He should have been cognizant of what was happening to the Mother and stepped up sooner. Though what would he have done?

Until the recent—and to an immortal a couple of decades was very recent—rending of the universe brought about by the death of his mate and his reaction, he and his cousins had very limited interaction with each other. Maybe by some weird quirk of fate, that disturbance, and their coming together because of it, would be what might save them. They all now understood if they were to survive and one day thrive again, they would have to rely on each other, and help all, working together to balance life on the Mother. It was possible they could join forces and find a way to stop the killing of their people without killing off those who unknowingly, or uncaringly, were destroying the balance.

"We need to do us some deciphering and discoverin' of what all has been done and to who and how much. As Chastity has shown by her appearance today, this is not restricted to the land, but also to the sea, and that would mean, also to those who ride the winds, we need information," Bear gazed at each to accentuate the point.

"Excellent," Rebecca patted her husband's arm, "but you're a little behind in the 'let's get to it' category. We are already seeking information, contacting those not here. Doe has sent out messages to the land people, Tatanka, Elk, Willow and such. Alex is talking with Iktomi's people and the others of the insect realm, Suzette was to contact those of the seas," and here she took a quick glance towards, Chastity who shrugged her lack of meeting or knowledge of the Otter, "and I am handling those of the air. Though my resources seem a bit limited, I have had a word with Eagle. And that, my dearest love, is where we stand."

Bear looked abashed, "Wow, I really am behind the curve here, though I do have Sung coming and he is bringing as many of his people who will follow. I have invited our own to come as well." He indicated the inclusion of Alex and Rebecca, both of the Bear clan. "I've talked to the Sheriff and he is willing to do his best to help calm the fears of ranchers and townsfolk alike, but we are going to have to help provide food so no one feels the need to hunt. Well, not any more than absolutely necessary. We don't need a war amongst the People again."

"We are going to need far more than assembled today." Bear looked at his little army that could, taking stock. "Chastity, can you contact more from the sea from here? Or do you need to be in the water to communicate? And can you survive this far from the ocean?" Bear knew he was showing his ignorance of a cousin but he required knowledge and if that meant sacrificing a little pride and ego, so be it.

"We are one of the very few species that can live in either salt water or fresh. I was sent because of that and since in either incarnation I can breathe, survive, for long periods of time. Though I prefer the weightlessness of the water," she grinned patting her enormous belly, "far more comfortable with a little assistance to offset gravity. But, yes, I am here to help and contact with my people and those of the sea is possible from the river out back."

"Then we all work together. As you all seem to have this end under control, or at least moving in the right direction, you don't need me." He said to his wife and granddaughter, pride and love filling each word. "I want to have a meet with John and go over my ideas on how to handle the humans when it comes to an invasion, no matter how small of wolves and bear. Probably be a good idea to contact the Cat families as well. We don't need a war over territory which is about to shrink in size."

Evan didn't notice if the others took note of his leaving—they had immediately begun to engage in their own plans and how to gather information more efficiently—and it didn't matter, he had a mountain of work and smoothing over of fear to do, before Sung arrived with the packs and his children ambled their way in. They had to save as many species as possible if they were to revive the health of the Mother. And that was another thing, he needed to get up into the mountains and find her to assess how bad off the Mother was. Too many problems and a dearth of solutions. He needed a beer. Maybe he could stop off for one before meeting up again with the sheriff.

Sheriff John was back in his office doing whatever paperwork small town sheriffs needed to do, Evan knew, because he had told Evan that was where he was headed. The two embraced as if they hadn't seen each other in years, though truth be told, it had only been a couple minutes, but friends were friends.

"You kinda got me in a pickle here," the Sheriff began as Evan made hisself comfortable.

"Well, don't have to be, if'n we handle it right. Now I got Sung's solemn promise," he said before John shushed him down. He may not need to affect the local idiom around the Sheriff but he did out of respect for the man.

"Now, damnit Ev, you know and I know what we both know about Sung—or what I think I know though have a hard time believin'—but to convince the townsfolk, and especially the ranchers, that he can control the packs, well," he scratched himself all along his balding head, almost as if trying to get a thought planted and hoping for a good crop.

"What I'm thinking," now it was Evan's turn to do some shushing, "is, what if I buy some cattle, I dunno, maybe a hundred head. Some from each of the local boys, spread a little green around, with a promise if they lose any more, I'd cover the costs of that as well. Would they be more likely to get on the wagon with the rest of us? Hell, tell 'em it's a government program, from the feds, maybe they'll think twice about refusing or interfering if they think the big guys are paying for this."

"They might, but you'd have to come up with the cash 'fore hand and put it where it can't be touched by anybody but them's they trust, the local bank or farm bureau, with signed guarantees against loss. And that would leave you wide open if they decide they lost more'n they got." He put his feet up on the desk as if to keep them out of the pile he was smelling as it grew where they sat.

"Course there would have to be an accounting, signed, legal like by all parties. We could use Louis, down the bank, he's 'bout as close to a city accountant we got round here ain't he?" Evan nodded his head in the direction of the one bank in town, "folks trust him, don't they? And I'll have that fella Oscar act as the government man, he's just odd enough people'd be more inclined to believe. "

"Yeah, I guess so. Louis'd be a goodun 'cause you're right, folks known him a long time, if we can get him on board, they'd be more disposed to come along. But where you gonna come up with that kind of cash? 'Specially without nobody knowin' the where or how of it?" The sheriff knew Ev was not a rich man, hell, he wasn't really a man, come to that. He had that house, but he would never sell that not even to save the world. It had been one of the only things that kept him alive when She died. 'Course She was back now; another thing John just couldn't rectify in his head. This kind of stuff just didn't happen and yet, it had.

"Don't worry about me and the money, money don't mean nothing to me and mine, we'll come up with it once a number's been settled on. Will they go for it?" That was the crux of it all, if he was going to have to fight the town while trying to save the Mother, one of them was going to lose. And he couldn't afford for it to be him. But he didn't want the town to suffer neither. Shit, he needed a beer.

"I think they will, though they're going to be awful concerned about the safety of the kids, and womenfolk, and dogs and such," John counted them off on his fingers.

"Shit, ain't been a human killed by a wolf since at least 2005, we just got to make sure it don't happen here, simple." Evan shrugged and grinned as if he believed it, but it would up to Sung to get across to them if they wanted to survive as a species, they would have to control their aggressions. Simple. Evan knew they were not stupid, or dumb, animals but quite clever, smart. They would understand it if it was explained by their protector. And he had some of his own coming, maybe they could act as security, he grinned to hisself.

"I'm going down the street for a beer, want one?" he knew, but manners triggered the question.

It was the middle of the afternoon and he figured the bar would be practically empty and he figured right. Just the one fella down't end of the bar with a beer and a short one in front of him. Evan was pretty sure the fella hadn't moved in almost twenty years. He wondered if the guy was still alive.

Meg popped her pretty little head out of the back room at the sound of the door closing and smiled a great grin before running over to him and grabbing him in a bear hug. "Where you been? I've missed seeing you, thought you'd start coming 'round again now that yer back from the dead. Been what? Almost ten years since you showed up again, right?" She was grinning as if her favorite grandpa just walked in after not seeing her in forever. Yeah, she was happy.

"Been kinda busy livin'," he laughed, "and getting used to my new life, though kind of the same as the old life, only better."

She opened the beer and set it on the bar in front of him, he nodded his thanks and pointed at the lone afternoon bon vivant at the other end of the bar. She smiled and went to refresh the glass and bottle.

It was a quiet place, except for a short vacation from sanity, he chuckled to hisself. He should pop in a bit more regular, not regularly, just stop for a pop now and again. There was a lot to be said for a quiet place to sip on a cold one while life moved at its own pace outside. Like an oasis of peace in a crazy world. Keep the TVs tuned to something non offensive or thought-provoking, sports was always good for that, and you sit for hours and never find yourself worried about the state of world affairs. Or your own, for that matter. Yes, every town should have a beer joint with a good barkeep, a decent juke, turned down so you didn't need to shout your order, a damn good burger and quiet.

The door swung open on rusty hinges and the scree of metal on rusty metal pulled the eye to the offending. Some sounds cannot be ignored and this one grated on the nerve to the center of the cerebellum. Evan took the requisite peek and hung his head with the cliché standing at the entrance, staring right at him.

"Hey Frank," might as well meet this nuisance head on. "Been a while, thought you'd found greener pastures to shit in." Well, good manners only got you so far, and Evan was just not in the mood for this. What had it been? Almost twenty years since this mountain decided to block the sun on his life. And the guy hadn't aged a day. Hmm, that was an interesting point. Someone had been keeping their antagonist in prime condition. This could not possibly be coincidence. The universe didn't work that slick.

"Well, I'm back now," the idiot grinned and made to move toward Evan.

"You got a bad memory? Don't you remember what happened last time? Got your feelings and body hurt before you took off like a scared kitten. Why you want to come back and start up where you left off? Why don't you just go back out that door and back under whatever rock you crawled out from?" Yup, Evan was in no mood for this and if the big, dumb ox wanted to dance again, Evan would punch his card. She'd be pissed but maybe he wouldn't tell Her.

"Maybe things won't go like you remember them, this time. Maybe I can take my payback one ounce at a time," he cracked his knuckles, it was an immature and annoying habit that he, apparently, couldn't break himself of.

"And maybe you should just close yer trap and let a fella drink in peace," came from the quiet man down at the end of the bar.

Evan didn't know who was more shocked, him, Meg, the guy or the mountain, but a feather hitting the floor would've sounded like a bomb.

"Damn, every time you show your ugly face in this joint a fella can't hear himself not think. So, shut the hell up, go someplace else and let the rest of us enjoy some quiet," the words thrown, he downed the brown liquid with one gulp and glared at the mountain, challenging him.

Evan knew he had to do something or this guy was going either to the hospital or the morgue, and he didn't want either. "Looks like you ain't welcome here," Evan made to stand up until he felt the hand on his shoulder. His fellow imbiber stood next to him, steady as Pike's Peak, he smiled as he pushed Evan back onto his stool.

"I got this."

He stood no more than five and half feet as he planted himself in the path of the rolling landslide and pointed at the door. Big Frank barked one huge guffaw before he reared back to knock this pipsqueak into the next month. As he came with a roundhouse the little fella ducked under it and flicked a quick whip action at Frank's groin and the mountain crumbled.

As the little man made his way back to his bottle and empty glass, "You ain't the only one been in a war," he muttered to Evan as he passed him, "Vietnam, 67 to 70, three tours. And a little Taekwondo." He quietly took his seat and motioned for Meg for a refill. Even threw two twenties on the bar and smiled, Meg knew.

Evan took the long way home, stopping by the Sheriff's office to inform the man that he had a sewage problem in his town and he should be aware of it. He whistled as he made his way back to the craftsman.

"You look like a bear about to break into the Bear dance," Rebecca said as he strolled out back. "I can assume things went well with the Sheriff?"

"Well enough," he kissed her check and took a deep breath of her scent while closing eyes and holding that fragrance as long as breath would stay in him. "anything happening here while I was out?"

"Yes, Suzette is back and she needs to speak to you, she said it was urgent and she wanted you here so she wouldn't have to repeat her news," She was worried, She had never been good at hiding what she was feeling or thinking, "it's not good news, she is extremely distraught."

"Yes, I am," came from the soft voice behind him.

The Darkest Hour

Dark clouds began to roll in from over the mountains bringing cold and rain, pushing down on all who would dare to be outdoors. The moods of Bear and company darkening in reflection of the weather as Suzette told her tale. It was a mirror of what they all had seen and heard from the People throughout this part of the world, and what they feared was the truth throughout the rest of the Mothers domain. Sickness, destruction of the habitat, babes still born or sick and dying soon after. The numbers were dwindling.

It was almost impossible for the gathered not to wallow in despondency, the news laid them low. How could humans not see what they were doing to their own home? How could they not feel the balance shifting dangerously out of control. This was as bad if not worse than when Evan had caused the crack. Reality was bending and the People were the only one's suffering. Or were they?

Humans had to be suffering as well, they were no different than the people, they were animals just the same. Were they not becoming sick? Were their babes not sick? Were they not dying? How could you watch your children die and not demand something be done? Had they become so callous, so obsessed with power, desire, greed they would sacrifice their own? To what God did they bow in obeisance?

Evan wanted an accounting; he would know if humans suffered as the fauna did. And if their children died in the womb or shortly thereafter, if they hungered and cried in the night, if the female's breasts were as devoid of milk as the Mother, why was nothing being done? He had to control his anger; he had seen what happened when he did not.

Suzette was drained by the end of the telling. Evan poured her a stiff bourbon to rejuvenate her spirits. She thanked him knowing it would do little but little was not nothing. She was always filled with life, vitality, love, and hope. It broke Evan's heart to see her lost in anger, despondency, bitter after seeing the condition of her children and those of the cousins. Rebecca sat next to her and pulled her into an embrace, rocking her like a child and murmuring reassurances and love. It was all she had; it was all any of them had.

Chastity had remained quiet, taking in all being said. She knew, she knew to the bone what these People were feeling, she had felt it for so long it was burned into her soul. "I feel in my heart your words. I hear them and know them as my own, we have lived them so long. My people once roamed all the oceans and seas, free, you could not travel anywhere and not be greeted. Now we hide in the shadows while humans race their boats through shallow channels and dump their excrement into our home. Maybe now that all see what is being done, we can join together and rid the Mother of this pestilence."

"No, if it is war you seek, you have come to the wrong camp." A crack of thunder and brilliant explosion of light seemed to put the exclamation point to Evan's words. "Not all humans are evil, not all are callous. Most, I would venture to say, suffer from a lack of being aware. They are wrapped in their own struggles and don't notice the needs of others. They desire empathy but don't know how to convey or receive." He shook his head as if the action might clear away that which stood in the way of a clear path. "No, we have to find a way to appeal to their sense of decency, family, love, the connection between all who live through the Mother."

"Well, then, maybe we need to consult the Mother directly." Alex had been quietly listening and taking in all being discussed. She felt the pain, the emotional distress of Suzette to her core, but she knew more suffering did not alleviate the current pain. She didn't know much about Chastity—hell, none of them did—but she didn't like the way her thoughts were going. "I know you've been hurt by humans, all of us have been, but violence is not the way. Hate begets hate. Violence only escalates and the score never evens out." Her tone was even, not filled with anger or vitriol, but the words were granite and carried much weight. Evan had never been more proud of his granddaughter than he was right now.

"I understand, we are peaceful people, sometimes, though..." she let it hang and then die.

"We understand," Evan picked up the thread, "it must be almost impossible to see your children killed, mutilated, all for nothing, for no purpose. But we discovered that violent reactions also serve no one. We hope you will lend your experience, your knowledge, your patience to the cause of us all."

Silence wrapped them all, time stopped as if they stood on the other side of the veil. No one would push the Manatee. They could all sense her grief as deeply as they could Suzette's. So, they waited, giving her time to calm her reaction.

"I am sorry, sometimes I let my emotions run rampant and the sight can be ugly. The unbearable pain clouds your thinking, you want retribution, your pound or ton of flesh, but nothing is solved, no healing comes from sending another into extinction. Please forgive my grief driven passion. Of course, I will lend my assistance to any plans you come up with, I am yours." She hung her already drooping features in shame.

"Leave us retire to the house," Rebecca's eyes never left the black clouds heading directly towards them. Everyone grabbed whatever item was closest to them and bolted for the safety of the home.

The storm pounded the landscape with rolling thunder, brilliant flashes of lightning, and pounding rain. The only occupants that weren't bothered by the torrential onslaught were Chastity, who lived in the water and so felt quite at home, and Suzette who could not seem to bring herself out of the deep depression brought on by the suffering of her children. She could feel it in her bones, to the core of her being, each one that passed due to stupidity and avarice stung like a deep knife wound. She could see her own extinction coming, a death by a million stings, with each passing cutting deep in her soul.

Rebecca could feel the woman's pain as she clutched Suzette's body close to her bosom, the couch shaking with each explosion of thunder. Suzette's children might be a thousand miles away but she could sense each child as if in her own lap. They might not be happening every second but they were occurring with some regularity. Oil spills, dumping of sewage, garbage, bilge water into their homes, making them uninhabitable. Killing off their food supply, dying by a thousand, thousand cuts of regulation. This had to be stopped, Suzette's thoughts and mood rode the storm, her anger building, righteous indignation took root and she wanted nothing more than to strike out at whoever or whatever was nearest to her.

As if sensing the rage boiling deep in her adopted Aunt's soul Alexandra planted herself on the floor at her grandmother's feet and wrapped Suzette in her arms. Rocking, humming a tuneless melody of love and support. Where the empathy came from the Mother only knew, but Suzette could feel the tension, the pent-up anger dissolve as if being filtered through Alex and her grandmother. The soft purring signifying her release and rest.

The storm subsided as Suzette calmed into sleep. Evan made a questioning eye contact with Doe, Chastity, Alex and Her, but their glances seemed to indicate it was all just coincidence. He might have agreed if the incidences of twenty years ago weren't so fresh in his mind. Could it be possible that the Spirit Animals had more power than they thought? Could their emotions contain a powerful medicine they were unaware of? As if reading his mind, Doe shrugged as she gave a small shake of her head, 'no'.

The knock on the door roused them all from their private reverie. Evan grinned welcome as the Sheriff, without waiting for response, let himself in. "Everybody OK here?" He took in the gathered, his eyes resting on the slumped figure of Suzette leaning against Her. "Mighty big blow, we have some wires down, utility trucks are on the way, tree branches blowed from here to hell, nothing too horrible, but enough to scare a few of the locals. We, as you know," he took in Evan and Alex, "don't normally get these kinds of storms, but they seem to be happening all over the country." He may have been speaking to all but his eyes never left Suzette.

There was a definite connection between the two, everybody could feel it. And though they may not be in favor of the relationship—again, Bear had almost destroyed the world with his heartbreak—they all knew it would not last forever, just a little happiness on the long immortal road. They both had earned some joy, no one wanted to be the one who tried to take it away.

"This happening all over here?" Evan snapped attention from where all had allowed it to go, his hand signifying the general area of their little town. "I don't recall big storms coming our way lately, just this one." He took in each for assurance, all seemed to be in agreement, though now his mind began a new trip down a different road than had brought it here. "what have I been missing?"

" Well, I might've misspoke a bit, not here, here, but all over the foothills and piedmont. Usually, the mountains protect us from big trouble, now it's running wild all along the front range. Actually, it is happening all over the world. It's like the weather's gone a little crazy. Reminds me of my ex," John shot a glance at Suzette, hoping it was alright to talk about another woman he had known a lifetime ago, she didn't seem to notice, curled up in the embrace and love of Her and Alex, "she was changeable as the weather, worse. No, it seems the weather is as changeable as her. No rhyme or reason, just calm to destruction. Places what never had big snows, floods, or devastating winds, now got 'em coming every other week, seems. Somebody is pissed and they're taking it out on the rest of us." He glanced at Evan and then the others to assure he had not offended by seeming to implicate Mother nature.

Unknowingly, Sheriff John had sparked an awareness of the Mother, though not in the way he thought. Now, all shared a knowing look. Evan, or maybe all of them, needed to hightail up into the garden in the forest and check on the Mother. Then, get as many as could come to a damn big pow wow and hash out some solutions or the whole damn world was going to go out either in a blast or just die off. Neither of which appealed to any of the assembled.

"Sheriff, you remember me telling you about Sung and our plan, don'tcha?" Evan knew time was of the essence, and for an immortal that was indeed a concern.

"Biker fella, good in a fight, yeah, I liked him, seemed an honest sort, why? Seems we set up a cattle buy for him and his packs, if I recollect. Wasn't easy convincing them ranchers and Louis at the bank but you ponied up a goodly sum, if I recall. He still coming, ain't he?"

"Yes, he's going to be showing up here within the week with maybe more'n a few packs of wolves in tow. As I told ya, they'll listen to him and he'll do his best to keep them out of everybody's hair. We got to run an errand and I need someone who kind of knows the lay of the land to make sure nobody messes with them. And can tell him where we've gone, though he will figure it out for himself, but just act as a liaison. Plus, you'll be in charge of hauling the cattle we'll need to keep them wolves fed. You still got yer trailer, dontcha?" Evan clicked off all the necessities on his fingers.

"Yeah, I'll do all I can. She going with you?" he asked nodding to Suzette, "she don't look too good, maybe she should stick here, I can keep an eye on her, make sure she's alright and took care of."

Evan knew, he understood, but it would be up to Suzette to decide if she wanted to stay or go. "We'll see how she feels tomorrow."

"I can stay with her, as well," Chastity threw in the pot, "I'm afraid I'm not much good where you'll be going. If my People need the Mother, she usually comes to visit us in our natural habitat. I'm not really a mountain creature," she looked abashed but truth was truth.

"I need to go," Suzette whispered, barely heard but understood.

John understood and he wanted to tell her 'NO' in no uncertain terms. He wanted to say, 'look at yourself, you can hardly stand. You cannot go where these others are headed.' He wanted to wrap her in his arms and give his strength, his love, his support, so she would know it was alright to stay here, just this once. She could let others carry the load just this once. But he respected her too much to stand in her way. He thought far too highly of her to treat her like some fragile child. He knew he would rebel with greater vehemence if someone did that to him.

His eyes, his face could not hide the love, yes, he realized, the love he had for her. Hell, they had never shared a kiss, held a hand, talked quiet in the night, but he knew. He also knew how impossible it was, he knew it could never be. They truly were two completely, as completely as two beings ever had been, different people. And it was shattering his heart. He could only hope she would come back in one piece, with her heart, her life, her joy intact.

He had no idea, or maybe he did, he had to admit, what all they would face in the future but he could see what was happening around him and the town, hell, the world. They was headed up into the mountains again, and he was pert sure there would be no violence, but the mountains held their own dangers, he knew. He scratched where the mountain lion had damn near ended his life. Still, he wanted to go, to protect, but his job was here. He was a man of honor and duty. He would do what was asked of him. He walked over to where she sat next to Her, reached for her hand, pulled her up into his embrace and whispered into her ear where only she could hear, "you come back, ya hear. You do what Evan tells you, you let them take care of you and you come back." He didn't trust his voice any further. He shook Evan's hand, they shared a deep, understanding look, he walked out the door to his car.

"I'd like to go, too." As usual they had forgotten Glen. He always faded into the background when all the commotion was happening, Just as he had at the bar, Evan thought. He was a good kid, and a wonderful Spirit for his people, but he was what he was and canines, once out of the needy puppy stage, tended to blend into the fabric of life, until they were needed. Then they could exert themselves as protector, playmate, love.

"I think I am going need you here to help hold down the fort," Evan knew before the thought formed in his head this would not go over well, Glen hated being left behind, if anyone was going anywhere, Glen wanted to go along. "I need you to be there to help the Sheriff. He tries to understand all of this but it just doesn't fit in his well-ordered mind. You have a connection to Sung no one else has. He really likes you and trusts you and he is going to need you as well." Evan hoped the promise of spending time with the Wolf—someone Glen truly admired and loved—would be the treat he could leave to lift Glen out of the funk that was coming with separation. "Sung will need your help," he reiterated, hoping it would lift Glan's spirit.

Glen nodded his head; he wasn't happy with the decision but he was overjoyed with the prospect of spending time with Sung. His eyes showed the turmoil of being left behind yet knowing he was being given a gift that he dearly wanted. Such is life.

Chastity, lost in thought, and for the most part now lost to the rest of them, made her way back to the small river that ran through the meadow behind Evan's house. She had never had much love for humans, they'd done too much damage to her children. She was a shadow of herself, her power diminished by the passing of so many, the survival of so few. Killed by recklessness, by uncaring. How could these others be so accommodating to this sheriff? It was obvious they held him in high regard, but why? He was not of the people. He was a white man, not even of the indigenous who had made the Spirits strong through their belief. No, he was of the light ones who took. They used their numbers and superior technology, not to benefit, but to subjugate, to enslave or eliminate those who stood in their way. Their way of ruling the entirety of the world. Yet, they all seemed to trust the man! Even the Otter, who should know not just from what they did to her people but to the humans the same color as she. Yet, she was obviously enamored of the man. Chastity needed the water, required time alone with her thoughts and the relief of the river.

She would allow the river to wash away her anger, her hatred of mankind, she would pray to the Great Spirit to absolve her of what she was feeling. But how could she not, the suffering had been centuries in the making, even though her people had helped man when he was lost at sea, when he would have died without her people to show them the way to safety. Man was unkind. The water flowed over her tired body. Her thoughts rode the current away from her.

Rocky Mountain High Relaxing

The mountains felt taller, steeper, working their muscles more than they should. The forests deeper, more copious, and more barren of game. The packs were beginning to snap and growl at each other as the hunger gnawed at their bones and guts. Sung had to find food, and quickly.

Usually, the forest this far from the tree line would be teaming with life this time of year. Where were all the rodents, rabbits, an elk, a deer? He wasn't asking for a banquet just something to settle the hunger of the, now, five packs assembled. It wasn't an army, fifty or so, but they had to be fed. The need to hunt visceral, as necessary as the consumption. They could eat what they scavenged, but they would not lower themselves for long

He heard them before he saw them, he scented them before he heard them, his stomach growled with anticipation long before he would sink in the first tooth. A small herd of elk making their way to autumn pasture to fatten up before the coming harsh winter. He moved ahead of the packs to recon and saw them, maybe thirty, with some elderly straggling behind. They wouldn't know there was a small legion of wolves tracking them until it would be too late. They could take the three fighting to keep up with the younger, stronger leads. They would be doing the old ones a favor, a quick honorable death. A death that would serve to keep others alive. And not just the wolves but the elk calves would benefit as well; scarce food would go further without the need to feed the dying. If the packs allowed the old and infirm to live, they would only endure pain and agony before they starved and finally froze to death. Yes, this was the way of the Mother, the way of nature and life, it was kinder.

He quietly growled and the others came to join him where his superior senses had found sustenance. He growled and yipped his order, to leave the front of the herd, concentrate on the three holding up the rear. It would provide plenty for all here and the others would live to provide another day. The packs moved as one, silently surrounding the old elk and with a howl attacked. It was quick, as painless as they could provide and filling for the victors. It would buy Sung another few days. It should be enough.

The terrain was beginning to have a familiarity to it, he'd come this way when the troubles had called all who could come to Bear's aid. Yeah, they were close. He only hoped Bear had everything in place so they could settle in. Bear had mentioned them settling in on the property behind his but Sung didn't like it. Too open, too flat, not good hunting ground, unless you were human in a truck or four-wheeler hunting wolves, then it was perfect. No, Sung had come by a pasture surrounded by thick forest halfway up a particular mountain just to the west of Bear's place. He told Bear about it and they agreed it should be far enough from town they would not be a threat to the townsfolk and the pasture would provide grazing for the cattle Bear was certain he could provide. Great plan, but plans had a way of sneaking up behind you and shoving good intentions up your ass.

Sheriff John drove his four-by-four up the logging road bouncing until he was certain his guts were going to come out either his throat or his ass. Pulling the long trailer behind wasn't helping the ride nor were the dozen nervous beef cattle mooing their discontent as they suffered the same jarring action. John prayed he could find the spot Evan and Sung had picked out, God knew it was far enough from the town and deep enough in the woods to avoid detection from any unless they stumbled across the damn cattle. But they were surrounded by a few million acres so he hoped, sometimes that's all you had.

He looked across the cab where Glen sat happy as could be, smiling at the joy of being out in the wilderness. If he was still upset about being left behind, he hid it well. The bouncing and jarring of the truck didn't seem to bother him one bit, he had his head out the window and laughed to beat the band. That was one happy kid. He gazed at the trees, the sky, the birds, and the varmints skittering through the forest. Kid just wanted to hop out of the cab and run. John didn't think he'd ever been that happy in his life.

He worried too much; he worried about Suzette. He worried because he really had no idea what the others were up to. He worried about his town. He worried that he was too old for this kind of shit. He worried that maybe other predators would come and attack the herd leaving Sung's experiment hungry and mean, but Evan had assured him. With a few packs of wolves wandering the territory, all others would stay away. One or two wolves and a bobcat or lynx might take a shot, a mountain lion would for sure take on a couple wolves, but a pack thirty or so strong, nothing would bother them.

John had had his run-in with a mountain lion, had the scars to prove it, but he had to believe even they would be smart enough to stay away. If the timing was right, John wouldn't have to remain up here more'n a day or two before Sung showed up. He could use the time alone. He had shocked himself by the depth of feeling he'd discovered within himself for Suzette. It wasn't that he thought digging a black chick was wrong, he just hadn't had any interest in any woman since the ex had left, taking the boy with her and anything she could pack in the U-Haul.

He had his job, his town, and he was happy. And now he had a couple of new deputies he could trust. Fellas he'd know'd in the Navy and a former Navy Seal who decided she just wanted some peace after a lifetime in the service. Retired now and looking for a cushy gig where they could bang a couple heads, when necessary, and make new friends. They'd feel like they were still contributing to society, and have folks be happy to see them if they showed up at the local watering hole. They was good folks—one divorced, one widowed, one never been either—three contented human beings.

The logging road came to an end in a 'man-made' pasture. The loggers had clear-cut the area and never replanted. Stumps, like headstones, popped up out of the tall grasses and prairie flowers. It was purty in a sad way, but he could be happy here with just him, the kid, and the cattle for a couple days.

The air was filled with the scent of forest, pine, dirt, pure mountain air, scat, decay, life, and death. It reminded him of his childhood running through these mountains. It amazed him the power of the memories, the strength of the pull on his emotions. How he had forgotten how much he loved being, almost, alone in the mountains.

It mattered not one iota that these same mountains had tried to kill him a few times. He'd been lost when a freak snowstorm came through and had to hole up for a couple days in cave that was not much more than an indentation in the rock. Another time he got lost up near the tree line, took almost a week to find his way back down and home, his folks thought he'd been staying at a friend's house. And then there was the mountain lion, he scratched at the memory of the maddening itching while the wound healed. He loved these mountains and longed for this time in them.

They found a flat where they could park the truck and unload the cattle. They'd have to be cattle boys until Sung showed up, protecting and keeping the herd together in the general area. He almost wished he'd've brought along a horse. Problem was, he didn't have one, hadn't rode one in since he was a teen—weird, he thought as he had lived his life in cattle country—and the thought of sitting in a saddle for a couple days made his ass throb. Besides, cattle were open-range kind of animals, they got skittish when they couldn't see their neighbor a quarter mile away, the dense forest surrounding the man-made hole in woodland would act as a fence to keep them within sight.

Nope, they had the extended cab, one could sleep in the front, one in back with the stars for a rook and the silence for a pillow. If shit was about to start again, he would clutch every bit of peace he could find before it did.

It was dawn of the third day, with boredom having taken up residence in the camp right next to them, that they heard the howls. Still a distance away, the wolves were giving directions to where Glen and John sat. Glen was a good companion, he didn't talk much, would engage if engaged first, was happy to just stare at the night sky and did his chores without complaining. John found he required more camaraderie from his fellow humans. The howls were welcome.

They increased in timbre, as they decreased in distance. John could feel the tension increase with anticipation. Would Sung really have the ability to rein in several packs of wolves and protect Glen and the sheriff? Evan sure seemed to believe he could. 'Course, Evan wasn't here, now, was he?

The first wolf stuck its head out between tree and bush, tongue lolling out the right side of its mouth. It stared hard at the cattle for the briefest moment before turning its attention to the man sitting on the open tailgate of the truck.

John sat motionless wishing he knew exactly where Glen was, hoping the kid would be aware the gang was coming in. Glen wasn't stupid and he knew why they were there, he would be cautious, his senses sharp and his eyes wide-open or so John hoped. John sensed him before he heard the sound of boot on rock, Glen was on the driver's side of the truck making his was, slowly, towards where John sat. Good.

Two more wolves crept out of the timber, a third coming in from the right, a big one, over a hundred pounds easy if John was any judge, black as the inside of a well at midnight on a moonless night. John, Glen, and the cattle were surrounded. If Sung didn't show up and get this under control soon, soon would be too late.

The cattle caught the scent and began pacing, kicking up dirt, snorting, bellowing distress, stampede stamped on each cow. Though as they looked for escape, they were hemmed in by the dense woods. Things were feeling tense and about to explode when the biggest wolf John could imagine strutted out into the clearing.

It was lean, hunger filled its eyes, but there was more, though thin it was well-muscled, this would be the Alpha and, John hoped, Sung. He was shocked that he thought it, he still had never completely come to terms with the thought all his closest friends were Native Spirit Guides from ancient lore. Glen took off like a shot directly toward the huge canine.

The other wolves growled, snapping their jaws, making to intercept when the great wolf snarled, backing them off. As Glen jumped to hug the beast the air shimmered, John rubbed his eyes, and there stood Sung with Glen hugging him and slapping him on the back, huge grin planted firmly on his face.

John was shocked by Sung's appearance. Not because he had actually witnessed the change from wolf to human but by how thin he was. He still had the cut of the biker John had met, but the girth was gone, his face sunken, his clothes hung on the man. John swore he could almost see through him, as if he was disappearing. He did his best to hide his astonishment, though Sung was still as sharp as ever and he saw.

"Yeah, been a bit of trip down here," he joked still hugging Glen close, "and things were getting a bit slim before we began, but I managed to bring close to a hundred with me," and now he more resembled the cock-sure biker dude that had become a friend. Pride in accomplishment could fill out a man, as surely as a good meal. He eyed the cattle lowing as far from the gathering wolves as the forest would permit. "Those for us?"

"Yeah, but from what I see," Sheriff John sighed, "looks to just be a down payment."

"We'll not be greedy," the slender wolf said, "but damn it is a gift that will be greatly appreciated." He licked his lips. "We'll make them last as long as wolfly possible. None of them will die in vain. I know this might seem a bit barbaric, but it is nature. These animals serve no other purpose but food, either for you and yours or me and mine. I guess that's why I could never get why ranchers were so selfish. Man, they got tens of thousands of these and we only would take a few, but they hate us anyway. Shit, we left them alone, and their families. Shoulda been enough."

"I get it. Well, you eat your fill, that's why Ev bought 'em. We ain't here to judge, we're here to help." John called to Glen to join him in the truck, last thing he wanted was the boy getting a taste for fresh kill. He'd know'd dogs that would pack up as sure as any wolves, he wanted to keep the kid pure. And he knew he should quit thinking of the kid as a kid, but some things take time.

The two sat in the cab while the wolves picked out a half dozen of the cattle. It should be plenty to satisfy them for the time being. Wolves didn't need to eat every day, so he hoped this would tide them over for a bit. But he was going to be busy making runs up here if Evan didn't come up with some kind of plan besides spending every nickel on beef cattle.

Evan and the others returned to the spot where he and Alex had hung out, talking, and waiting for the Mother. He reminisced about taking her on the trip around space and their walk on the beach. The walk where he discovered she was more like him than he had ever thought. It was up here on this outcropping they'd sat really getting to know each other that the Mother had taken over Alex. That one had upset Evan more'n he'd thought. The remembering still brought a pang of anger and appalled him that she would do such a thing. He understood why, he just didn't like the doing.

Now, he was up here with Rebecca, Alex, Doe, and Suzette. And she weren't doin' too well. She rode him most time, not much room for awkward or shame when you're feeling poorly, especially when you coulda stayed home. He knew she felt in her heart she needed to be with them, she was a stubborn one, but he also knew the shock she had endured seeing the condition of so many of her children. As Spirit Guides and the protector of their tribes they did their best to watch over, but sometimes the lives they watched over, both animal and human, got a bit chaotic and you lost track of time. Especially when time was not in your normal lexicon.

And who knew the weather would get so out of hand, that pollution would affect so many, that man would be so damned irresponsible. He wanted to let them all stew in the shit hole they had dug for themselves, but he'd have to let his own suffer along with, and he was in no mind to do that.

Somehow being up here with these folks, his family—and yeah, they were family all—he just couldn't hate nobody. If they had learned nothing from the craziness before, it was that they were all connected,

Mitakuye Oyasin, we are all related, cousins. He would inform his people that Deer were off the menu, most didn't eat much meat anyway, just the black bears, but he didn't want them going after Doe's people, or Otter's for that matter. From this time forth unless you came across a carcass or one who would be better off with a quick kill, you leave them be. He knew the Mother made them what they were, but that don't mean a man, or a bear, can't change its ways.

Time stood still up here in the forever, they could afford to rest, take in the beauty, be a family and try to let Suzette heal a little before they found the Mother. He required to assess what her condition was, confer with her, and make plans to stop the insanity of man.

Getting to Know the Odd Side of The Family

Oscar pulled up in front of the craftsman. He would've preferred to have flown, but there were the humans to consider. Can't scare the normals when you hope they will be of some use. Though after the fiasco of trying to find where they'd left their 'getaway' vehicle out in the hinterlands of Arkansas, he had considered just leaving them to their own devices, but it was not the way an avian behaved. These two were not exactly Daniel Boones in the woodlands. All trees DO NOT look the same! And they had been lost for almost a day seeking said vehicle while dragging the chains with them, as Anna Marie refused to leave any litter in the forest.

And then he spent the next three days in the same cramped vehicle, of course it was a subcompact, with these two chuckleheads, he was ready to eviscerate both of them. She refused to drive over fifty-five miles per, as she was trying to save the planet by increasing her mpg's from thirty-four to thirty-six, while they bickered about finding vegan or just vegetarian. One would give her the runs, the other was almost impossible to find in the south.

He could have grasped both of them, one talon each, and flown them here in two hours. But they would've flipped out, screamed, struggled and he would've had to let them go from an inordinately high altitude. Well, he corrected himself, he wouldn't have had to, but he would've anyway.

The house looked empty, shades drawn, no sounds, no scent of a decent meal cooking, nothing. He knocked to no answer, rang the bell to an empty echo before deciding to check around back. Nothing, nobody, deserted.

He was about to head back out front and see if the two environmental warriors had extricated themselves from the car when he spotted an overweight man shuffling up from the property behind Evan's abode. He was not familiar in the least, but there was something, a familial kind of feeling emanating from the fellow. If he wasn't one of The People, then Oscar had lost his Owl Sense. As the massive creature closed the gap, Oscar doffed his chapeau and called out, "Hello, I'm seeking Mr. Beach, you wouldn't happen to know his whereabouts, would you?"

"They have all gone off on errands to save the world, I was left to let the sheriff and anyone else know, I have done so," it was a woman's voice and Oscar had to reacquire center.

"So, will he be back soon?" Apparently, information was a valuable commodity and he was going to have to work for each morsel. Speaking of which, he was starved, Owls do not abide a vegetarian diet and the sight of him gobbling insects or the odd mouse or bird would probably have been off-putting to the hippies he had collected.

"Hard to say, though I dare say Glen, their rescue pup, should be back soon, he has only run up to the mountains with the sheriff for a couple days and it has been just about that long." Huffing gulps of air from the exertion of walking up from, well, somewhere, she sat on the elongated picnic bench.

"Shall we wait then?" Mayhap he could leave the annoyances with this fine woman while he took a little feed break out of sight of the humans.

"We?" She asked suspiciously.

"Yes, I have a couple companions," and the commotion of them arguing around the corner of the house announced their entrance, "Brian and Anna Marie." He waved a hand at the two young, radical, zealots apparently on a mission to discover where he had gotten to.

They waved a tired, half-hearted hello as they made their way to where she sat and flopped down on the ground rather than take the chairs available.

"Could you do me a small but remarkable favor," Oscar sidled up next to the large woman, "unless I am very mistaken you are one of us," he winkled conspiratorially, "and as I have dragged these two half-way across the country and therefore have not eaten in several days," again the wink with nod added to be certain she would understand the problem at hand, "I just need a little time to be myself and find something to eat."

"I'm sorry, I am not quite understanding what the problem might be," either she was not what he thought or was dense as a post.

"I couldn't eat what the umanshays did and could not etlay emthay see atwhay I eat," he nudged her with his elbow.

"Are you having a stroke? Do I need to call someone or thing to aid you?"

Geez, lady, he wanted to scream what the hell is wrong with you? Instead, "I am of The People and they don't know about us, I can't let them see me transform to myself so I can eat or they will shit their pants," he whispered in her face.

"Why didn't you say so? Of course, I shall babysit the children while you go kill something to fill your belly," how could one person be so judgmental to one of their own kind. Oscar did not care. He was hungry and everyone on the Mother seemed intent on making him crazy. He needed some Oscar time!

"I have to run an errand you will be fine here until I get back. This is," well, he hadn't a clue who this is and stopped in his rhetorical tracks.

"Chastity, I am a Manatee," she said right in front of the norms.

"How exciting! You're on the endangered species list, did you know?" Anna Marie was fully engaged, as if it was the most natural statement anyone had ever made to her.

And with that Oscar made his exit.

"So, you're really a Manatee or were you just messing with that guy?" Anna Marie asked, a coy smile playing around her lips indicating she got the joke; in case it was. "He's wound a little tight, if you ask me, but he did get us here, wherever that is." A nervous laugh escaped unsure lips. Anna Marie wasn't certain what was going on but she didn't want to upset the applecart, number one, and number two always best to humor those with visions of grandeur or otherwise. Besides, how this woman identified was none of her business, she had dabbled in sexual eccentricities once or twice herself.

"I am the Spirit Guide of the Manatee, what you see is my human manifestation so I may fit into your world and function without you knowing," She grinned and her eyes disappeared in the wrinkled countenance her smile caused raising her jowls.

"I don't think I quite understand," said the very liberal human not wishing to upset a member of another race or species. She was dead set against racism, speciesism, or any ism or phobias and she would swallow her horror or discomfort to prove it to anyone. She did not see color, sexual orientation, sexual identity, size, physical or mental challenges, religion, she hardly saw humanity, just a blank slate defined by political beliefs, morality (hers), values and acceptance of others as equals. She was superior to none, and that was where she based her belief in being better than most.

"We, The People," she gave a wave of her arm to include all who were not there as she was the only representative of a vanishing race, "are the spirit guides of the original people of this planet. We aid those who believe, watch over our own children, heal with knowledge, teach by example and lesson, we are the true first nation, the very first inhabitants of the Mother."

Anna Marie's blank expression betrayed her complete lack of knowledge of the indigenous peoples of the North American continent and their beliefs. Strange for someone who claimed such deep liberal roots, it was usually the first, and easiest, step into liberal philosophy. But she believed, and here was her leap of faith, that what the woman was trying to say is she was a teacher, a guru, swami, a Rabbi, if she remembered anything about the few weeks she had converted to Judaism.

An exasperated sigh before Chasity aksed, "Are you familiar, at all, with Native American beliefs? How the Mother was created and then created all the children? Their concept of spirit guides? Any of it?" Chastity was tiring of this game. She assumed, and we all know how that usually turns out, that all knew of the spiritual beliefs of the first nations. Ah, well. "I believe Mr. Beach," best tread lightly with the uninitiated, "has some books inside that will explain better and more thoroughly than I." With great effort she rose from the bench and shuffled her way towards the rear door, Anna Marie and Brian being dragged along in her wake.

After staring at the children's book for several minutes Anna Marie's eyes traveled to where the corpulent woman stood patiently waiting for the information to process and register in the child's brain. Anna Marie smiled, it was not in humor or because she got it, it was because she feared the woman must be insane and she didn't want to do or say anything that would incite a violent reaction. Identifying as binary or male/female, was one thing, believing yourself to be a supernatural spirit creature was beyond the pale.

Brian sat next to his ersatz girlfriend/revolutionary not comprehending a thing. He just couldn't see that the material in this obvious 'young reader' had anything to do with reality or Chastity. Or, especially, them. These were fables, tales, myths and legends, they had nothing to do with reality. They were the stories of uncivilized, primitives. Why should they care? And the light began to glow as the winds of change blew on the spark of recognition and understanding.

"Wait," he giggled conspiratorially, "are you trying to get us to believe that you are one of these?" He pointed at the pictures in the book which she couldn't see but knew and thought of Oscar and what he'd said back in the forest. Were all these people going to be nuts?

"Actually, I don't care what you believe, truth is truth. That is who I am, as are those who reside here and, as a matter of fact, Oscar, with whom you rode across the country to get here is the human manifestation of Owl."

The bang of the back screen door announced the entrance of another player on this undulating stage of fairyland.

"Well, have we all been getting along swimmingly?" Oscar, having fed on whatever he had caught, was now in a more positive and gleeful frame of mind.

"Where in the fuck have you brought us?" Young Anna Marie found her voice.

"Hmm, it would appear someone has been speaking out of school or certainly to the wrong grade level," he glared at the Manatee.

"Sorry, I thought they knew or had some kind of clue. I know you said they didn't know who we were but I assumed you meant specifically." she glared back haughtily, "and if they didn't, when were you going to inform them?"

"OK, this game has gone too far," Anna Marie made to get up from her seated position and bolt for the nearest exit.

"Just settle down, no need to fly off the handle, this can all be clarified, and completely normalized," Oscar was imploring with hand motions for her to remain seated, though Anna Marie was having none of it. And he realized almost instantly there was probably no way to 'normalize' anything at this point.

"You brought us to this insane asylum, for what? Because we were trying to save one of the last Maple-Leaf Oaks on the planet, we are not insane! We," and here she finally seemed to remember Brian was her partner in all this, "are attempting to save this planet and all who reside here before the corporate bastards destroy everything. We will not have our pure intentions toyed with nor mocked. Certainly ,we will not be put under observation. We are leaving!" And she made for the front door and her awaiting chariot.

Chastity, though not quite certain exactly what was happening knew she might have made a faux pas and wished to correct any misconceptions, stood, blocking the exit to any other room. Also, there had been something about the way the young girl child had said 'under observation' that screamed for attention. "Please sit," she commanded, "and we shall endeavor to sort this all out." She was large of proportion and larger still of domination. All returned to their previous positions. Really, they had no other choice. While the human manifestation was of a peaceful, serene creature, she could be quite intimidating.

"Oscar, please inform me of any and all pertinent facts you may have conferred on these two innocents," both Brian and Anna Marie relaxed slightly knowing that, at least, someone in this nut house knew them to be innocent!

"I was hoping the others would be here and between all could explain who we are, what we are, or how these two pure of heart environmentalists could come to our aid. They are truly committed to what they do and we need an army of them, if we are to succeed in the same endeavor as they have immersed themselves." He attempted to say what he was attempting to avoid saying.

"Well, that's not going to help," she flipped a finlike hand to indicate his long-winded avoidance. "We will need absolute honesty here, and apparently I am to be the purveyor of such." She smoothed out imagined wrinkles in an imagined dress, "you two will need to open your minds to alternative realities you may have never considered."

"Is this going to involve drugs?" Oscar couldn't tell if Brian feared or hoped.

"No," Chastity thundered, "though if recollection serves Bear might have a short supply of the weed about somewhere."

"No," now it was Anna Marie's turn to put the kibosh on the idea, "we need our wits about us to know if truth abides!" She wasn't certain where the term came from—a movie, maybe—but it seemed to fit the occasion. "What is it you are trying to get us to understand or believe, or whatever. Are you trying to tell us you truly are some kind of magical beings who come from the spirit world to stop the destruction of earth by humans and you need our help?"

"Kind of," Oscar shrugged his shoulders with an 'eh' kind of expression.

"Well, why didn't you say so instead of dancing around the truth? If that's all this is then we're in! Now, where's the pot?"

Oscar and Chastity just stared at the two and then each other. "So, you buy into the fact that we are not human but Animal Spirit guides and you're OK with that?" He had to know.

"Sure, why not? We've bunked with some pretty weird characters and marched, protested with some of the most off the wall freaks you can imagine. You want to be spirit animals, we're down with that!"

Anna Marie got up to go see if there was anything in the kitchen worth eating or if she would have to graze out back.

"True dat," quoth Brian hard on her heels.

"Well, that went better than I thought it would," Oscar said with a lack of conviction, "We have a couple human contacts who can help us enlist more, I think."

Of Hopes and Dreams and Plans

Big Frank sat on the picnic table absently chewing on his meat and cheese sandwich, he took a swig from the pocket flask that was his constant companion. He should've been more concerned the boss would catch him, he could lose his job, his pension, yet he couldn't seem to make himself care. He just sat and stared at the mountains in the distance. Something was pulling his attention hard like a magnet and his eyes was the iron. There was something going on up there and it was all he could do not to hop in his truck, say fuck it all, and drive up there to see what it was.

Which was funny, the thought niggled at the back of his almost empty mind, he'd never much cared for the great outdoors and specially them mountains. He'd got himself lost up there when he was not much bigger than a tree stump, just wandered off into that forest while his folks picnicked at a campsite. Walked through them woods for a couple days trying to find a way out, but every Goddamn tree looked like every other Goddamn tree, and every stream run through the same spot of forest. He never knew if'n he was going in circles or the forest was trying to et him. Either way, he hated it.

On the third day he saw that big tan dog sniffing around trees and bushes, like it was looking for something, or someone, so he followed it. Didn't seem to notice him, though every once in a while, it would turn as if to make sure he was on its tail. They walked like what seemed forever. He remembered thinkin' at one point, maybe it's taking me somewhere where it can kill me and eat me. He didn't care, he was tired of being lost, tired of walking, just damned tired.

Yet, he knew, deep in him, that that damned scruffy thing wouldn't hurt him, it was like as they was connected somehow. Like the dog was leading him to freedom. Or death. Either way, this bullshit was gonna end. Damn dog disappeared just as they come out the woods. He sat on a rock hoping that thing would come back and play with him, instead it was a State Trooper what found him, took him home where his pa whooped his ass for making him miss work, got his ma all riled, and got the whole state searching for his dumb ass.

He never forgot that dog.

And the dog never forgot him. Coyote used to come round just to see how that kid was faring. Right up to the time everything had gone nuts because of Bear and his dead mate. For some reason Coyote'd forgot about the kid, lost his connection with him, couldn't sense him at all no more. It was weird one minute he coulda come right at the guy like an arrow, next it was like he was blind to the kid. Almost like somebody done come up and took the leash out of his hand and he was now invisible. He missed that kid, though he couldn'ta pointed him out in a police line-up, couldn't pull up a picture of him in his mind, like as someone was blocking his memories. Or maybe the kid just hit an age where Coyote had lost contact, it happened a lot with humans.

The two small animals hiding in the bushes smiled at each other. Nobody would ever guess they had been the nexus of all the troubles plaguing the earth. It wasn't that they were bad or evil, just tired of their treatment by the others. Soon or late a body gets done with being treated like they was low life forms just because of the way they was made. One sly and wily enough not to have to work too hard to fill its belly, the other ostracized because of the way it protected itself. You don't want the stink, don't mess with the black and white mink.

Big Frank's eyes were riveted to a spot he couldn't see up near the tree line. There were not thoughts running, skipping, or jumping through his head, just that spot. It called to him like the sirens of ancient Greece called to Odysseus. He didn't know what or why it called to him but it took every ounce of energy he possessed not to run all the way to the top of the mountain. Maybe once he got off work he'd go back to the double-wide, pack up some clothes and head up there. Hell, he'd hardly been out of the trailer since when? Damn, years, he'd been just between the trailer and work, never went out nowhere, never did much of nothing. Just sat in the lazy boy, drank beer and whiskey, and worked. Like he was waiting on something, maybe death. Damn!

He'd had these feelings of connection to something or someone outside his body since being lost in those same forests. The feeling had changed over the years until almost twenty years back when they had changed completely. Whereas he had felt the connection to something that watched over him, like a guardian angel, now the feel was more controlling. Even though he could sense it, know that it was no longer protective but antagonistic, he couldn't fight it. Certain people just pissed him off.

Like that old man at the bar. He had never met the guy before that day, years back, but every time he'd thought of him, saw him, or, especially, when he was in the same room, Big Frank's blood would boil and all he wanted to do was squash the sonofabitch. Something he had found to be far more difficult than he ever would have thought. 'Wonder whatever happened to that old sonofabitch,' the thought meandered but didn't stop to stay and blocking their latest run-in.

He stared hard trying to see what was up there, ten miles away, in them mountains.

Coyote stopped mid-step, something caught at his attention as he crept through the underbrush. He was seeking two things, Bear, and a bite to eat. He hoped to come across a little something, something someone had left behind. People thought he was lazy 'cause he ate what others left behind, but he always thought hisself an environmentalist, recycling what others left for garbage. He was doing the Mother a good turn by not leaving trash just laying around.

He'd heard tell the humans would toss out whole sides of meat just 'cause they was a wee bit out of date. In Coyote's world ain't no date on nothing but the growling in his stomach. Funny how he would feel hungry, 'specially on this side, he didn't need to eat, none of his kind did, guessed it was just habit. Just as he was 'bout to get to quittin' and head up the tree line he smelled something o're by the crik, perfect, he could get drink with his meal.

Someone had left the rear hock of an elk without even bothering to cover it up, just left it here like a dinner on a plate. It had been there for a spell but time only gave game some seasoning. The water was cool on his throat though not as refreshing as what Bear usually had in his hip pocket.

He knew Bear was up here in the high altitudes and he had to wonder what brought Bear back up to this side of reality. He had been sticking to the human side for more'n a decade, human time, and seemed content to do so. Now, here he was, and not alone. Something happened somewhere and it was about to latch onto Coyote's tail, 'less he could stop the blamin' 'fore it stuck to him like Skunk stink.

That's when the familiar tug caught at his attention. Just for a sec, not long enough to hone in on. It was somewheres down the mountain, that he could tell. Had the taste of someone he once knew, or pissed off or, something. And then it was gone. Well, he could think about it after dinner, while he went off in search of finding what he'd done when he ain't done nothin'.

Forest was quiet today, shit been quiet for months, like everybody done took off on vacation, or in search of food. So dry up here you wished there was a crik or pool around every copse of trees. He'd never seen anything like this and when you're an immortal, never is a long time. The weather was upside down and angry. Didn't know from one minute to the next if it was gonna try to blow you off the mountain, bury you in ten feet of snow, or try to burn your ass as you ran hell bent for water away from the fire tornadoes. Never, been like this and he hoped it'd never be agin, but only time would tell that. And when it come to time, he could see real good behind but couldn't tell what was around the next bend, and he'd like things to settle down. Him and his been taking a punishing between trying to survive and humans blaming them for every missing kitten or puppy. Yeah, they'd been hungry, but not that hungry.

He required a sit down with Bear. He hoped against hope Bear come supplied when he come up this way. Coyote hadn't had a sip nor a toke since the troubles. Shit, this can't be about that again, could it? They'd stopped the destruction of that town and the rest of the world, well, the others had, Coyote had kept in the background acting as reserves in case, well, you know. Shit, he couldn't even convince hisself he wasn't just a coward hiding behind the womenfolk. But that had all been cleared up, Bear had fixed what needed fixing, and everything was back to what had been. Or was it?

Coyote scented Bear, well, he scented the pot and knew Bear was close. All he had to do was follow the breeze.

They were sitting on the edge of an outcropping overlooking an infinite valley as the sun was deciding whether to drop the final half inch or so. Wouldn't make no nevermind to any of the assembled as they all could see just as well in the dark as in the light.

Bear was here with that pretty Otter, what the hell was her name? Suzette, yeah. Though she didn't look too good just laying on her back soaking up the days heat, a gift of the rock. Another pretty young woman was talkin' quiet with Bear's mate, if Coyote remembered her correctly from a few long days ago. But shouldn't she be dead? Oh, that's right, come back alive as can be and one of The People! Shit, he'd forgot. Now, how the hell did that happen? Only one Spirit guide per family but now Bear got two, no, wait a minute, the younger one watching over Otter, she was Bear too! How in all? Well, it weren't up to Coyote to figure the ways of the Mother and Great Spirit, just be hisself.

Bear noticed Coyote standing in the shadows of a tall pine taking in the scene. He looked confused and about to turn around when Bear called out to him, "Well, you gonna stand there countin' noses or come join us?"

Ain't no turning back now, he straightened hisself and strode into camp. "What's going on up here? Having a party and don't invite the life of?" He tried to sound cocky but came across as pitiful with hurt feelings.

"We're up here seeking the Mother," Bear's tone flat, not betraying any more than was necessary.

"Bout her?" Coyote indicated the Otter laid out on the rock.

"A little, but most about her people, my people, all the people, I'm guessing yours is just as affected, unless you want to correct me?" Bear eyed Coyote suspicious.

"Nope, you speak truth, me 'n mine been takin' it hard last life cycle. Shit, I got kids never knew nothing but hunger and want since they was born and they died hard. It's taking a toll. You seeking to fix that?" Coyote's misgivings coming to the fore. He didn't believe Bear nor any of The People gave two whits about him and his crew, but Bear had always been a good soul and treated Coyote fair in past.

"One step at a time," Bear cautioned. Same old Coyote, same old impatience. "We're up here to find the Mother and this is the last place she came to me. We want to see if she's alright. If she ain't, we got bigger problems than original thought. We think humans maybe done more damage faster and to more'n we knew. Now we got to see if'n it can be fixed or if we are truly in the last days." Now Bear pulled a joint out of the bag he hid on hisself and rummaged until he found the lighter. He sparked the end, took a deep toke and gave thanks to the ancestors, those who was no longer here, extinction had taken a hard toll over the centuries, it was always right to remember those who hadn't made it this far. And to remember you might be next. He offered it to Coyote who thanked him with more enthusiasm than he'd meant to, but what the hell, be grateful.

A pall hung heavy pushing down on the group. There was no conversation, no laughter, trading of jibes, just worry. Bear putting thoughts to words and stating what they all feared made it all real. Immortality might have run its course.

"Interesting you showing up just as things begin to find their ugly side again," Bear was not suspicious by nature but nature has a way of evolving.

"What you trying to say, Bear?' Coyote growled, "don't know I like your tone."

"Don't think you want to get yerself in a dander and do something you will definitely regret," Bear's tone was soft, but the warning was solid. "I'm jest noticing you seem to have a knack for popping into a situation that is quickly deteriorating and then losing yerself when the rubber starts burning and the road gets bumpy."

"I come back when shit was hitting the fan pretty hard last time, if'n you remember," now hurt feelings joined forces with indignation and Coyote thought about crossing a line he knew wouldn't let him come back.

"Yeah, I remember you come back and then made scarce," Bear was not in a forgiving mood, He'd been up on this outcropping for a month, Bear time, and his back was giving him hell, old injuries decided to remind him of bad days, and he was just cranky with the way life was going.

"Was nothing for me to do, hand to hand ain't my forte, sneaky is. You guys was fixin' to have a beat down and I'd a just been in the way," Sometimes truth hurt worse than the beating.

"Ya-hey to that," Bear let out a huge belly laugh and tossed another white stick to Coyote with the lighter hot on its tail. "just a little ball busting, getting a little squirrely sitting up here waiting and needing to jump start saving the world."

"Always saving something, ain't ya?" Coyote said through held breath with the last two words riding an exhale. "But you got one helluva tiger by the tail this time, ain't so sure you can pull this one off. Humans're fucking the Mother quick as they breed. They don't seem to know they live here, but they won't if they keep on the course they're on. And ain't another neighborhood to be escaping to. We all know that! You only get one Mother, you best respect her or you're going to be starving in some hole wonderin' how this happened." He spit to get the taste of his own words out of his mouth. Bear tossed him a bottle to finish the job.

"Damn, if she don't show up pretty soon, we're just going to have to load this on our shoulders and hope we don't completely screw it up," Bear looked into the forever hoping to see her coming this way.

Rebecca came over and put her paws around his massive chest and leaned her head into him. "I'm worried about Suzette," she whispered into his ear, "she doesn't show much of any signs she's improving. I fear for her people, for her, for all of us." She wiped a tear from the end of her snout and sucked a sniffle back in.

A change in air pressure and slight warming of the temperature signaled arrival. A slight breeze indicated movement; the sigh told you where she stood. Bear shoulda know'd he wouldn't see her coming but he was damn glad to feel her here. "My poor, beautiful child," the words ethereal, as if the bushes themselves uttered them.

Bear turned and saw the ghost of the Mother kneeling next to Suzette, her tears falling freely onto the face of the small black woman. Suzette was losing hold on her identity as more and more of her children lost their grip on life, as they sickened, she could not hold onto who she represented. She was the proverbial canary in the coal mine.

"I guess I don't need to tell you why we are here." Bear's voice raspy with emotion, with longing.

She turned away from the visage of the woman to look at him. It had been less than two decades since they had last met, a split second in immortal time, but she had aged considerably. The dark circles under her eyes exposed her weariness, the fact that she could not seem to maintain substance. It required all her strength to hold together. At one point she trembled and the mountains shook perceptibly.

"My children, we are at a very dangerous moment in time. Honestly, I never thought this was possible. The Great Spirit sleeps or is far too busy controlling the rest of the multi-verses. We are but one child among billions. If we are to save ourselves and all the rest, we must act now," she sat in an indentation in the rock formation as if it were a throne.

Alex ran up to her, tears streaming down her face and threw herself onto the lap of the stunning woman. "Is this?" Asked the Mother.

"Yes." Bear could hardly get the word past his lips. The thought of losing everything, everyone he loved this time forever, was crushing his heart.

"She is so small, so precious," she scratched the head of the small bear cub nestled in her lap.

"In human form she is an adult, but time is what it is," Bear explained unnecessarily.

"If only all could remain in this state none of this would be happening," She tore her eyes from the cub to take in all surrounding her. Bear, his mate, Doe, Coyote, Otter, all so thin, with a pallor of frailty. Her heart breaking at the senselessness of it all.

"What do you all propose to do?" her words were more solid than her visage, she was not going to go quietly into the nothingness of space. They would fight, fight for survival, for their last breath if needs be, but fight they would.

"Well, to be perfectly candid, we came to consult you. Of course, first we had to see how you were, now we know, we are open to any ideas you might have." Bear took in all the others with his gaze to nods of accord.

"Our main difficulty is," came the whispered voice from Suzette, "we almost need a war, where we can beat back mankind and all his destructive ways." They all nodded once again, leaning in to see what she had in mind. "But we have all been created to assist, to teach, to stand as examples, to protect. It is the way of The People. We are not warriors; we are the peacemakers. Humans have seldom listened or heeded the advice of those who caution and plead for peace."

"What we need is a human who will be listened to, someone strong enough, with the power to command, to force them to do what is necessary not only to save themselves but our children alongside them," Coyote was all in. He knew what they needed and they wasn't it, they had to create an army of humans to kowtow the other humans into doing what was right.

"You propose to give one human or small number great power. To have all others follow them as they command. What do you think would happen if we allowed such a thing?" Bear knew, but he wanted Coyote to think about the disaster he proposed.

"They only respond to power, to a strong leader who commands. They consider reasonable to be a weakness. We are talking about the survival of the Mother, of all our children, of us!" Coyote attempted strength but weakness and fear coated every word. Bear understood, he had seen the dwindling numbers, the skeletal wolves, and bears. He could see what this was doing to Suzette, but there had to be some other way.

"Are there reasonable humans? Ones who command through respect? Respect for truth? For the Mother? For life?" Bear was searching for a glimmer of hope in a hopeless situation.

"There has got to be someone, or someones," Suzette, bless her, sounded almost optimistic, she smiled, and though worn to the bone, sat up to encourage. There had to be someone and they had to find that someone before it was too late. She gazed upon the glimmering features of the Mother, almost transparent, ghostlike, praying to the Great Spirit she would know of someone who sheltered on her.

The Mother's visage became slightly more solid as she considered. Could hope and dream actually win out? "You have children all over the surface of my body, ask them to search for those who speak truth about what is happening. Tell them to scour the land and sea, find us a spark of hope to blow on and see if we can't start a fire!"

"No," Alex blinked her eyes as if coming rising from dream, "We don't need what they do to themselves and have done since the dawn. What we need is an army of children, innocents, the ones whose futures are being most threatened. We need to bring together the children of this world, and not just human children, but ours, the cubs, the pups, the calves, the infants, hatchlings, fawns, every single child of the Mother. Bring them together to demand that their elders do right by them, by us, by all."

Bear's paw touched the paw of his mate, pride filled them both, this child, this perfect wonderful child, the fulfillment of their love, she would be the hope of the world, of the Mother. It was the perfect idea. The children of every species demanding life from their parents, their societies, from those who brought them life. They would demand full payment on that promise.

"Humans won't don't listen to their pups," Coyote pooh-poohed the idea with his attitude. "do you have any idea how ridiculous this all sounds? It's not even pie in the sky, it's delusional dreams and absolutely impossible."

"Well, maybe that's exactly what we need, a grand, meaningless, stupid gesture that will finally get the attention of those who hold the power. Maybe it's time we showed ourselves to be what we are. And more importantly what we can do!" Bear said quietly as he warmed to where he thought Alex was headed. "You are thinking we need to join forces with the children. We don't have to show ourselves to the adults—who wouldn't believe what was right in front of their eyes as they have proven by what's brought us to this point—but to the children. Those who are not yet jaded and cynical but still prone to believing in the unbelievable. If we could organize them, we could force the leaders to listen and act!"

The others, including the Mother balked at that idea. Coyote howled his indignation. "So we're going to just pop out of myth, and for the most part only Native American myth, land in some poor girl or young boy's lap and say. 'Ta-da! We're here and we're real and we've come to help you!" He howled again and rolled on the ground with the audacity and sheer insanity of the plan. "The parents would never believe the children; it would be considered some kind of mass hallucination. No, it's too outrageous, too ludicrous.

"Think Bear, you expect the children to convince the adults, those same adults that kill because someone of their own kind is a different color, or believes in the same God as them only prays different, the people that kill for an inch of land or a drop of water or just to dominate one and other, are going to just stop their despicable ways because their children say 'oh, mommy, oh daddy, please stop destroying our future? Do you have any idea how absurd this sounds?" He was almost screaming his indignation to force the idiocy of this through their heads.

"Maybe that's why I like it," said Mother thoughtfully, "I mean, not exactly, but I love the concept of the children demanding their right to live. I like bringing in the cubs, fawns, chicks, all. The children are, literally, the future. Your friend the sheriff came around, didn't he?" she stared hard at Bear.

"Well, yeah, but this is a much grander scale with so many possible negative repercussions, I don't know," he began to back away from the idea when his granddaughter interrupted.

"What have we got to lose? Look at us, we are slowly disappearing and, as you told me a long time ago, ain't no coming back from extinction. Why not attempt one grand idiotic, last stand." She smiled at all of them, " all we need to do is to convince almost every child of every species, of every color, religion, and territory of human, to join in and save the world, simple!"

" I still think we should try something that would present less exposure to the mental stability of humans before we completely blow their minds. And I have an idea," he scratched his paw under his chin in thought.

After a few moments of silence Coyote broke the quiet into a thousand pieces, "And that would be what, Bear?" he almost shouted his frustration.

"I'm not exactly sure yet, I want to take a little time to see if what is hatching in my brain is even possible. If you'll all give me just a little time and patience," he let it set right there. One thing Bear knew is you didn't go off halfcocked without some information and a chance in hell that an idea would work.

"Well, Bear figured out what needed done last time and he is the protector, the healer. We have relied on his strength many times in the past, maybe this time we should rely on his wit and guile." The Mother seemed pleased Bear had an idea that would not involve violence nor harm. She was all in, though only for the nonce. "But remember Bear, we do not have an eternity for you to work with. You need to do your experiments and do them now. Since the dawn of the universe, we have never before felt the press of time. Now, it pushes on our backs and conscience! And I don't like the feel of it."

Bear pulled out the bottle, which never seemed to empty, took a long pull, before handing it to his mate, who grimaced but took a sip. Doe was game and chugged a few swallows, before tipping the bottle so a sip could pour into Otter's mouth. She then handed the bottle to Mother who took a long pull, coughed once, and handed the bottle to Coyote. Mika shook his head, glared at each of them, before taking the bottle and declaring, "this is utterly ridiculous, we need muscle, not subtlety." chugged deep and threw the bottle back to Bear who handed it to his granddaughter. She was of age.

"Well, I guess all for one and one for all, we live or die in the service of Mother."

"And the brain of the Bear," Alex whispered just loud enough they all heard, handing the bottle back to her grandfather.

"Yeah, and that's never been tested," Coyote whispered.

"To the future!" Bear knew it was dumb, but they needed something to hang on to, some hope. Sometimes hope is all you got, and when it's all you got, you run with it. He chugged two deep swallows and put the bottle away.

The Wily and The Effluvium

The two small animal spirits hunkered down in the small copse of bushes and watched the big man eat his lunch. They knew he could feel something pushing on his consciousness but he had no idea who or what might be behind it. They snickered as they watched. He was feeling Coyote, they knew, as Coyote had been attached to the guy since the guy was a cub. Now they had control of him. What the hell, Coyote wasn't using him for nothing and they needed somebody big to do what they couldn't.

And they was tired, tired of being chased away from human and animal alike. They didn't make themselves the way they was, the Creator had when he made the Mother. But they'd been chased, harassed, bedeviled, and vilified since the dawn. They was done.

They'd had a little taste of what could be when they was able to use the crack Bear had so conveniently provided when his mate died. And they'd almost won that battle. Others might have walked away defeated but not these two. They was wily, thieving, and willing to do anything to protect their own. They knew the Mother was on the precipice, but nobody gave two shits about their people except as pests to be extincted. Well, payback is a bitch. Fox was created to punish those that was arrogant or careless. These folk and their kind was the definition of such. Skunk never done nothing but take justifiable revenge against those who would do him or his harm. Well, the harming was on the other foot now.

The big man scratched at their pushing on his brain. He knew something wasn't quite right but he hadn't a clue what or why. He was perfect for the trouble they was planning. They'd leave Sung alone with his mighty pack up in the forests. With him up there, he'd be well out of the way. There was nothing he could do to help those down here, 'sides, the way he looked, and his big, ol' pack with him, they could hardly defend themselves let alone cause mischief to two very determined and smart spirits like those hiding in the bushes.

The big human turned his head and stared directly into the bushes as if he could feel their presence. They'd better back off a bit. If they got heavy handed, he might buck and then be lost to them. They just had to keep the hate boiling right below the surface, so each time he ran into Bear he'd be ready to explode. They knew he couldn't harm Bear, that wasn't what was required of him, just keep Bear a little off balance so he couldn't think right or concentrate on what needed doing. The big human was just a distraction, if he got whupped and beat down, then he got whupped. And if he died, he died. Just another human on a Mother with too damn many of them scurrying all over her as is.

Skunk turned to Fox, "We have to stay together on this, no trying to break away once things get ugly."

"Of course," Fox replied, his visage serious, almost with a pained expression that Skunk would think he would turn on his co-conspirator. " I would never betray you!" Though the hint of a grin betrayed he'd considered.

"There is a long history of many of the People pretending to be one with me and then turning their backs the moment I had to protect myself or my people. It is not my fault that I cannot pinpoint where or on whom that defense should stick," Skunk knew folks didn't like him. They acted as if he stunk all the time not just when he was defending. He didn't begrudge others their fangs and claws, or their size and muscle, that was how they survived. Well, he had his way and it worked just fine. The difference? Nobody died of the stink. "I'm sorry, I shouldn't have slurred you."

"It's OK, I'm used to it. If people have hated you because of your 'weapon' they have done the same to me because of my cleverness. No, we have to stick together or we will become extinct together." Fox might have considered for a moment betraying his friend, it was in his nature, but he also knew neither had the strength, size, or capability to do what they planned alone. They needed each other equally.

Of course, once they had accomplished the takeover, that was another story. Leopard can't change his spots and a Fox gotta do what is natural to his nature!

Big Frank could feel someone watching him, like some itch at the back of his head he couldn't find to scratch. Shit, someone was tailing him and he didn't like that one bit. Sneaking sombitch without the cajones to show theyself. Where was the bastard? He turned his head slow so as not to startle whoever might be hiding and spying. God, how he hated cowards, if'n you got a problem come face it man to man. Standing up and stretching, casual like, he tossed what was left of his lunch towards the garbage can off the parking lot missing the can completely. He didn't give one shit, he had more important quarry to hunt.

There was something about that copse of bushes, he was sure something, or someone, was hiding there, but they was doing a hell of a job. Maybe Big Frank would wander over there to take a piss. He laughed to hisself. Yeah, that's what he'd do, see if a little piss could roust whatever was hiding there. He took another swig from the flask and shoved it inside his vest pocket.

Sauntering over like he got nothing else to do he made his way to the bushes. Hmm, if someone was hunkered down in there they wasn't spooking. He'd still do a bit of kicking around and see what flew. Pulling his zipper down he relieved himself into the thicket. Man, did that feel good, he hadn't realized how much he had to piss until now. And nothing or nobody took off. He was just spookin' himself.

He shoved his stuff back inside his pants and zipped up. He looked down and swore under his breath, he'd been so distracted looking for whoever would take off running he'd pissed all over his shoes. Dumb bastard! But, he'd been sure someone was here.

He looked back up to them damn mountains. Man, there was something calling him there and it was taking every ounce he had not to just run up there. 'Course, weren't no way he could've run much past the end of the company property in the condition he was in. Too many cigarettes and too many nights with the boys, but he sure as shit could drive up there, maybe tonight.

"Frank! You gonna stand there gapin' at the damn scenery or get yer ass in here to work," it was Jim, the foreman, pain in the ass.

"I'm coming, can't a man have an after-supper smoke in peace?" He said it before he realized he hadn't had a smoke and didn't have one in his hands. Ah, fuck 'em, that guy wouldn't notice shit.

"And leave the damn flask in yer car or I'll have to write you up!"

Shit, maybe that asshole was more observant than Big Frank had given him credit for.

Skunk and Fox reappeared in another copse down from where Big Frank had pissed on himself. No animal with any self-respect would hunker down in, sleep in, or live in its own or another's excrement. They wasn't coming back to the scene of the brine, as it were.

"We may be losing some control over this one," Fox admitted to Skunk, "Coyote might have a much stronger leash than we had thought."

"Or just remembered he had this pet from when that large thing was small," chuckled Skunk, though it was tinged with worry.

"Either way we need some kind of backup plan in case this one cuts loose," Fox stared at the retreating figure of Big Frank, concerned they were losing hold of their greatest distraction. If Bear and the others were allowed time and peace, they would find a way to overcome what these two had set in motion.

"I can't help but wonder if we are endangering the Mother with this plot. I mean I know we have been derided, treated like degenerates, and scorned, but we are not the only ones and if we allow mankind to continue its course are we not harming ourselves and destroying our home?" Fox was having a crisis of conscience she hadn't seen coming or considered. "Shit! We could extinct ourselves if we're not careful!"

"The Mother has been through this many times in the past, climate change is part of change which is part and parcel of life, but she always recovers and resets, she will again. She is the one who made us what we are, she can't be upset when we revert to nature. It's natural." Skunk shrugged, "It's not like she is going to extinct us because we are what she created!" He was growing tired of Fox's timidity and doubt. If they were going to try to change the order of the world, turn the totem, then eggs would be broken and some of the people would suffer, they knew that from the get-go. Fox's intrinsic decent nature was threatening the whole damn plan!

She would have to have a contingency plan just in case she skunked out.

Reality, Line Two

As the wolves finished off their 'banquet' Sung sat quietly talking to Sheriff John and Glen. John listened intently to what Sung was suggesting and quietly asking questions. Glen was distracted by the yipping snarling and gnashing of teeth coming from just the other side of the truck. Though Glen represented all dogs, most of those were domesticated, civilized, tame. He was not used to the viciousness of wild wolves. If the sheriff had been worried Glen might turn feral from hanging around the wolves Glen's reaction to their dining habits had dissuaded him of the notion.

"Glen, try to focus, pay attention, son," John tried to force Glen's concentration away from the carnage and to the task at hand.

Sung saw a distraction was in order, he locked eyes with Glen. Glen took the lifeline and sunk himself in the overpowering presence. "They do what is natural to them; and used to be natural to yours until man domesticated your lot."

"Well, I'm glad we don't have to kill in order to eat. Doesn't it bother any of you that they are viciously slaughtering living beings for food?" Glen was aghast that his friends seemed to not care about the cows being destroyed and eaten.

"All creatures do what is natural and necessary for them to survive. And remember this, yours may be domesticated, tame, when comfortable in their cushy homes surrounded by their human families, but give them a slight change of circumstance, their environment, as it were, and see how long it takes for them to revert to their natural proclivities. Survival is the overriding instinct in all of us. My people may seem barbaric to you as they devour these cattle but they care for their family, when not threatened or starving they will back down rather than attack. We only take another life to survive."

"What about these cows or any other herbivore, they don't kill anything to survive," Glen was not going to give in on accepting all life was built around the taking of others.

"Glen, herbivores eat plants, plants are living breathing entities. They are born of a seed, they grow, and if left to their natural course will die. Or be eaten by these and others who become fodder for the carnivore. It is the circle of life." Sung needed Glen to understand his people were no different than any others, "Look, do you like chicken? Hamburgers? Hot Dogs? Ham sandwiches? They all were alive at one time. What you are reacting to here is witnessing the culling. As the saying goes, 'nobody wants to see how the sausage is made'.

"But they're eating it raw, just ripping it apart!"

"Yes, they are, it is how we have done for a million years and how yours used to dine. I realize you don't want to know but if you'd stop, calm yourself, meditate and remember, you would find out your people were right behind mine. Actually, the sheriff here would probably allow that his people were just as barbaric as mine when they were first born. And in many ways are just as vicious today, only in a more civilized way." He grinned as he nodded to the sheriff.

"It just seems wrong," Glen couldn't let it go.

"It is all perspective. If you are the one who hasn't eaten in weeks and your belly growls and knots painfully, you see things one way. If you are what's about to fill that belly you see it differently. And that includes plants. Humans see plants as non-sentient, but they are tied into the same essence of the universe we all are," Sung spoke quietly hoping Glen would see that they were all connected.

"But they don't feel pain, fear, love, compassion like we do, they aren't alive like us," again Glen clung to the life raft of his preconceived concepts. If everything felt everything just as he did, as the sheriff or Bear did, well then you couldn't morally eat anything or walk on grass or, or anything!!

"How do you know that? They breathe air, they are born and die, they 'live'. They just aren't mobile for the most part, but if you would take the time, surrender yourself to the soul of the universe, you might see they are not that much different than we." Sung shook Glen companionly by the shoulder, "And they serve their purpose just as these cows do, as all living things do. We are all made of the same stardust and energy, and to that stardust and energy we return."

As he spoke the sheriff noticed Sung appeared to become more solid, as if the conversation gave him purpose or made him more real. John couldn't wrap his head around all this spiritual mumbo jumbo. Was Sung really what he claimed or was John losing his grasp on reality. And if he was what did that mean about all the others? Suzette? He shook his head attempting to clear the muddying waters.

"Is it the mountain air or the sun setting or my senile mind but you seem to be growing more substantial, younger, stronger. How is that possible?" John required a rock to hang onto before he slipped beneath the waves.

"My people here are growing stronger, therefore so do I, but they represent only a small fraction of all those who roam the mother. Too many are hanging on by a claw, too many will die for no reason other than the avarice of humanity." He wore his worry like a thick cowl. It bothered the sheriff to see this magnificent, confident creature being worn down by outside influences, predominance's he had absolutely no control over. He would sacrifice almost anything to save his people, his children, but his sacrifice would mean naught if he was no longer around to watch over them.

"So, does anyone know what Evan and the others are up to?" And there was the solidity he sought, Evan.

"My belief is he and the others have gone off in search of the Mother, to counsel with her. To find out her condition and see if she has any ideas on what they might do to convince humans they are destroying her and everything that takes life from her," Sung's intonation did not instill confidence.

"Wait," the sheriff felt himself slipping once again, "You are sayin' he went off in search of the human persona of the planet Earth? That there is an actual Mother Earth, Gaea, kind of person? You've got to be kidding me! Ain't no such animal!" He had been pushed a mile past believability. Yes, he had seen what he thought he had seen when the wolf became the man, and Evan had become a Bear, Glen a Dog, Suzette an Otter, oh, fuck it, in for a penny, though that pound was hard coming.

Sung could almost see the wheels break loose and begin to spin in the sheriff's brain. "Sheriff, think of all the wonders you have witnessed. How can you possibly deny your own eyes? You're not prone to delusion or hallucinations, soon or late, you're going to have to believe your own observations." He shrugged. You can deny what is right before your eyes until you are dust flowing through the blackness of space but truth was truth. You either believed yourself or you believed nothing.

"Shit! I jest thought the same damn thing. If I'm to believe anything I have to believe my friends. No matter how whacky or absurd they happen to be," he could only shake his head. He had seen some crazy shit in his life but none as insane as what he had witnessed since getting tied in with this group. Nor had he had as much fun. He was living a fantasy and at his advanced age he hoped it wouldn't end anytime soon.

Of War and Peace

It was 1968, mid-June, right about 85 degrees and not a cloud in the sky. The humidity was kicking up as the day grew older but the long-haired kid standing by the side of the two lane didn't seem to notice. He sat on his duffle and stared across the flat expanse to his west as if he didn't have a care in the world. Because he didn't. He was on the road to lose himself. To ease away from the last year and a few months. He'd gotten his discharge papers, went home, could no longer fit in to the place he'd been born and raised, so took what the government had given him and what he'd sent home from the jungle and started walking. He coulda bought a car but he was in no hurry. He'd walk until his feet got tired and then lay out his sleeping bag and look at the sky.

He'd had enough of what he'd seen and didn't want to see no more. The sky was pure. He didn't believe in no god, not after what he'd witnessed man doin' to himself. But the sky, the sky was as perfect a place as he could imagine. Blue in the day, black at night, clouds, stars, hope. He laughed, hope, what a stupid word.

What did he hope for? To not watch any more death. To not smell it, taste it on his food, how it permeated his skin. He had no idea what he was searching for, but he knew what he didn't want.

This land out here breathed of its own, it talked to him and told him possibilities, reflected his story. He thought he could lay down here and melt into it. He was tired. So, he sat on the duffle with his thumb hanging off the end of his hand and just not caring.

He didn't hear the pickup stop on the gravel; he did hear the toot of the horn. It was an old Chevy pickup, bit of rust around the rear wheel wells and dents to show it had lived hard but was still purring like a newborn. The fella driving it with the farmers tan waved him in. He couldn't tell how old the driver was but thought somewhere between late twenties and the grave. He'd worked hard as evidenced by the muscle in his arms, the tired in his eyes and the wrinkles the sun had gifted. He smiled as the kid got in.

"How far ya headed?" the question floated over on the breeze as the farmer spoke out of the side of his mouth, head turned, easing back onto the blacktop.

"Don't really know," the hippie said, honest.

"Runnin' to or from?" It was just as honest. No judgement just surveying the lay of the land.

"To, I guess," if this conversation was ever going to get off the ground it was going to have to pick up some speed.

"Any idea what you're looking for?" as it was now evident this young man was on a quest of sorts, though the Good Lord only knew to where.

The young fella's eyes filled to overflowing as the pure honesty of his answer surprised him as much as anything in his existence, "Life".

Doing his best not to look over in case the young man might be embarrassed by his, obviously, startled response, "Well, I got a place you can bunk for a couple days if you're in need of a little rest. Ain't much, but it's quiet, so quiet a man can hear his thoughts without nobody interrupting them."

"Thanks."

What the farmer's idea of 'ain't much' and the hitchhiker's were definitely at odds. Here about forty miles west of where he'd picked the young man up was the prettiest little farmhouse surrounded by acres of spring crops. He had no idea what, as he'd never grown a weed, but it just reeked of life. The farmer's wife, Jody, was younger than the man himself by about ten years. She was pretty, in an offhand kind of way. She didn't wear any makeup, that the young hippie could tell, she was dressed in a well-worn summer smock which only added to the pretty and the slight bump where the dress began to tighten around her belly gave truth to her condition. From the way these two interacted he couldn't tell if they was in love or just made good company, but they appeared content. This place was heaven, he knew he was going to hate walking away from it.

They had a quiet dinner, each sharing as much of themselves as was proper. Nobody prospecting for any information that was none of their business. He did mention to Jackson—he'd finally found his manners enough to ask for a name—that he had served over in the Nam but preferred not to talk about it. Jackson was not a prying kind of man. He showed Earl—turnabout was fair play—the small bunkhouse attached to the barn where he could stay. A bed, washbasin, outhouse out back, perfect.

Morning came early, Earl had slept the sleep of innocents, the best night's sleep he'd had since long before he'd shipped out. He felt rested for the first time in years as he stretched and made his way to the farmhouse in search of a cup of coffee.

Jody had a couple of eggs, toast, and coffee on the table as he entered. He nodded his thanks and sat.

"You can go ahead and eat," she told him.

"Aren't we going to wait for Jackson?" Manners can't be unbred out of man.

"Oh, he's been out in the field for more'n an hour already," she glowed when she smiled.

Earl walked over to the window she was looking out and saw Jackson out in the field bent over and pulling weeds, hoeing the earth, making room for the crop to grow. He watched for a few minutes before he sat back down to eat.

"He sure is a hard worker," admiration filled his words.

"Well, he worked so hard to get this place, begging, borrowing, promising, he feels it's his duty to me, to him, to God, to everyone who believed in him, to show they wasn't wrong. He works to keep a promise to himself and all who went before," now Earl saw the love, and not just the love, but the great respect she held that farmer in.

"Think he'd get mad or think I'm out of line if I went out and asked to help him? Not that I really have any idea what I'd be doing, but I could learn," he didn't know where the idea came from, but he fell in love with it as soon as the words jumped from his tongue.

"I guess if you went out and sunk spade in the soil, he wouldn't be too broke up," she smiled appreciation.

Earl's thoughts traveled the long road back to that beginning as he stared hard at the brown expanse before him. He thought of Jackson and Jody and their kindness at taking a lost soul in. Of showing him where life was. They were good people, never shoving their beliefs on another, just living as examples. He thought of the kids, four for them, three boys and the girl who were supposed to take over the farm when the folks got too tired to plow.

Johnny, the eldest, had ejected from a car as he and friends were celebrating graduation. Broke his neck, died instantly. Ronnie had taken it hard and taken to the bottle and then harder stuff. He was alive but couldn't quite get his shit together enough to care about the farm. Quince had an artistic streak and an irresponsible main valve and the girl, Jennifer, had married a stockbroker from Denver.

Earl had fallen in love with the place the moment he saw it, and Jody and Jackson saw that. They wanted the farm, this piece of land that Jackson had worked so hard to get and harder to keep, to continue, they willed it to him. And now it was dying and Earl could do nothing about it.

Maybe it was Karma, payback for the war. Maybe he should have stayed back in the hometown and taken care of his folks, working a job he hated for forty years before drinking himself to death, maybe he was a shitty farmer and maybe it was just the way things went. He wasn't the only one suffering through this drought. And he had to realize he didn't have the kind of power to affect the rest of humanity and the weather. Shit, he was just so tired, and beat down by it all. He wanted to start walking again, but he'd promised and that was sacred.

She watched him as he stared at nothing and everything. As he watched all he had worked for, lived for, the land that held his blood and hope withering, dying without sound, fading into oblivion. She wanted to cry for him, for all of them, her own as well, but she couldn't. She had work to do, she was seeking a way to save her Mother.

Though wasn't she his Mother as well? And wasn't the land, this land his child, also dying as he watched? Maybe, just maybe, they could help each other.

"Excuse me," she was careful not to startle this hunched, sad, once tall, and proud man, "my name is Willow. I was passing by and couldn't help but notice, feel, your desperation. Maybe we can help each other."

Earl gazed at the diminutive woman with oversized ears—which instead of making her appear odd actually only increased her attractiveness—who had appeared out of thin air. She was pretty, no, cute, one wished to pick her up and stroke her fine hair. He couldn't say why, he had never wished to do that to any human being but there was something about her that begged to be cuddled. It took several moments for him to overcome the shock of her statement and the fact she had somehow come up through barren, brown fields, apparently on foot. Just passing by, through barren, wide-open land. And he hadn't seen her approach. He guessed he'd been so wrapped up in the sadness of his dying dream he hadn't noticed her coming here. But where in all hell had she come from? He was three miles from the nearest blacktop and that was ten miles from the nearest main road that came from or went to anywhere. And that anywhere were a couple towns that couldn't have held more'n a thousand between the two!

"I'm sorry, what?" Weren't much but solitude bankrupts the verbiage.

Willow immediately realized she had made a faux pas. Humans weren't used to folks showing up unannounced. "I was passing by and the sorrow emanating from you just pulled me in. I know that sorrow and thought I would offer help." Though she knew there was little she could actually offer.

He stared at her, there was something in the way she spoke, as if English was not her normal tongue, though she spoke it well. "Not unless you can make dead oats and sunflowers come back to life," he wanted to weep yet the stoicism of farming for almost half a century sustained, "Sorry, been a bad couple of years and this one is the worst. There is nothing left, my hope died with the crops."

"Love this land, dontcha?"

He laughed until the laughter got away from him. He howled to the sky, the wide-open, sun filled sky, blue from horizon to horizon, nary a cloud, a drop of rain, just heat, hard, throbbing heat, pounding down on the scorched landscape. When he finally ran out of insanity, he caught his breath and sat on the hard, hot ground. He was done. "If you could've seen it in full bloom. It ain't big, but it's the prettiest place on God's formerly green earth. It was all I ever needed."

"You mean when it looked like this?" The air shimmered and he saw. There were the sunflowers climbing to the sky, several acres of oat plants, green turning to gold over to the left, his little garden of vegetables for his own personal use, just to the right of the front of the house, looked about ready to burst.

The tears flowed in rivulets down his face, he covered his face but only for a moment as he wanted to witness the miracle before him. He didn't know if she was witch or illusionist and he didn't care, this was his passion as it should have been. And then, just as quickly, it was gone. It was the Wizard of Oz, gone from the striking vibrant colors of Oz to the black and white of Kansas.

He stared at the brown ruin in front of him and then at the diminutive woman standing next to him, arms crossed just below breasts, nose twitching as if scenting. A tear raced down each of her checks before disappearing into the parched ground. Almost as if she could feel the crushing despair in his heart.

"What did you do? How did you do whatever you did?" He grasped for words, for the right questions, but his thoughts scrambled and scattered before him like dead tumbleweeds before the hot, dry wind.

"Would you like a chance to get all that back?" She ignored his pleadings. She had proven to herself how much this man loved and needed this land. He would do whatever was necessary to bring back life to this land.

"Of course, I would. My God, I don't know and I don't care what you did. I'll sell my soul to have what this was." He didn't have money or much of anything but this farm, but he would give her that if he could just spend the rest of his time surrounded by the beauty he remembered and she'd just shown him.

"Think you could break away from this for a time, if it meant you might get your wish?" She knew she tantalized and it was cruel, but only slightly so. He had to be willing to sacrifice all he was and what he believed if he was to be of any use to her, The Mother, life. And she couldn't guarantee anything she just knew in her soul that anyone who loved the Mother as much as this man did, had to be able to help them. And that meant he could help himself.

Somehow, instinctively Earl seemed to know what she was asking. Was he willing to give up his own life if it would bring life back to this farm? To all the farms. To this earth he had loved since he'd come back from hell. He knew the answer. "Will we be gone long?" Will I live to touch my land again? Or will I be buried under it? He left unsaid

"Depends on a lot of things," she spoke the words and forced herself to believe. "Do you have a vehicle?"

Ironing Wrinkles

Bear was thoroughly convinced in his own mind that what had come to him, the grand plan, was impossible. But they needed impossible right now. Mankind had always proved problematic. He killed for sport not just survival. He warred not just with his own kind but with nature herself, as if he could truly rule over all of creation. He dumped his refuse where he slept, excreted where he lived, despoiled the very land that gave him life. But there had only been so many of them, now they had multiplied until they covered the Mother like a massive, pulsing ant colony, except the ants knew better than to destroy that which provided life. Not man.

Man acted as if there were millions of Mothers throughout creation and he only required a ride to the next one. He was wrong, so very wrong, and deep down, where rational thought dwelt, mankind knew it. That's what made him so dangerous. He knew he was slowly murdering all in his path and suiciding at the same time but didn't seem to care. His appetite was insatiable. So, if gluttony was to be his legacy let it be written, he lived and died by the fork.

Evan wanted to punch somebody, but he'd turned over a brand, spanking, new leaf since She'd been returned to him, not just whole, but as one of his true family. Bear had to control his impulses and urges, even if it caused his head to explode. He would do whatever he could to bring good karma on their association of do-gooders!

Yes, it was worth whatever it took to save this planet, this land of plenty. They would save it despite man. Their job was to save the Mother for all living things, mankind be damned. Sometimes a bear's just got to do what a Bear's gotta do.

He knew he couldn't do this alone and had thought about engaging Sung or Doe, maybe Tatanka or Elk but they weren't in much better condition. Nope, for the experiment he would rely on bears and bears alone. As soon as they got back to the homestead, he'd take off and try.

They popped into the backyard of the house. He had never seen anything that filled the heart like this old craftsman. He loved his mountains, the pines, and the snow, but this was home. He and Rebecca—well, if everyone else was gonna use the proper he ought to, too! —they had raised their human children here, they had spent their human lives here. It was good.

He was taken aback by the presence of the young couple lounging on the grass, staring at nothing. The scent of cannabis hung heavy on the still air. Both looked up as the small bear clan appeared in human form as if out of thin air, they giggled and returned to their contemplations.

"Ahem," Evan cleared his throat to garner attention of the trespassers, "I hope you don't mind my curiosity, but as this is my home, might one ask who you two are and what you're doing camped out in my backyard?" They didn't have the scent nor feel of one of The People so he had to assume they were just human vagabonds who saw the empty house and yard, and decided they'd camp.

The young man eased his head up from the soft grass seeking the source of the words, shook his head to clear a few of the cobwebs, and then stared at Evan. "Sorry, someone brought us here, told us to wait, found some pot and food, then said he'd be back. Oh, and the large woman who claims to be some weird spirit animal or whatever," he giggled again shaking his head, "said she was going to hang out in the river 'til you got back. I guess you're back." He rolled over onto his stomach to attempt a dismount from the earth or to stand, it was hard to tell which.

The young woman pulled her head free of the gravity that held it firm to the Mother's breast before breathily stating, "good pot, man." She lay back down, gravity winning this bout.

"OK," Evan said to the forefathers who were more present than the two grass people, "let's see if we can find who invited the invasion and get some of this straightened out!" As he made his way to the back door, he chastised himself for leaving the good weed where someone might find it. Spirit guides could handle the good stuff; humans would, well, just lay on the Mother hoping they didn't fall off into space.

His hand reached for the bottle before pulling back, nope, he'd need to maintain if he was to get to the bottom of this without ripping someone's head off. The bang of the front door called his attention and he followed the sound, with Rebecca and Alex close behind, both finding far more humor in this than Evan did. But they didn't know what his plan was or how much this was interfering with its implementation. For some reason both of them found Even's discomfort amusing, which irritated him that much more.

Oscar stopped in his tracks just inside the door at the sight of the three coming like a freight train towards him. He had never wondered about what a bug might feel like just before windshield but he thought he now knew.

"Good day," he began before Evan's look froze him.

"I can only assume you are the perpetrator who dumped the two stoned hippies in my backyard. Explain!" One should never poke the bear.

"Well, it is all quite simple really," began Oscar, his large eyes searching for an escape route but finding he had closed the door to the cage behind him. "I found those two out in the forest chained to trees, as it were, and I thought, as we needed human interlocutors to abide the cause and all, well, what they lack in intelligence and thought, they more than make up for in intensity, heart, emotion, and fervor. They believe in the cause celebre and are willing to sacrifice all to achieve the same ends as we. They just require a bit of guidance, a mentor, as it were." He gulped what he hoped was not his last swallow.

"And you thought I could take up mentoring as I have ought else to occupy my time?" exasperation replaced anger and frustration and Evan turned on his heel to retrieve the bottle, almost colliding with the two coming in the back door looking the worse for wear. Not so much hippies as vagabonds who'd taken to the trade early in life.

"Nice place," they both said together hoping to calm the savage bear.

"Don't even," and the hope aborning was crushed. "Everyone out back." An order to be followed, not questioned.

After they had all settled themselves on chair, log, stool, and ground Evan began the introductions. He may be on the verge of pissed, but he was never rude. Just as he completed naming names and omitting pertinent spiritual information, Chastity sauntered up from, one could only assume, the river. How she could spend all day submerged in water and never appear wet was one of the mysteries of the universe.

Anna Marie and Brian both greeted her warmly as one would an ancient and favored aunt, one whose mental facilities were somewhat in question.

"She thinks she's a manatee," Anna Marie whispered to Alex who was sitting at her right side.

Alex giggled and nodded knowingly.

The brilliant sunshine called to the six-foot-tall Sunflowers and they responded enthusiastically blocking out all who might be spying, and anyone thinking to listen in would be discovered as Bear's sensitive ears would pick up the rustle of stalks. This left only the front of the house unprotected from spies. People had the wrong idea about plants, all species, that because they were immobile, they were not sentient. All plants had some level of sentience. They could sense the presence of malevolence, communicate between themselves, and protect those most vulnerable even if it meant sacrificing others. The weak gave way so the young could live. No different than wolves, elk, or most mammals. They would gladly sacrifice so the species could continue. They also, if one knew the signs and was paying close attention, give warning to other species. They could be the best guardians a mammal could hope for.

Chastity eased herself onto the long wide bench placed there for her comfort. A cool breeze helped moderate her temperature. She could survive out of the water for long periods, if necessary, but she preferred not to endure more tribulation than absolutely necessary.

"I take it you all have met?" Evan studied the giddy youths as they poked each other where they thought no one would notice, gawking at Chastity in a rude manner. "Might I ask what you two find so humorous?" Evan was in no mood for stupid right now. He had a plan in mind and this was holding up the attempt.

They feigned seriousness, though without success, before straightening up before his powerful, intense glare. "It's just that she told us she thought she was some kind of spirit animal for manatees and then gave us some pot. It was hysterical, good pot though." It was Brian the most grounded of the two though only by a fingernail.

"Correction," Oscar butted in, "Chastity tried to explain she was the spirit guide to the manatees and I gave you the pot, well, it was Evan's pot, but I procured it."

"I don't give a shit about the pot, where it came from or who is so high they can't maintain a conversation. I want to know what these two think they know. What they actually know. And of what use they are to the problem at hand. Can anyone please answer any of these questions so I can get on with the experiment that might actually alleviate some of what is happening to the Mother?" Tired and worry combined to make short the fuse on his temperament. He wanted to straighten this out and he wanted it done now.

"If I may," chimed in Oscar, "a quick story. I found these two wood urchins chained to a tree..."

"A Maple-Leaf Oak," interrupted the young wood urchin earning her hard stares from the assembled, "sorry, but that is what they are and they are endangered." She spoke the word slowly, irritatingly slowly, to emphasize what they apparently weren't grasping. Her sacrifice, her willingness to die for this tree, to martyr herself. And Brian, of course.

"Fine a Maple-Leaf Oak. You could sense the commitment, the devotion and heart, the pure, honest willingness to give her all..."

"OK, OK. I get it, they were committed, or should have been," Evan muttered under his breath, "so you thought you'd bring them here where they could commit more mayhem and disruption."

"Well, no," Oscar seemed genuinely hurt by the accusation, "I thought that since they were so dedicated," he purposely avoided the word committed, "they might know others whom we could conscript into our service. As we all seem to be on the same road just not traveling in quite the same direction, as it were, they might be encouraged to join forces. To fight the grand battle, all hands on deck, sort of thing."

Silence can fill a space, no matter how large, to such a capacity it drowns out all other sound completely. Deathly still covers the territory absolutely.

"Now, you two, what do you have to say for yourselves? What do you think you know about the situation we all face? What do you actually know? And how to do you anticipate being of service to the betterment of all." Alex knew that tone of voice, it was when her grandfather had had enough jawing and wanted facts. And would settle for nothing less.

"Well, Anna Marie..." began Brian before Evan stepped on him.

"I didn't ask what the other knew but what YOU knew. I don't care what propaganda you've had shoved in your head. I don't care what bullshit you were willing to swallow because you wanted to bed a pretty girl, you aren't the first to try that approach, you won't be the last. I asked what do you, YOU not her, think you know about what is happening on this planet and what you seriously expect to do about it," he waited.

"Well, anyone can see that the climate is changing. Storms are becoming more violent, more frequent, and more dangerous. The Jet stream is wavering as it has never done forcing winter storms to intensify in constricted areas while those who used to get snow by the foot receive barely inches and those who never saw snow receive it by the foot. Rain comes so heavily in mountainous regions that flash floods are happening within moments of the rainfall and destroying towns and cities. The Gulf Stream is being strengthened and condensed so it flows farther north towards Greenland and Iceland quickening the thawing and dissipation of the glaciers and hence, the polar ice cap, increasing oceanic levels and flooding low lying areas forcing more people to crowd inland and decreasing the expanse of farmable land. And if something isn't done to reduce the stress on this planet, most living things will roast, drown or freeze." Brian was surprisingly lucid as he counted off the disasters happening and imminent on both hands. Catching himself and Anna Marie off guard. Anna Marie stared at him for several long seconds with admiration aborning on her face.

Evan nodded his head in appreciation before taking the girl, Anna Marie, into his gaze. "And you?"

She stammered and stuttered still taken aback by Brian's lucidity, "The Maple-Leaf Oak is almost extinct as we speak, less than six hundred still remain. I know species are facing extinction all across the world. Though I haven't a clue what we can actually do about it," she admitted.

"So, the stunt out in the forest was just that, a dumb stunt," Even's gaze remained locked on her eyes.

"We had to do something and a stupid stunt is better than no stunt!" She slumped where she sat and appeared about to cry, "I was just so frustrated that no one seemed to care we, as humans, were destroying our home. I screamed from the mountain tops, I showed them the data. I had been studying this since I was in high school, I have a PhD in environmental science and a minor in Meteorology. I've studied this stuff for fifteen years! They just don't want to hear it. It didn't matter if it was stupid or pointless, or a completely absurd fool's errand, we had to do...something." Her eyes pleaded with him, with the wife, the granddaughter, the pretty woman and the large one, even to Oscar, they had to see she meant well.

Evan opened the bottle and reached in his vest pocket for a joint, this was going to take some patience and time. He couldn't fault her heart, but her head could use a bit of adjustment. He had to, once again, adjust his thinking and assumptions about people. The girl was obviously less flighty than he had originally thought. A scientist, eh?

He felt Her hand on his shoulder. While he'd been engaged with the two She had come over to sit next to him, now She was telling him to calm himself. Through Her touch She was conveying more than could be said with words or chastisement.

He could hear Her voice, soothing, reassuring, 'they are only children,' She voicelessly spoke, 'they will always be children but they mean well. They have no idea what it is to live forever, they are but minutes in our day.' The slight tightening and untightening of her grip told him She was only coming to grips with what it meant for Her. And She'd been at this for a couple decades now. She was telling him he should respect the fact that what these two did today or tomorrow would have no bearing on their own lives, they would not live to see the end result. They did this for those who would come.

He smiled. She was so wise, wise beyond Her years or his, he chuckled. She, of course, was right. The fact these two whackadoodles were willing to put their today on the line for people they would never live to meet said something very admirable about them. Now, he had to figure a way to harness all this goodness and light into a cohesive plan to include them, put them to good use.

And really, was his plan any less insane than chaining yourself to a tree?

"I understand, you want to do something but let us not waste time and energy on miniscule solutions when we need miracles," he lit the joint—not his best stuff but something the kids could handle better—and passed it around. He offered the bottle, though before any could accept, Alex, with a huff and a shake of her head, strode inside and grabbed glasses for all. They would, at least, be civilized. She brought out a pitcher of water and another of lemonade for those who preferred teetotaling.

"What have these two told you and why do you believe or not what they have told you?" He pointed to both Chastity and Oscar, who appeared about to protest when Evan's glare stopped the words in his head.

"Alright," Anna Marie, the supposed leader of this pack of two, took a deep breath to clear the rest of the smoke from her head and concentrate her thoughts, "Oscar brought us here, across the country, promising he would introduce us to like-minded people who could help save the planet. We came, only to find this woman who claimed to be some kind of Native spirit guide, or something, and then we got high. No, we don't believe her, she is very nice and seems harmless enough, but we think she is a little off kilter. Why? Because who could possibly believe that such a thing exists outside of myth, and if it was true why would she suddenly appear out of nowhere to save us. Why wasn't she doing that all along?"

Bear sat back to think for a moment taking a long hit off the joint and a swig of his bourbon. "What if I told you we are all Native Spirit guides and we've been here all along?"

"Then I would ask you the same thing, why have you waited so long to come to us? Why haven't you stopped this madness already?" She sat back smirking at her cleverness at disemboweling his premise.

"Because you think we are gods or magical in our powers, we are not. We have been here all along, guiding, helping those who wished to be helped and taking care of our people. But keep in mind, 'our people'" yes, he used air quotes, "are animals. Your kind, for the greater part, though not indigenous folk who are closer to the Mother and to us," he made a hushing motion with his hands before she could interrupt, "don't care about my people. To them we are just game, some to be hunted to extinction, if possible. Humans, for the most part, do not care about those they consider below themselves.

"Your kind believe themselves to be the rulers of all they perceive without the responsibilities of caring for those they rule over. We, Spirit Guides, attempt to steer humans in the proper direction, to live in concert with the Mother and all her children. But you cannot even seem to realize you are all one species. You separate into countries, tribes, clans, colors, beliefs and any other minute detail you can find to show you are different, rather than find similarities." He sat back once again to collect thoughts that had tendencies to flit and fly like startled sparrows on a feeder, especially when he wanted to be elsewhere doing other things.

"I know you will say, but not all. And that is true but too many and their shortsightedness will extinct us all. Our people see it. We are, literally, the canaries in the coal mines, the bears on the ice flow, the wolves scrounging for scraps, the birds battered by storm and the manatees sliced to the heart by humans who can't see three feet into the water to see what harm their 'fun' causes. It is their 'right' to destroy, but not to preserve. Their 'God given right' to rule but not to care about themselves, us, or future generations who will bear the burden." He ran out of steam. His words weighed down by sorrow, despair, and heartbreak he hadn't known lived so deeply in his soul. It all felt so hopeless.

But where there is hopelessness there is the balance of youth, a belief all problems are solvable, and the hope born of promise.

Alex took a hard pull on her own bourbon, something she had acquired a taste for, as it was a family tradition, before she spoke. "Sounds like the end of the world, don't it?" A little dark levity in a crisis situation.

"And what do you supposed Spirits plan to do about it?" This time it was Brian who brought along the snark.

"Something completely stupid, meaningless, and hasn't a chance of succeeding," was all Bear would say.

For Every Action

Suzette felt herself being lifted gently and carried a short distance then laid back down on a soft, comfortable bed. She floated in and out of consciousness wanting nothing more than to lose herself in oblivion. Somewhere a voice told her to hang on, if she were to let go all her children would be without her guidance and would soon disappear from the Mother.

But that was impossible, her people had lived on the Mother for millions of years, they couldn't just disappear. But in her heart, she knew the truth of it. They were dangerously close to all the people becoming extinct. Something had to be done. But what? She was too tired, had carried her people as far as she could, who would help?

Bear. He was a good bear, a smart, resourceful bear, he had finally figured out what had happened last time they were threatened he would do it again. He had to. What would this world be like without the people? What if every otter from every part of the Mother suddenly disappeared? Every wolf, every bear and cat, fish, whale, dolphin, dog, coyote, all gone. From every corner of the world. What an empty horrid place this would be. Bear had to figure this out, and soon.

She drifted on subconscious currents throughout the universe. This was such an odd feeling as her People, the Spirit Guides, did not sleep, they couldn't. Who would watch over their children while they slept? They would be naked to the world without the watchful eye, the strength, and wisdom, of the People. It horrified her to consider such a thing. Even in this semi-conscious state. She had to break free of this stupor. Who watched over her children now?

She felt someone crack open her mouth and dribble a dram of something on her tongue. She swallowed, and coughed, whatever it was it burnt a bit going down, but it reminded her of someone. It was bourbon and the someone was Bear.

She forced an eye open and forced his face into focus. Concern colored his features and his deep, sunken eyes gave testament to his exhaustion. He attempted a smile but it only deepened the creases on the antiquity of his features.

"Did it help?" his voice more thought than words.

"I'll live," she said with far less vigor than she intended.

"I have a crazy idea and I need to run it by someone who has the analytical mind to consider the insanity of it along with the possibility it might be our only chance. Are you up to listening to the craziest, most whacky idea of all time?" Now he did grin and some of his youthful vigor returned. He had hope.

And if he had hope, she could do no less than listen and find hope in herself.

She did listen intently and what she heard horrified, shocked, and intrigued her. It was such an outlandish plan she thought it might just work. The main question was, could they actually do it. It would take every Spirit Guide from every belief throughout the world. And those who didn't believe such things, those who had grown too 'civilized' to believe that animals had souls or that natural animal spirits could guide, give strength and aid those who requested, wouldn't make any difference. It mattered not what they thought or believed as they would not subtract from the energy needed, they just wouldn't add. What mattered was how much strength all of the People could pull together to make this outrageous proposition work. Could they pull from not only their people but also the humans who still held faith in something greater than themselves and all living things being connected. And would the Mother allow such a thing.

She tried to consider it from every angle. It was true they needed something impossible, some grand, preposterous, senseless, absurd gesture that would send shock waves throughout the land. Something that aroused the great majority of humans and spurred them into action.

And if it failed, then everything would die. But, if they did nothing, everything would die. So, what did they have to lose? Bear wanted to try it with his own people first. A test run to see if it was even remotely possible. If he could accomplish it on a small scale then he could increase in size and scope until the final test. And if he succeeded, then all could. They needed to build their strength, their spiritual power. She could not be laying about with barely the energy to lift her head or sit up. She had to be strong, not just for her people but for all of the creatures that lived on the Mother.

Bear was one for grand gestures, if you were going to fail, fail magnificently! You want to get someone's attention, then get in their face, let them know you exist. And then don't. She laughed in her head as she considered the audaciousness of his plan. It had to work. It wass a dream come true, literally. It was too insane not to. She wished she could go with him to see the progress, but she had her own battle to engage. She had to heal herself and her people.

Sung watched as the wolves devoured another cow. This time they played with it before the kill and ate slowly, not of necessity but to add pounds and muscle. They grew stronger with each passing week. More packs had come, Sheriff John and Glen continued to truck cattle up the logging roads, as the wolves extended their territory. John began to wonder if this experiment was growing too large, would get out of hand, though Sung reassured his friend he could control all. It was who he was, John had to believe as he watched Wolf grow stronger, as his packs did. His coat shone with health; his eyes gleamed with purpose. And the respect the wolves showed, none would challenge him, they were subservient to his every command, even those not voiced out loud but somehow understood. No one hunted his children up this far near the tree line, they could have peace and time to return to prime physical condition.

At night while the packs would curl up together to sleep, Sung, Glen and the sheriff would sit around a fire and wonder how all the rest of the Spirit Guides where faring. Though mostly they wondered what Evan was up to and if his half-formed plan was coalescing and baring fruit. Shit, they just wished they had some concept of what he planned so they could help.

"I sure would like to know what everyone else is up to," Sung wearily allowed.

"That makes three of us," John said as he slapped Glen on the knee to assure he was part and parcel of this company.

"Maybe we should run down the mountain and see what we can discover. I should check in at the office to see if all is quiet and let them know I'm still on the job," smirked the absent sheriff.

"I need to stay here. As our company grows, there are bound to be quarrels and scrapes over territory. My people are not used to being this close to one and other. We like to have a little distance between us so no one is encroaching on another." Sung took in the large concentration of wolves in such a relatively restricted area. They were hale and hearty, filling out with the regular diet but soon they would want to roam, it was in their blood. He needed to be here to hold this group together. If they all of a sudden took it upon themselves to go off hunting, he knew where they would head. They had a taste for beef now and beef didn't have to be chased for a half mile. Cattle filled the prairie lands of southeastern Colorado in herds and were easy pickings. If this large a contingent of wolves started thinning those herds there would be no holding back the ranchers. They'd be hell bent on killing every wolf they came across. Sung, Glen, the sheriff, and especially Evan, hadn't gone to all this trouble just to make better targets for pissed off ranchers. No, it was imperative he stay with the packs until Evan revealed what he had in mind.

"Me and the sheriff could go into town and nose around a bit," Glen didn't think he could ever think of, let alone call, the sheriff, 'John'. "I'll talk to my children, shit almost everybody has a dog, or should, and they listen to everything humans say. Plus, there are millions of strays and feral canines who will talk to me. They see all. I would speak with them." Glen admitted to himself silently he also wanted to see all the others. He really loved the sheriff and Sung but a dog likes to hang with all the folks. He missed Suzette, and that pretty Doe. Most he missed Evan, Alexandra, and Her. They were his family, they had adopted him and taken him in. He owed them everything and he missed them terribly and worried about them constantly.

It was a lazy afternoon when Glen and Sheriff John drove into town. The sun blazed in a cloudless sky, the heat driving most indoors to air conditioning, or to pools and shade. Even the dogs were hiding under trucks, shade trees, and porches. No one was out unless absolutely necessary. A hundred and ten on the prairie can do that to folks.

"Can you drop me off at the house?" Glen asked.

John didn't have to ask which house, he knew, the house that had become a home for Glen. He wondered if Glen would ever move out of that back room, he guessed not. They were his only family now. Not that he'd had one before, at least not one he remembered, but Evan'd taken him in, fed him taught him, loved him. And Glen was loyal. If there was anything to this Spirit Guide stuff John could believe Glen was Dog personified.

He dropped him off with a wave and a promise to stop by later in the eve for a cold one, then it was off to the jail where he hoped it was quiet enough for him to catch up on some paperwork.

He radioed his, now trustworthy, deputies that he was back and would be at the office for the rest of the afternoon if they needed him. He picked up the stack of communiques piled on his desk and began leafing through them. He couldn't believe how the stress of the job had dissipated once he hired on these old friends. Having reliable folks at your side made all the difference in the world.

The usual mix of dispatches from across the state and region. A trespass here, a shoplifter there, nothing earthshattering. Just folks bored and beat down from the heat. They'd get arrested, spend the afternoon and night in a nice airconditioned jail and pay a small fine, less than a hotel would cost, then be on their way. Small towns from the Rockies to the Mississip were pretty much all the same.

Then one of the reports caught his eye. Some big guy had been caught speeding and decided he wanted to give the deputies a few towns east a run for their ticket. They'd run him down before he killed anybody but then he decided he'd like to try his luck in an adversarial aggressive way. Them County Mounties'd called backup and it'd taken six of them, three county Mounties and three Staties but they'd drug him off to the hospital for a bit of patching before locking him up for more'n a night. He was not going to be let off with a small fine, he would talk to the nice judge in a week and see how that run down the road turned out. John sighed as he put the paper back on the desk, rubbed his eyes and picked up his phone to call the Sheriff a few towns east.

The fella had refused to give a name or hometown and the plates were from another car, they couldn't identify him and he wasn't going to help. John was pretty sure he could be of some assistance.

Glen was greeted by a house full of folks, only a few he knew. So, Evan introduced him to Anna Marie, Brian, Chastity, and though they'd met a while back, Oscar, who he remembered from before and they all settled back into the yard for a proper welcome.

"How is everything up top," Evan asked and Glen knew what he was and wasn't saying. He wasn't quite in a trusting mood yet as far as some of these was concerned.

"A-OK," Glen smiled, "Sung seems to have everything under control. He's doing real well and sends his love to all of you. He's fit as a man half his age and working on getting stronger. He just is curious and would like a word when you get a moment."

"I'll pop in on him and have a chat." That's when everything stopped. The world stood still as an excruciating moan rose from the house next door and caught on the wind demanding everyone's attention.

Doe jumped up and ran over to check on the source, though she knew. The wood screen door banged hard against the wall, as she barged through to find Suzette laying on the living room floor unconscious.

Doe knelt on the hard linoleum and attempted to feel Suzette's pulse and head for fever. All watched in silence as she seemed to slip from human to Otter, to human to a combination of the two, as if her physical nature couldn't settle on which aspect she was supposed to be. It was something out of a horror or sci-fi movie.

"We have to find a way to stabilize where her physical form is. Right now, she seems to be fluctuating between present tense and the other side. We need her to become either Otter or Suzette and treat whichever takes control," Bear was attempting to put into words something they had never run across in their long lives. One always knew who and where you were and your physical representation showed that.

"Well, how do we do that if she doesn't know. How do we stop her from bouncing back and forth between the two?" Doe didn't mean to sound petulant, but her concern for her friend was overwhelming. She wanted to help, to lend strength, to hold her in one place but she hadn't a clue where to begin.

Bear was a creature of chances. Sometimes you dove into the deep end to see whether you could swim, this was a deep end situation. He gently moved Doe out of the way and waved the rest back to give himself some room. He had no idea what he was attempting or if it would work, but he had an inspiration. As gently as a man of his size and structure could he picked the small woman up from the floor and held her as close to his heart as possible. He could feel her heart beating against his chest, a rapid staccato, a drum beat to an impossibly fast reel, her breathing hard, shallow, and fast, her form flowing from human to spirit to animal to all three. He concentrated his every thought, his strength, his love for her—yes, he loved her, she had been a friend for years now and had been there when he needed—and pushed into her with all his great might his need for her to heal.

Spirit animals are not magic, they can't create things out of the ether, but they can lend strength, they can support, they can complete, heal, a torn soul. This was what he attempted. To use the force of his will to repair whatever was happening within his friend.

He soothed, murmured hope and reassurance. He forced his breathing to slow, to match what he wanted her to do, squeezing and patting her back in rhythm to life, to the breathing of all living things. Doe, Rebecca, Alex, and Oscar began a slow rhythmic chant, wordless, more rhythm than melody, more melody than lyric, it wasn't the words that mattered it was the love of the chant toward the intended. And she began to calm. Bear called to the Mother and the Great Spirit to hold her as well, to lend their power and the gathered's need for her decency, her goodness, her joy to life. To let her know how empty the world would be without her kind, her children, the playful, joyous creatures they were. This was what they sang. She had to find the strength within herself to hold onto what she was so her family would live. Children without a parent to guide them, to love them, were not long for this world. They all needed her; he needed her. She calmed, her breathing settled into a steady in and out, her heart beating a counterpoint to his own, he could scent the streams and the ocean on her. Life filled her. She would be alright.

The room let out a combined breath they hadn't known they held. Anna Marie was weeping and didn't know why, Brian held her close, tears streaming down his own face. They both appeared horrified by what they had seen but understood and felt the love of all for this woman. They were overwhelmed by the shear weight of that love, overwhelmed by the need.

Tatanka stuck his head in the door and Bear could see Elk over the great one's shoulder. "Ah, there you all are, everything OK? We've been looking over all the properties for you, we need to talk." The seriousness of his proclamation broken by the relieved laughter of the living room.

The rain came during the night while the small company sat outside consuming snacks, drinks, and smokes. They sat talking, enjoying the company, though not the subject of conversation. The rain saturating the dry, cracked ground, refreshing the overheated beasts and humans. It had been several months since a rain quenched land and beast and it felt good, physically, and spiritually. It was spring and the rains should have passed through with regularity, soaking the crops, the lawns, the souls of all who lived, worked, and relied on that relief. There had been torrential showers through the end of winter, flooding towns and forcing creeks to become rivers, rivers to overflow their banks and homes, businesses, and crops to wash out to sea.

Even worse was the loss of life. Of course, humans focused on their own losses, dozens had died, drowned in their homes, trying to drive through raging rivers or attempting to save friends and children. And still they refused to see what their actions were doing to the Mother. Some listened, but their voices were drowned out by the raging of business and selfish interests. Something had to be done and it looked as though it would fall on the shoulders of the few gathered here. It was time for Evan to divulge his plan, but he wanted Sung here when he did.

He sent Glen to find the Sheriff and then drive up to retrieve the Wolf, they would need everyone's input. Evan felt confident but only so far.

In the meantime, Anna Marie cornered him alone in the living room, "What the hell happened next door?" She had been waiting as patiently as her revolutionary heart could but now, she wanted answers.

"Things are happening to the climate, to the animals, birds, insects and life of this planet, we are trying to stop that," he thought this had all been explained already.

"No, I get that. What happened with that woman or whatever she is." Anna Marie was still in a state of terror from what she had witnessed.

"As we have explained, we are the Spiritual representations of animals. We stand guard for our children and we help those humans who take the time and energy to believe in us and ask. When we stand in the world of man we take on the manifestation of man, when we reside in the spiritual realm we take on our true selves. We believe because Otter's people continually dance on the brink of extinction, especially in today's world, and she is weak right now, she couldn't tell which world she belonged in. It is a very dangerous and, as far as I know, unheard of condition. We got lucky but we have to save her people if we want to save her." His neutral tone belied the worry that was evident on his features.

"Well, why didn't you say so! Do you have a computer with internet connection and password that will allow me access?" For the first time since he met her, she seemed conversant with the real world, though he wasn't exactly certain what she wanted.

Alex walked into the room just as Anna Marie made her request. Seeing the confused look on her grandfather's face she took over, "It's in the den," she told the woman, "I'll get the password and anything else you might need." She smirked over her shoulder at her grandfather who could only sheepishly smile his thanks.

Bear went back outside where what he understood was still being discussed to explain his plan once Sheriff John, Glen, and Sung returned. He would need all the strength of every spirit animal, from the smallest insect to the greatest souls, Tatanka, Elk, Cougar, Rhino, Elephant, everyone would have to work in concert if they were to have any hope of succeeding and convincing man they had to stop their destructive ways. If not, they would destroy the Mother and every living thing that she harbored on her. The enormity of what he planned, and what would happen if they failed threatened to overwhelm him.

Glen, getting ready to head up to retrieve Sung, noticed Evan sway as if a single reed in the wind and stopped as if to ask him if he was alright. Evan shook his head and waved him on his way. "Find them and bring them here, we will need all counsel."

Glen ran as he had never run before. Seeing Evan in even a slightly weakened state had shaken him to his core. Evan was the strongest of all of them. He was the protector, the guardian, when all else failed he would succeed. He always had. Maybe this time it would prove too much for him. He chased that thought far from his mind. He had to believe and he had to find the Sheriff right now and then the two of them would run up the mountain and bring Sung back.

Evan had swayed when the epiphany struck. He could not expect anyone to get onboard a train when they had no idea whether it would run and where it would go. What he did know is it would take Glen a little bit of time to find Sheriff John, for the two of them to drive up to where Sung watched over his packs and bring him down. That would provide plenty of time for Evan to bend time just enough to get up to where his people were most concentrated and attempt what he would explain to the others, assuming it worked.

"I have to run an errand," he poked his head in the door to the den, noting Alex and Anna Marie absorbed in whatever was showing on the computer screen. "Let your grandmother know." And he was gone.

Bear transported himself to the Canadian Rockies well outside the purview of man, approx. twenty kilometers SE of Lake Louise in Alberta Province. There would be dozens of Grizzlies in the general area. What the hell, if he was going to attempt this why not find the biggest meanest bears around. He liked their attitude.

He stood in the small open meadow and sent out his call to all in the area. He would wait here where they could see him, sniff around a bit and then, once they knew who he was, they would come.

After about forty-five minutes and his second smoke, he wanted to be calm and relaxed when he attempted his insanity, they began to show up. Each giving the other enough space not to feel crowded in, they didn't want any kind of war over territory, knowing they could, when necessary, occupy the same general area. And since it was Ursa Major who had called, it was necessary. Soon there were thirty-seven, it should be enough for the experiment.

Drawing them into a circle around him he projected into their minds what he was going to attempt. A few smiled at the audacity and others chuckled at the possibility of being somewhere without humans. They all agreed, as bears enjoy a good joke.

He pulled them into him psychically, so he could feel each one individually and as a group. In his mind he tied each to the other so now they would be one entity. It felt as though he had loaded a thousand-pound bag of rock onto his back. Mentally he sagged just for the moment, but he was Bear, the strongest, the protector, he stood erect in his mind. Picturing exactly where he wanted to take them, he pushed through the veil. With a soft hiss, a pop like the opening of a very large pickle jar and the scent of dill, they were through.

He opened his eyes to count, yes, thirty-seven, all accounted for and none the worse for wear. He checked each physically and mentally and they all seemed content, happy to be in this garden of Eden. They spread out, taking in the sights and lack of human scent. It was pure, pristine country, unspoiled by mankind. Bear was satisfied now his plan would work, though he only had brought thirty-seven. Each one of the People would have to start small and then work up to the numbers that were going to be asked of them. He felt confident this would work, though his assessment of what would be needed, for all of them to work together, in concert, forgetting and forgiving all past indiscretions, might prove the hardest hurdle.

He needed to get back and talk to the rest of the gang but didn't have the heart to force these cousins to leave just yet. He could bend a little time here and let them enjoy a few days or a week here. Hell, it might do him a world of good as well. He'd still be back before Sung, Glen and the Sheriff returned.

Down The Rabbit Hole, Indeed!

Willow couldn't tell if Earl was quiet by nature, quiet because he wasn't used to being around women, or had adopted the habit out of being alone for so long on his farm. She had eked out a few sentences concerning his past. Only a few and all about the farm—as if his life began the day he came to it, nothing before. It was as if he didn't exist before he showed up. He said nothing about how he'd come to live at the farm, come to love farming and that piece of earth. And, finally, how he'd come to inherit all. And for as little as said abut the farm he didn't say anything about much else. That piece of the Mother was his entire reason for being. He loved it more than a man could love a woman. He would, and had, given his life to it gladly, without reservation, and now, yeah, now, all he had was dust. He had not the words to describe that loss nor the desire to find them. She felt for him, she knew the loss of that which you loved most. She had felt it every day since time began.

"You hungry?" the words, like the crops dying as they passed through them, were empty of life, devoid of feeling, just something he thought he should say to be polite. He'd stopped being hungry for food, it was a mere necessity. His hunger was deep and unfulfillable. What he craved lived in the corner of his soul just outside where the dream had died. Though the thought of a burger appealed.

Willow wasn't certain how to answer the question. She knew humans had to consume foodstuffs to keep living, her people had to consume foodstuffs to keep living. She also knew that in certain regions of humanity her people were sometimes on the menu. She was a vegetarian by nature, though as a creature of spirit rather than physical substance she required nothing. But manners were manners, so, she thought she should be agreeable to consuming foodstuffs. As long as it grew in the ground and didn't move or talk.

"Sure, I could use a bite, but I should warn you I don't eat the dead bodies of once living things," she thought that should cover the ground nicely.

Earl sat silent for long moments as the two-lane rolled beneath and the sun moved a quarter inch towards the top of the mountains. "Well, isn't everything we eat some form of living thing? I mean we plant seeds which are then fertilized by the by nutrients in the ground and water and they grow into vegetables, grain, grass, and such. They just aren't mobile, but from my observation and some papers I've read, they can communicate with each other, warning of fire, man, and other disasters. Then, those further along can try to protect themselves or drop seeds deep into the soil so the next generation can survive. Not sure I've ever seen the difference in one or the other. But I'm not one to force my beliefs on another, we'll find some grub for both of us," he nodded to himself, satisfied he'd made his point.

Willow sat in stony silence somewhat shocked by the man's reasoning and logic but also because he had uttered more words in five minutes than he had the entire day. She smiled, though she knew she was still not going to eat the flesh of someone she knew. Theory was one thing, but she knew many cows, pigs, and chickens. She knew others of the people ate her kind; she would gracefully abstain.

After driving through the night, the sun was just peeking over the horizon when they pulled up in front of Evan and Her home. Apparently, it had rained sometime in the night. Earl got out of the truck and knelt on the wet grass almost as if in prayer. He hadn't seen wet grass in so long he wondered if it still existed anywhere on this once green earth. He wanted to lie on it, roll in it, feel the cold wetness against his skin, instead he stood, refusing to wipe his damp hands on his jeans to dry them off. He would hold onto these few raindrops as a talisman of hope.

It was quiet on the home front and Willow was unsure if she should go up onto the porch and knock or skirt around back and make themselves comfortable, wait until the rest woke. She couldn't be certain they were here, but realized if she stopped, closed her eyes, and concentrated she could feel them. There was the familiar vibe of those she knew and loved and also some very odd energy coming from those she would be meeting. And from the number she could feel and the unknown, apparently there would be a meeting. They would wait in the backyard and allow all the rest to sleep.

Coming around the corner of the house she was greeted by Doe as she, coffee in hand, made her way from the home she and Suzette had appropriated. They hugged carefully so as not to spill a drop of the life-giving black liquid and Willow introduced Earl to her. He stood stock still, as if frozen by the woman's beauty. He finally stuttered a hello before turning red about the ears and neck. Doe smiled inwardly at the reminder of the affect she could have on human males. Her kind, her children, took beauty for granted, it was nice when someone stopped to admire any of them.

"Everyone still asleep?" Willow ventured, "and how many everybodys are there?"

"Well, the usual suspects," grinned Doe as she scrubbed her short tan and white hair, "plus some very interesting species of the People and humans."

Earl's ears perked up at the strange references, maybe he heard it wrong. Probably distracted by the most beautiful woman he had ever seen. Life on a farm on the eastern edge of Colorado did not lend itself to multiple interactions with beautiful women, but, he reminded himself, here he was in the presence of two striking women met in the last twenty-four hours. Life could be weird as they used to say back in the late sixties!

The slamming of the wooden screen door announced another presence coming out the back of Evan's home. Another lovely young woman greeted the three with a nod and a yawn. She carried a pot of coffee, and a platter of bear claws, fruit, and fish in hand. Who ate fish in the morning?

"Morning, Alex," chimed the two women with Earl as they made their way over for morning hugs and a bite of breakfast from the heavily loaded plate.

"Willow! This is a fantastic surprise and a lovely way to wake. Coffee?" She asked as she hugged a welcome to Willow and nodded at Earl.

"Please," they both said together.

Alex set the platter on the picnic table and with a quick questioning glance back at Earl she went to grab more coffee cups. She passed Evan coming out as she was going in and nodded to where Willow and her friend stood, apparently not knowing whether they should sit or grab some grub. They hadn't exactly been invited but then Willow seemed to make up her mind, grabbed a handful of the mixed berries and a banana from the platter before plopping herself down on one of the ever-present chairs. Earl, deciding when in Rome, did the same, only he added a bear claw. They had eaten sparingly the night before after their conversation in the truck.

Evan grabbed the largest bear claw as he made his way to the upright log which was his usual spot to rest. He threw a silent question at Willow after he hugged her and welcomed her back. She replied with a crooked grin and dancing eyes. If Evan knew one thing it was that Willow was as good a soul as there had ever been, literally, and if she brought this human into their circle there was a reason. She would tell them in her own time.

And human he was. Evan could scent the human from where he sat, but there was something more. A scent of the mother, the land, this man was as tied to the Mother as any of them. Curiouser and curiouser, it promised to be a fascinating morning.

The largest man Willow had ever seen came up from the meadow behind Evan's house as if coming down from bed. He looked well rested though his weight seemed to drag on him, and he scented of salt water to her well-heeled nose.

Tatanka, Elk, not small by any means, and Oscar joined the group— she remembered the three from their earlier skirmish— accompanied by two humans of questionable intellect and integrity or maybe they were completely stoned this early in the morning, and lastly by the return of Alex accompanied by Her. Willow knew the woman must have a name but she could only think of Her in the terms Evan had originally set down. For a woman who had been dead for more than a decade and then resurrected she looked well rested and radiated a beauty from deep within.

Earl stared at the middle-aged woman hot on the heels of the younger beauty he had briefly met. The woman looked to be in her mid-fifties, he guessed, though he was no expert on women or their ages. She was stunning in a midwestern, plains sort of way. Not a runway model, not primped, painted, or pampered, more like all excess had been burnished and only the purity remained. She was the perfect picture of a middle-aged, middle -class, prairie housewife, slightly wrinkled of face though not wearied or frazzled, dressed in a floral smock, simple, timeless, something women had worn forever and would until the end of time. He felt as though he stood in the middle of a Hollywood movie set full of beautiful and handsome actors, though none of them gave the impression of being coddled.

The party was complete. Or so Willow thought, for just as Evan seemed about to make introductions for the new arrivals, the squeak of screen door opening attracted all attention to the home next door. A small, very dark brown woman was making her way, slowly, gingerly, wool blanket wrapped around her shoulders, though the morning was warm, towards the assembled.

Doe got up to rush to the small woman's side but Suzette shushed her away with both hands, a scowl, and then wrapped herself tightly in the blanket as she made her way to the comfortable Adirondack chair by the quiet firepit.

"Oh, go on with whatever you were about to do," she chastised all, "I ain't gonna die, not now, not ever. I had a spell but I am up to whatever task you all decide we need to do. I have children to think of and they don't need no worn out, tired, weak Spirit guide that can't protect them. I am Otter, now get on with it!"

Early stopped the bear claw just as it was entering his mouth, What had she just said?

"Well," began Evan, not willing to doubt or argue with this strong willed, petulant woman, "it would appear our little group has grown once again. Willow if you would be so kind as to do the introduction of your friend, I will tell you who has joined us while you were out and about."

"This is Earl. He is from over in eastern Colorado and I thought, from what you had said we were seeking, he would fit right in with this band of mischief makers."

"Earl, I welcome you to our family. Would you care to share yourself, who you are, that is and would you smoke with us?" Evan was being purposefully formal. He wanted each of them to come into what they were about to learn of their own free will but some ceremonies needed to be done to cement the friendship.

"I'm not sure what you mean by smoke." Earl was not a prude by any means, he was, after all, a child of the sixties, but getting high, and here he gazed across the table to the two young people laying on the wet grass, first thing in the morning was not his usual way to start a day.

"We are of Native blood," Evan's casual wave took in all assembled, or most, "We share the pipe to cleanse the soul, and bond the friendship."

"Oh, of course, I am somewhat conversant with the ceremony and I would be honored to share in brotherhood," Earl had met many First Nation people in his travels before settling down on the farm and had dealt with more as a farmer at market. He knew, and more importantly, he respected.

"Alex if you would do your old grandfather a favor," Evan put on his best frail, old visage for all to enjoy, as if aging right before their eyes.

"Of course, grandfather." She was back with the box almost before they stopped giggling.

All shared the pipe, Earl washed himself in the smoke as he had been taught and offered it to the relatives before handing it to Tatanka, one of the largest, most powerful men he had ever met. And as a farmer he had met many. Evan was pleased and a bit surprised by Evan's knowledge of the pipe ceremony.

Once the pipe was cleaned and put back into the case they all leaned back with their coffee, juice, or other beverage of choice so Earl could properly introduce himself.

"I served in the war and came home to find home had left me," he began and Evan nodded in the knowing. He had served in that same damn war, lost hisself for a minute till the acid, but that was his story not Earl's. "I wandered, not knowing what life held in store for me, if anything. There were times when I thought I couldn't go no further. I was lost, alone, my friends and family didn't know me anymore, I didn't know me anymore. The damn war had changed me, changed who I thought I was, stolen my life sure as if I'd got myself killed over there. I wasn't much use to anybody, not even me." There was no pity in the words, no woe is me, just the facts, emotionless. "I'd thought about just ending it, get out of everybody's way. I remember laying on the ground,

I was naked, but it was warm, like the land held me in her arms. I stared at the sky, the stars, the night, the immenseness, the grandeur smiling down on me and just started crying. I had never felt that lost and alone before, not even in fucking Nam. Pardon me," he apologized, "I curled up in a fetal position and prayed for death. Instead, I felt the land, soft and yielding like a mother's breast, and it comforted me. Ain't that the damnedest thing you ever heard?" He shook his head staring at the ground missing the smiles of knowing from all in attendance except the two young people.

"I felt like the earth was my mother and she would hold me and care for me until I healed. Next morning, I got up, put some clothes on," he laughed at the absurdity of the image, "and began walking. I guess I walked a hundred or more miles, never got tired. Again, it was as though the land itself was giving me strength, like she wouldn't let me fall. She would carry me if needs be, but the need never come. Until this farmer saw me and picked me up in his pickup, took me to his farm, where I met his wife and kids. Quickly I realized he might could use a hand, he was working this land by hisself and the kids being too young, he didn't have no money to pay one. I needed," he emphasized the word, "the land and he was willing to teach me her ways. I knew it wasn't the reason he picked me up, but I thought it mighta been the reason I got in." His smile contained all the joy of that time, and then, he broke down.

"I failed her. I didn't do right by her and my crops failed. Rain wouldn't come. I begged and pleaded, I promised her if she would heal, I find someone else to take care of her. I heard the people on the television and radio talk about climate change but I thought they was just screaming to promote their agenda. Just liberals hollering to hear themselves holler. This was the earth we were talking about, how much could man affect something so grand. Well, I found out, alright, I found out as she was dying. Now, it's too late and all I needed, wanted, was for her to heal. But I listened to the liars on TV and radio instead of those trying to save her. It's why my farm is dying, 'cause I failed her." He pulled out a handkerchief and wiped his eyes. "That's when your friend found me crying in the field. She said if I came with her, I would meet people that would understand, that knew. That knew her, the land, and loved her as I did and maybe, just maybe, we could help each other."

The silence wrapped them all. The Mother so still not even a blade of grass moved. "Guess I'm a bit of a mess, I didn't mean to bring my sorrow into your house."

Willow reached across to lay her hand upon his shoulder, lending her empathy and strength. She thought he had spoken more words in the last five minutes than he had in his life. And what powerful words they were. And what strength he had shown is sharing them. He was at the end of his rope and reaching out for any help that might be offered.

"No," Evan reached across the table and placed his hand on the farmer's other shoulder, "you have come to the right place. You are going to learn some things, some things that will be impossible to believe, but if you want to learn and keep an open mind, hopefully, we can all help each other."

The peace was broken by the roar of an unmufflered engine as Sheriff John's pick-up came wheeling between the two houses coming to rest and startling the assembled. Two dogs sticking their heads out of each side of the backseat windows, tongues lolling in the breeze as happy as two dogs could be.

No, shouted Earl's brain, that was one dog and one great big wolf. As the wolf jumped out of the cab, Earl jumped up to stand in front of Willow and Doe to protect them from the huge beast. He was ready to fight this thing if he had to, but protect, he would.

"Sung," shouted Evan, "We got normals here!"

The wolf seemed shocked for just a split-second before turning and running toward the house next door, and banging through the screen door into Suzette's home, the other dog hot on his heels. Earl heard laughing and howling from the house before two men came strolling out of the house.

"We put them away," they grinned as they joined Sheriff John next to his truck. John looked at the two, shook his head and walked away. Tomfoolery, he seemed to say to himself.

"Earl, meet Glen and Sung, the last two of our merry little band." Evan pointed to the two leaning against the sheriff's truck. They both shuffled over to shake his hand. As they did Earl could swear both of them smelled him, it was the weirdest sensation. They sat at the end of the picnic table and each grabbed some bacon Alex had brought out just as the sheriff's truck was rounding third. Sheriff John shook his hand before grabbing a folding chair and setting it next to the dark brown woman wrapped in the blanket, reclining in the Adirondack.

"Earl has shared his story with us and asks if we can help each other," Evan said to all, "and these two young people want to save the world but don't realize how difficult that will be. They also seek allies. I would assume, and we all know how that usually turns out," they chuckled, though quietly, "that we are willing to accept all friends we can find." Nods of assent. Where the Mother was concerned all help was needed and accepted, "but that means accepting some very difficult truths." At this the sheriff let out a loud guffaw.

"Sorry, but I have been through this initiation before. Seeing can be believing, if I understand where you are going with this, but believing, really believing, accepting myth and fantasy as reality is a bit of a bigger leap." He smiled at the woman wrapped up next to him and laid a comforting hand on her hand in a show of devotion and admiration.

Earl had known interracial couples since the early seventies so wasn't as shocked as the sheriff might have expected. He might be a farmer but was hardly unworldly.

"Earl, you said you are cognizant of Native rituals, how much do you know about spiritual beliefs and traditions?" Evan stuck a toe in the water as Anna Marie and Brian sat up. They had been shown but still didn't really believe, assuming it more to be an effect of the really good pot they had smoked rather than fact or reality. They both grinned to see how the new guy would take this. Though Anna Marie had worked through the problem of Suzette as if she truly believed. She knew it mattered not what she believed. If Suzette was sick because her children were dying Anna Marie would figure out how to stop the dying. And she had some concrete ideas on the matter which she would pass on to Suzette once she came down a bit from the weed, which had probably not been such a good idea after staying up all night working the problem.

"Well, I know about the animal spirits, kind of, how the world came about according to their myths. Not a lot, but I kind of get it. Never been that religious or curious enough to delve into it. Guess I always just lived and let live, as long as nobody was shoving nothin' down my throat," he shrugged off his apparent lack of belief.

"What if I told you they weren't myths, but like many myths of old they were based in fact. They, the animal spirits, were real?"

Earl's laugh was cut short by the intense stares of those around him. Even Brian and Anna Marie sat up straighter with the force of concentrated attention that that one question brought. The morning was silent, no buzz of insect, no touch of breeze, it was as if the world held her breath.

"I guess like any good farmer, you'd have to prove that to me. I believe the earth spins on her axis because I can see the change of seasons, the sun crossing the sky. I believe in the life she gave me because I planted the seed and watched the crop grow. I believe you want me to believe because it serves some greater purpose, or you think it does, and, for some reason, you want me to believe it too." He stared at the ground, shook his head, and then looked Evan in the eyes before taking in all their faces and wondering what he had got himself into. But if he was going down in this insane asylum, it would be with truth on his lips.

Evan leaned back and smiled, "Fair enough," he said.

The world began to spin again and life returned to the large backyard. Had Earl passed some test? Was this some kind of initiation and if he said he believed whatever cow shit they were throwing would they have thrown him out? He had no idea, but the plow was down and the earth needed tilling.

But as he stared at all those seated around him the air seemed to shimmer. He rubbed his eyes to clear them and tried to focus just on Evan, Willow, and Evan's wife and granddaughter, all seated in a row along the picnic table with Evan on his log at the head. They blurred and he felt the earth shift. He picked up his coffee cup to have a swig and see if that didn't help but changed his mind. Had he been drugged? Maybe it was in the fruit. Though none of the others appeared high. No giggling at his predicament, no strange gestures of watching their hands make trails in the air. No nothing just them losing focus, or him not able to concentrate. He just knew something weird was happening and he didn't like it.

After a minute the world settled down and all had returned to their normal animal shapes. There was a massive bear sitting next to a rabbit of large proportion, book cased by two other bears all staring at him. OK, things were now out of control and he needed to be as far away from here as quickly as his two legs could carry him, but when he turned to go he saw the large wolf sitting and panting next to a dog who seemed to be smiling. They gazed over at the Elk and Buffalo standing next to a manatee—well, that's what he thought it was, he'd never seen one in person—with a lovely deer sitting adjacent to an otter covered in a blanket. A giant owl landed on the grass next to the kids. The only thing holding his wits together was the presence of the sheriff and those two kids sitting on the grass.

Really, they should have reassured him except they seemed to think this was normal. Maybe they couldn't see what he was seeing. It reminded him of a bad acid trip back when he'd just come home from the war. Everyone was smoking pot and he'd taken a hit of purple Owsley. No one was seeing the same things he did, it was four-way and he didn't share. Yeah, he just needed to hang on for a bit and everything would be alright.

"What you see is real," calmed Evan as if he could read Earl's mind. And, of course, he could. Earl was tripping and all his thoughts were being telegraphed and projected like a drive-in movie.

"WHAT THE ABSOLUTE FUCK IS GOING ON?" He shouted to no one in particular and the universe in general. He didn't care if he pissed someone off or if they thought him rude and out of control. They had obviously done something to him and he wasn't pleased in the least.

"We are immortals, Spirit Guides created by the Mother when she was created by the Great Spirit. We have existed since before mankind was evolved far enough along he could understand the concept of spirit. He needed to be led into civilization. We lend strength, guidance, wisdom, and knowledge, not that everyone listens or takes what we give. Certainly not enough of humanity," to which all nodded knowingly. Evan kept his tone flat emotionless, just the facts. He didn't want to convey urgency or demand, just having a conversation human to Bear.

"So, somebody dosed me, now I'm hallucinating and you want me to accept this all as reality?" Earl made to get up again.

"Thank you, that's what we've been trying to come to terms with." Cried Anna Marie and Brian in unison. "They keep telling us the same thing and we were just about to believe and you came along, now we know for fact. They keep dosing us, though why, we can't grasp," and with that they lay back on the lawn exhausted with relief. "The thing is," popped up Anna Marie, "We would've helped anyway. And we have found some possible solutions to maybe save the otters and some others, it's just so insane they keep this up!"

Alex gazed at the young woman with a look of betrayal. They had spent the better part of the night researching ways to help Suzette and she had sworn Anna Marie believed what she'd been told. Now here she was saying she'd only played along.

"No one has given anybody anything," assured the sheriff, jumping in to stop this train before it could get round the bend. "What you are witnessing is true, as far as I can tell. These folks are friends of mine, we have shared our lives for more than a decade. This is who they are," John had no other way to explain. You either would believe or you didn't. All he knew was that each one of these people had shared in a war of sorts with him and he was willing to accept them whoever or whatever they were.

"I just can't, it's all too surreal," the funny thing was Earl actually wanted to believe this, because if this was real, then so was everything that had happened to him. Everything he felt about the land holding him, loving him, everything he wanted to believe. If he could just let himself go.

"Look no one expects you to just jump up and say, 'Oh, joy! The world is a magical place and I'm one with the fairies,' who also exist, by the way. We are giving you the gift of cracking a door on what you think is real, which is, but what is also just as real. Just take a peek and sit back have a cup, a nosh, and we will talk." Evan was Evan once again, as were all the rest. Just a dream, a daydream, while he was completely awake and aware, sure. He was tired, he'd driven all night with the rabbit and now he was down the rabbit hole with Alice. Who the fuck is Alice? He required sleep.

"Is there a hotel nearby?" even to him he sounded exhausted.

How Smart is The Average Bear?

The sun was setting behind the distant mountains by the time Earl awoke in a strange bed, in a strange house, with strange pieces and glimpses of strange dreams floating in his head. It was a strange feeling as his feet touched the solidity of the floor and all came back like a slap upside the head. Damn! What had been real? What had been imagined? He didn't know and couldn't accept what he thought he'd seen and heard.

But what if it was true? What if these people were the representatives of Indian lore? Could it be that much weirder than folks who believed in fate, karma, ghosts, spirits in the night? The second coming of someone dead for two thousand years? What is reality? Screamed a half-remembered line from a comedy album a half century before.

He half stumbled down the stairs, his equilibrium thrown off by the confusion floating in his brain. He was foggy, confused, and just wanted to go back to his farm, turn some soil, watch the sunset and, literally, watch the grass grow. But that was all gone, wasn't it? As he passed the open front door he saw Willow sitting on the porch swing lost in thought. She was a pretty little thing, came the thought and he immediately chased it out of where it had lodged in the wrong part of his head. Though he liked the ears, they were, what was the term, elven, he guessed.

He pushed his way through the wooden screen door and silently asked if he could sit by her.

"How you feeling?" She asked a bit tentative.

"Like the world is spinning a hundred miles an hour and I'm standing still. Dizzy, lost, dreaming," he sighed.

"Yeah, I guess we can have that effect on humans. Usually, we only pop up when asked and then to only one or two folks who have need," she smiled apologetically

"Let's say I can put my disbelief and skepticism in a box for now and I'm willing to entertain the possibility that what y'all are saying is true, why are you here? You just said you don't normally do this, you know, show up and tell people you're real and shit. Why now? Why here? Why...me?" The sound of shoe leather on wood caught his attention, a habit ingrained in his psyche during the war.

Sheriff John stuck his head out the screen door and grinned, "You know, son, I have been a cop since I got out of the service, you'd think I would've thought to ask that same question at least once over the last ten or twelve years." Though Earl was in the same ballpark age wise with John, country sheriffs had a way of calling every guy they came across either son or sir, depending.

"John, I thought we explained during the last time we had to save the world..."

"Wait, you guys have done something like this before? How come nobody said anything on the news or in the papers," not that Earl was buying into the whole Native Spirit guide bullshit but he at least wanted his fantasies to be logical.

"We don't really advertise what we do, we're kind of like the Lone Ranger in that we don't wait for thank you's or interviews. As a matter of fact, we don't want people, as a rule, to know we actually exist. But sometimes rules need to be broken." Willow shrugged and when she did, she did this thing with her nose that Earl found disconcerting. "and it was a different thing last time, a tear in the universal fabric kind of thing, but Bear fixed it."

"Well, I tore it, it was my responsibility to fix it," Evan's head appeared from where he was bent over in front of the porch weeding.

Earl had wanted this just to be between himself and Willow but apparently it was going to be a party.

"Nothing to be concerned with anymore, it's fixed and the universe will remain whole!" Evan grinned.

"Wait, are you trying to tell me all life in the whole damn universe was about to end and you 'fixed it'?"

"That's a bit of an oversimplification but, kinda," Evan shrugged wiped the dirt from his hands and came up on the porch just as Alex and Rebecca came out the front screen door. OK, a family affair.

"This is actually a more difficult problem," Alex noted.

"More difficult than saving the universe?" Earl had had about enough and was looking anxiously toward where his pick-up was parked on the street.

"Hang on, hang on," cautioned Evan, " let me explain it this way. In our last adventure we were really the only ones who needed to know about what was happening. We didn't need to involve humanity except these few," he pointed to John, "well him and a couple others. It was a problem I had created when Rebecca," and it still felt odd saying Her name, "died from the damn cancer."

"OK, OK, well, she's not dead, are you saying she came back from the dead? Like Christ himself, rising from the tomb?"

"Not exactly, she came back from the dead like a gift from the Mother and Great Spirit to save Alex. I came back from the dead because I'm immortal, though we immortals can suffer death, it ain't really. We don't actually die, though we can be extincted." Evan shook his head in frustration, it was so hard explaining these things to people who couldn't conceive of the concepts involved. "Anyway, none of that matters right now because we have to find a way to join forces or ideas with some humans to convince the rest of the humans to stop destroying the Mother!" There!

"And the Mother you refer to always is the Earth?" Earl was grasping for anything resembling a straw or life preserver.

"Yes," jumped in the sheriff, "as she is the Mother to us all. Look, I don't care what your religion or your beliefs are. Forget the personification of animals or inanimate objects or clouds in the damn sky crap, we only got one earth, one Mother, as it were, and she is the one that supports all of us in one way or another. We can't keep dumping our shit in her oceans or landfills or dumping carbon into the sky. We are creating an imbalance in the whole damn thing. We, humans, have to be stopped. And, sure as shit, the damn politicians ain't going to do it, they ain't got the balls."

"That's a fact," said Sung as he and Glen came sauntering around the corner of the house. "It's not just humans that humans are putting on the extinction list, if it was, I'd let them, but they are killing everything as they go. Wolves, bears, manatees," he said as Chasity joined the group with Tatanka and Elk not far behind. "otters, shit look at what it's done to Suzette!" Now anger colored Sung's words. It was

Sheriff John that put his hand on Sung's shoulder to calm him. "Anyway, we have to find a way to shock mankind into doing what is right, because he sure as shit ain't going to do it otherwise. Long as they each got what they want for themselves now, well, fuck the future."

"Anyway," Evan stood up to take control of this situation before anybody else decided to start a war, "you have been brought here because Willow thought you had the heart, the love, the strength to help us help you."

"But I'm just one man, one farmer." Earl had never felt so small, so insignificant in his life.

"Well, these folks are more but they need our help. Our help to help our own kind and theirs." John was allowing emotion to rule his tongue and he didn't care. He thought of Suzette and the pain she was suffering, but refusing to quit. He thought of Sung when he showed up in the forest, thin, emaciated, hardly able to stand but still leading his pack. He remembered his childhood in these forests so lush, green filled with life, now not much more than tinder for the next huge conflagration. He thought of the stupidity of politicians and the greed of the powerful, of people suffering, dying, and still believing the lies. His anger found fuel and he wanted this man, this good man who reminded him of his own father, to get this, to understand, to stand with them and be a voice, another hand to help lift humanity out of its own sewer. Enough was enough and there was not enough left. They had to do something, what was it Evan had said, enormously stupid and tilt at some huge windmills. They required ludicrous, insane, and outrageous and some folks to help pull the wagon. And he hoped Bear had something nuts up his sleeve!

Speaking of nuts, John perked up with a brilliant, crazy idea. "Look, we don't have a lot of time for convincing folks here," he told Evan, "maybe you could take him and these two across like you did me and show them what it should be and why we need them," he ran out of words, they needed action not long-winded sheriffs

Evan stared at the sheriff as if he'd lost his mind, his expression morphing into one of consideration. Maybe the man had a point and he could kill two birds with one grand stone.

"Sheriff, you might have stumbled on an excellent idea," Evan smiled while John looked shocked that Evan was considering his suggestion, even thought it might be good. Then glanced at the others in an 'aw shucks' kind of move, even kicking the ground. Evan's smile grew wider, he knew the sheriff didn't like people to single him out, especially for being clever or intelligent. Humans could be so peculiar.

"Here is the plan for the moment. Rebecca, Alex, and I are going to shuttle these three across the divide so they can see for themselves what and who we are. I need to report to the Mother about my experiment anyway, so I can accomplish two tasks with one jump."

"You want a little company?" Of course, Glen wanted to go, he hated being left behind.

"Actually, no, this time I need all of you here you to consider something, if each of you were to try and 'corral' all of your children into one spot where would that be and how long would it take?" The twinkle in his eye told them everything they needed to know, this was a piece of where Evan was headed in his plan, but where was that?

"Wait a second, what are you planning?" Sung spoke up first though the question rested in everyone's eyes.

"I got an idea, it is pretty outlandish and dumb, but it just might work, but remember, each of you has to settle on a piece of territory that will not interfere nor cause a range war with any other species." He saw the apprehension on every face, "Look just trust me for a few more days, I wont' be gone long in human time but I need to run some results by the Mother, if she says we are good to go, we are going to need to move quickly." He wasn't quite ready to tell them what he'd done with his thirty-seven children. He wanted to run it by the Mother and do a quick check-in on the participants to see how they fared first.

They had trusted him before and he had worked things out, though almost too late and at a cost of some injuries and a bit of a torn-up end of town, but he had. Now, he asked for their trust again, nobody had any better idea, they had no other choice. Each in turn nodded their agreement.

"But don't be screwing around over there, things are getting pretty ugly here." Sung spoke quietly but with force.

Evan gathered his wife, granddaughter, Earl, Anna Marie, and Brian in a small circle, "Just relax," he said to their concern, "nothing will happen to you except you'll have your eyes opened for you on possibilities." And the scene shifted, the air shimmered there was a pop like someone opening a brand new jar of pickles and the scent of dill, and they were not in Kansas, well, Colorado, anymore.

The colors almost assaulted the eye. The green of leaves brilliant against the dark brown of tree trunk and ground. The blue of the sky seemed to shine of its own accord, every plant, rock, leaf, came alive with hues unknown to the human spectrum, yet here, they could be seen. You could feel the life in every organism, hear the burble of the streams as if the water laughed and sang on its way down the mountain. And that was another thing, they had been standing on the plain at the feet of these grand ranges, now they stood thousands of feet up their slopes.

All three of the humans sat hard on the ground overwhelmed with life, sound, and sight. None believed the earth could hold this much sentience, they had only known what the earth had become. The rich vibrant colors, the scents assaulting their noses, the total silence as if every living thing had been removed from existence was awe inspiring. They were the only occupants of this perfect, beautiful world. Anna Marie was weeping with the joy of it all, Earl wrapped himself in his arms staring at the huge Bear towering over him as if he had landed in his concept of Heaven. He could see, feel, hear, smell everything, the most minute scents filled his olfactory senses exploding and filling his head with colors, taste, sounds, who knew scents contained sound? He thought he might die from joy and bliss. Brian crawled over and clung to a giant pine apologizing for what, no one knew, but he was overjoyed for the opportunity.

"Where are we?" Earl whispered the words to the Bear as if it were the most natural thing he had ever done.

"The best way I can explain it is, we are on the other side of the veil. There is the reality you and every human knows, every living thing lives on that side of the veil, here is where we come from. We are the only beings allowed in here, we are ourselves here," he pointed as his own visage and that of Alex and Rebecca's. "This is where all of that life, that life that is in such danger on the other side, originated and its roots are."

"Why can't we live over here? There is no sign of decay or death." Earl pled.

"Well, because each is a distorted reflection of the other. This one is more pure, more pristine because no one is actually here and destroying what once was, though what happens on the other side affects what happens here. As such these plants, this beauty contains no nutrients, no life-giving sustenance as there is no need for it here." A great sadness threatened to overtake Evan, "if something becomes extinct over there it ceases to be here, there is no Spirit left. We are but reflections of what lives, what has a soul. And all living things have a soul, an energy, if you will, that lives on once that thing dies. Plants, animals, birds, fish, all living things are tied together as a family of life. If anything becomes extinct, so do we, their spirit guides. Animals, trees, insects, dinosaurs, birds, plants, everything that gets obliterated on your side will no longer exist anywhere." The tear found its exit and rolled down the massive snout.

Earl wasn't sure he had ever witnessed anything as heartbreaking as a twelve-foot, one ton bear crying, but there it was. And a hole of empathy in his chest opened as if it wanted to take in all the pain and suffering of the world. It would kill him but he didn't care, if he could sacrifice himself so the world could become this again, even a pale reflection of this, he would joyfully give his last heartbeat. But he knew he couldn't. He stood, his legs shaking, his eyes spilling tears, struggling to form words. "What do you want of me?" and he realized in that moment that he had excepted the impossible. He had to believe in his soul, in his heart, and intellectually all of this was possible. There was magic in this world and he wanted to believe in it, to be a part of it.

"Enjoy all this for a bit, I have something I have to do and I don't think I can accomplish it here. Alex and Rebecca will look after you three, though you won't need anything here. You won't be hungry or thirsty, you have nothing to fear from anything in nature as the only nature here are spirits." He turned to walk away.

"But where will you be?" Now it was Brian who whimpered like a child watching his father leave during a storm.

"I have an old friend I need to talk to. I have an idea, a plan, and I want her opinion," the Great Bear grinned and walked away.

Wrapped in the sounds of the forest, the five sat in silence lost in his or her own thoughts. Alex and Rebecca talked quietly between them while keeping watch over the three humans.

"Do you really think this is all real, not some kind of hallucination?" Anna Marie had crawled over to where Earl lay on his back staring at the pines above.

"It is as real as anything I have ever known, more real than what I left." His words had such weight, they were as solid as granite and true.

Anna Marie looked to where Brian was lost in the study of a brilliant red, yellow, gold, and green leaf. "Hey Bri, Bri," she hissed, "what do you think? Is this real or just really good pot?"

He sighed remorse that she couldn't see the truth, "Anna Marie, did we smoke pot before we left? Any time this morning? No pot is that damn good it would last all night and then into the day especially with this real of hallucinations." He said it as if it was the most obvious thing in the world, and she realized, it was. Her scientific mind kicked in, what one observed with their own eyes and could correlate with the observations of others had to be true until proven otherwise. She didn't think anyone could prove otherwise.

"Do you have questions? Need reassurance, would you like to go walk around for a bit?" Rebecca spoke like what she was, a grandma. Yes, she was also a large female bear with her cub sitting across from her, but she was still grandmotherly.

It was quite the interesting visage, thought Anna Marie. And if you can't believe your grandmother... "Yes, I would love to go for a walk in these woods," she answered. Now, having accepted, she wanted to observe all she could, collect what knowledge presented itself and maybe solidify her theory on how to help Suzette's people as well as the others.

"Well, then let's all go exploring and see where we wind up," Alex giggled though she had an idea of where that might be.

The air shimmered ever so slightly, Bear felt it, though not as strong as he should have. He turned to see her sitting on a boulder nearby. She looked wan and tired though she smiled at him and waved him over to sit by her.

"Well, Bear, what brings you back to the good side?" She grinned to take any sting out of the words.

"I went to the north woods and gave my insanity a small test."

"Yes, I was aware. What is your belief?" The words were almost a sigh carried delicately to him on a slight breeze.

"My belief is it needs to be tried a few more times, each time increasing the numbers and distance between each group. I have to see if I can transport a large number, not necessarily within shouting distance, at the same time. I'm not certain we can move everyone at once, but it is worth the effort to find out. I don't think we have many options left. It should be attempted with everyone on board," he shrugged not wishing to impart confidence he didn't hold.

"I see," she said, with a wan smile, taking note of his depreciating manner, "the grand, stupid, impossible gesture." Again, she gave him a coquettish grin to remove any sting from the words.

"There is no one human or human federation that we can go to with the wherewithal to achieve the end we need. That is, to stop mankind from destroying everything of worth. It's almost as if someone or some spirit is pushing them past the point of reasonable or responsible thinking. As if mankind has been infected with some kind of virus towards self-destruction," he shook his head and glowered at the reality of their situation, "There have been some pushing, fighting to stop the madness but they are children and no one will listen to them. They attempt to prove that all the people, from all the nations, are just pawns of others in power. Why in the hell is it always about power with humans?" He tried to tamp down his anger but it was a trial. Everything beautiful and of worth was being destroyed and for no good reason. Mankind could have the greatest existence he wanted, to live in his vaunted Garden of Eden, to end hunger, want, to live in joy and harmony with all the creatures of the world, to stop destroying and truly begin building.

"What do you honestly think your chance of success?" Her breath was heavy, she carried all of life on her shoulders, think of that, thought Bear. "and remember, Bear, every action requires an opposite reaction, all actions require cost. I can't say exactly what that cost might be, but last time your actions cost you a painful death and a decade or more to recover. There is no guarantee whether the price this time might not be the same or worse, a long suffering, maybe an eternity of torment, then death, you might not come back."

Bear thought about that, he had thought about it since coming back to life. How many lives did an eternal Bear have? And did it matter. If it came down to it, he knew he would trade the rest of his eternity for the lives of all the rest. Besides, he wouldn't be endangering his people, his children, because Alex and Rebecca would survive and they would care for his. He was tired but he had to try this one last chance at survival for all. "Last chances only need one percent to succeed," he grimaced.

"And ninety-nine to fail," She whispered.

"Yeah; think you're up to helping?"

"Think you all are up to trying?"

"I'm thinking there might be a way to increase the odds." He grinned to himself, Why hadn't he considered this option before? Mentally he slapped himself upside the head. 'You is one big old dumb bear!' the laugh echoed in his head.

Do Monkeys Have Wrenches?

"You have company," Mother said before dissipating into nature.

"Was that?" Earl stood stock still staring at the spot the Mother had occupied just moments before.

"Yes, it was," snickered Coyote as he scrambled out from under the brush. "Hey Bear," he said sheepishly as he brushed the twigs and dirt from his coat. "And Mrs. Bear, little Bear and company."

"Well, I guess my private meeting wasn't so private. I thought you all were going to wait for me." Alex only grinned a challenge back at him.

"They wanted to see more of this side and we just happened to wind up here," innocence thy name is Alex.

"We'll discuss this later." Bear was not happy and did nothing to hide that fact, though his family and the humans were only part of his dissatisfaction. "Yote, nobody likes being spied on. And I like it less than most. Who you spying for?"

"Now Bear," Coyote began, "I ain't spying, you got this all wrong, I was just trying to get a little rest between trying to keep my family alive, while watching humans destroy without conscience, and finding something to distract the mind. Maybe you should be aware that away from your little island of joy on the other side, shits been going down all over the Mother, no wonder she looked so poorly. Half of the land is suffering such drought they can't grow a weed; everything is dying and what ain't drought is massive floods. Look at Kentucky in your land or Pakistan or Europe! I got cousins over there and they are terrified. And so am I!

"The glaciers is melting, the ice cap is melting, the Mother is melting and you are very quickly running out of time. We are approaching the point of no return. And when that happens, we best make our peace with the Great Spirit, hope he finds some place to save a few species, and then kiss our asses goodbye!" Coyote threw the challenge hoping Bear would counter with whatever he was planning and it would be brilliant.

"I ain't in the mood for giving up, I'm in the mood for fighting for what is ours." His words were clipped, terse, "You three seen enough? You want to save the Mother or die trying?" He was tired of planning, tired of waiting and tired of losing hope. It was time to put this thing in motion whether the others like the idea or not. They had no other choices.

They looked to each other, straightened up, and nodded their assent.

"Let's go home and get everybody involved, now."

As they shimmered back to presence in the field behind their home they were greeted by the sounds of shouting, a cacophony of growls, yips, screeches, howls, and squawks. Apparently, the conference was fully underway and nobody was in charge. Suzette stood on a bench begging for quiet and order, Tatanka looked as though he was ready to wrestle a large woman to the ground while Elk tried to hold him back. Oy vey, thought the great Bear.

Taking a deep breath he strode to the center of the melee, though no one seemed to take any notice, held his hands up to make hisself seem larger than he was and shouted, "Enough!"

The shock of having Bear appear in the gathering as himself, and the volume of the shout, stopped all in their proverbial tracks. Suzette slouched where she had been standing, Tatanka stumbled back into Lawrence Elk's arms, and the woman Tatanka had been at the precipice of a donnybrook with glared at Bear but was wise enough to stand down. Sheriff John and Sung stood off the side with Glen grinning at the pandemonium, though they stood more erect at the sudden manifestation of Bear.

"What in all the seven levels of hell is going on here?" Bear was disconsolate, the Mother was being murdered, their children were dying by the hundreds, if not thousands, and all these supposed Spirit creatures could do was emulate mankind. "I leave for a few minutes and this is what you've become?"

"Actually, more like a week and half, local time," the sheriff demurred helpfully.

"Whatever! You are supposed to be creatures of morals, values, created to help, guide, and lend strength to those in need, not become the weakest and most pitiful of their ranks. What are you? Politicians?"

They, at least, had the decency to appear embarrassed.

"Now, what is it that has you going at each other like humans?" Bear was hanging on to his temper by a fingernail.

"We are attempting to figure out who gets to decide who is allowed to choose what territory everyone gets," said the woman with the black and white hair that Tatanka had been about to tackle.

"And to whom do I have the pleasure of addressing?" Bear decided on polite rather than attack.

"I am Orca, of the great ocean," she stood to her full height to emphasize her own importance.

"Well, Orca of the Great Ocean, I am just Bear and I really don't care who decides what, I just know we are running out of time and need to figure out how to work this whole deal out." He sat on his favorite upturned log to wait for all to settle. "Damn, does it matter? You all know where you belong, Elk is not going to ask for a spot in the great ocean, Willow doesn't give two shits about the deserts of Africa or the swamp lands of India. You all know where you live and what we need to do. If we are to have any chance of this succeeding, we will NOT," and he emphasized the word with all the Bear he could muster, "interfere with others." He sighed. "Look I'm not sure this will even work, I am going to need your patience, and your cooperation for a little while longer while I try a couple more experiments. It won't take but a day or two," he shushed them, his paws moving in a conciliatory gesture.

"I have been discussing with Mother the best chance to turn the destruction around and we agree we need an insane, preposterous, magnificently grand spectacle to garner the attention of those in charge of humanity. Our idea was to gather together every species of animal, fish, mammal, and bird with whatever power we might possess and move them to the other side of the veil. I just want to try once or twice more to guarantee this might work."

"Wait, wait, wait," jumped in Coyote who had crossed back with the family and the three humans, "you are proposing we move every single one of our children over to the other side? How will that protect them from what humans do here? You know whatever happens here is mirrored over there. Extinct is extinct no matter which side of the veil you're on," Coyote smirked at his own cleverness and his ability to pop the great bear's idea. "and there ain't nothing we can eat to keep us surviving over there, except to feed on each other, and then, ain't we just humans?"

"You done? Good. No, we are not talking about going over there permanently just as a way to shock humans to come to their senses."

"That's the stupidest thing I have ever heard in my life," spit Orca.

"I agree," spoke up the small bowling pin shaped man, "mankind has shown itself to be totally devoid of caring when it comes to any other species. He does not bother himself about extinction of others, I am not certain he gives a moment's thought to his own. He lives for the second he is in, now, not tomorrow, not a half hour from now. My people are hanging on by the tip of a fin, does mankind take note? HA, it is to laugh. Maybe we should extinct a few of them and see how that fits their idea of the future!" This little man was stirring a pot Evan had no desire to agitate.

"We are not going to war with anybody, that serves no purpose but death."

"Then we die taking out a few million of them with us. This whole concept is just stupid, as our friend Orca has so succinctly spoken." Evan finally knew who spoke. King Penguins took their name quite seriously and believed the title.

"Enough, maybe we should vote to see if the land creatures just fear mankind too much and are willing to allow extinction to happen. Is it the climate change, the destruction of your great land you fear? Are we all to join in to save the land creatures?" Orca taunted Bear.

"Really? How are things in the great ocean? The water still pure and salty enough to support all your needs?" He kept his tone of voice even not wishing to provoke her if she thought she was being attacked, but he had to nip this before the sentiment could grow.

"No," she admitted, "the sodium density is flagging with the melting of the ice caps and glaciers. Too much fresh water is not good for those of us saltwater creatures. And the amount of oil and debris is increasing every day. I take your point," she conceded.

"My point is simply this, if we do not work together to find some solution, the final solution will be the end of life on the Mother. So, the idea is to gather together each species away from the others to avoid conflict. Then, at the appointed day we, hopefully jump them across leaving a massive void of life on this side. I cannot believe that there aren't millions of animal, bird and fish loving humans who will flip out and take to the streets demanding action from their supposed leaders." He noticed the four humans here all nodding their approval of the plan. "I can't guarantee nothing, and if you all can come up with a better idea, I'm all ears. But understand we need something so shocking it will shake them to their toes."

"And what if it doesn't work?" asked Suzette.

"Then we all die together. Either way this is the only chance we've come up with and we think it is worth trying," Bear held his wife close not wanting to entertain the thought of losing her again. But, if she was going to die, this time he would die with her.

"Well, I love it," Earl chimed in, "What do you need for us to do? We obviously can't help with your part but maybe we can stir up a bit of good trouble while you work out your logistics." He nodded to Anna Marie and Brian who were now fully engaged in the idea of creating some chaos.

"And why can't we find species and subspecies that can occupy the same area. Ones that are not mortal enemies or predator and prey. We can work together in concert rather than worry about who is on the menu." Tatanka stood with his friend of so many centuries Lawrence, the Elk.

Bear thought he was right, there had to be many species who could concentrate their spirit guides to work in unison and bring them across. They had much to consider and not centuries to work with. It was time for the Native legends to come alive and save the Mother.

No one noticed the two boys playing catch out in the field behind Bear's home. It had been known for the last decade or so as a place kids could come put together a baseball game, football scrimmage or go down to the river to swim. He was just this nice old guy who wanted kids to be kids. So, these two drew no attention.

Yet the boy's attention was riveted on what the large group in Evan's backyard were talking about.

"What do you think?" asked the taller boy with the reddish hair.

"I think we need to go along with whatever they are planning, otherwise we will be too obvious and suspicious. Besides I want to save my children as much or more than they want to save theirs," grimaced the other kid with the shock of white in his black hair, "You see, I know something they haven't even considered."

"And that is?"

"If this all goes to shit, and the Mother is stressed to the point of extinction herself, all the larger animals will be the first to go. It takes too much to keep them alive, they need too much food, water, and land. The ones who survive are the small ones who know how to scavenge, to live on next to nothing. You and me and our children will inherit the earth. These bozos will all be extincted."

"But then so will we!" cried the fox

"No, dummy, the big ones go, and all of our threats go with them. See, as long as they're here we just get the scraps they leave, not the good suff. Not only that but they also feed off of us and our young. Think about it, once they are gone, we are the top of the food chain. We will rule, not some stinky Bear or Buffalo, us we finally get to be top of the world, not waiting for leavings from them. Hanging around hoping they leave a little meat on the bone," now Skunk was peeved and getting more pissed when he thought of centuries living beneath the weight of the much larger animals. Always waiting for them to drink their fill, eat their fill and leaving crumbs. No more spray and run, now he and Fox would get all the berries and nuts, the finest insects, and moles, they would make all the decisions, they would rule the roost.

"I get it," Fox spoke without much confidence but they were in deep and he needed to cling to 'the plan' for all he was worth, and the existence of his children. "But we still got to hedge our bets, right? I mean if everybody is going along with what Bear wants, and it seems like they are all in agreement, then we need to get our families together." He hesitated, waiting on a response from Skunk, "I mean, you know, just in case."

"You're not backing out, are you?" Skunk looked sideways at his partner in crime, "getting cold paws, or something. Remember if one goes down, we all go down. You, me, our children, our future."

"I know, but see, before there wasn't that concern, if it all went bad, we could just walk away, but now," he scratched his head with both forepaws, "if it all goes south there's a good chance we could go with it. We need for them to believe we are with them. We can always jump ship if this seems like it's going south."

"So, we hedge our bets, we play both sides. The idea is to have the advantage no matter how this all plays out," Skunk seemed pleased with the whole discussion and that Fox would grasp that they had the inside track no matter what. "And don't forget if it gets down to it, we have a monkey wrench to throw in the works, and he's a big monkey!" At that they both laughed though Skunk much harder than Fox.

Ya Pays Your Money. Ya Takes Your Chances

"This will all sound impossible," Bear cautioned.

"It has sounded impossible since you first proposed it, but impossible seems to be all we have," sighed Suzette. Her color was returning, no longer did she look ashen, almost like death itself, but a rich brown. Her skin had a sheen to it that denoted health. He wondered if what Anna Marie had suggested was having the desired effect. "There are millions of children spread out all over the Mother, you propose to bring them to one spot, each," she emphasized before he could correct again, "and move them to the spiritual side through the veil at one time."

"Yes, but it doesn't have to be the exact second or anything just the same day. And a day lasts for twenty-four hours," he explained, weakly, again as if this time they would all see how it was possible.

"Have you taken into consideration how much area each will need to gather in?" asked Sung. "You will need grazing land, forest, lakes, rivers, oceans all packed with the children of those gathered here. Where are you going to find that much room?"

"I have traveled the mother for centuries, not just my territory but throughout most of her. Most you have stayed within the vast area where your children live, and even if they are spread all across this world, they limit themselves, for the most part, to certain areas within that vastness. But there is so much more," Bear sounded exasperated. How many times would he have to explain the possibility of success before they stopped concentrating on the likelihood of failure?

"What you speak is quite true," chimed in Elk, "My children move throughout the northern hemispheres, thousands of miles, every year. The Mother is massive. Bear is right in that; we should not concentrate on our own concepts of territory but on the expanses of space afforded. Stop thinking of what you know and imagine what you don't!"

"Many of our children travel halfway around the Mother every year. We have cousins, some who do not fly but swim ten thousand miles a years, others who migrate eleven, fifteen thousand miles. And I do not exaggerate when I mention the Arctic Tern that will travel fifty-five thousand miles in a year, the Mother is vast, she can handle whatever we need as far as territory." Albatross grinned proudly as he recounted the great exploits of his cousins in the sky and ocean. Orca stayed silent but nodded her head in agreement, she knew the vastness of the oceans. She had swum around the great continents of land. Yes, the Mother could handle anything they threw at her.

"So, topography is not a problem, what we have to focus on is logistics. Now for some of you this will not present much of an obstacle, as most of your children do not roam, but there are others, like Dog and Wolf—yes, and you Coyote—", Evan quickly added before the spirit guide could expose his peevishness, "are spread out all over the world. I'm not sure we can get them all to one spot," Bear shrugged his impotence at this problem.

"Can you give me an hour?" Glen timidly put forth.

"What do you have in mind?" Bear's curiosity was now piqued. Was he going to try what Bear was desperately trying to find time to try himself? There was too much to do and only one Bear who wanted to do it all. Ah, the mantle of responsibility! Sucks.

"I just want to try something but it will take me a little concentration and strength, to see if this is even possible, just give me an hour and I'll let you know," Glen had a notion based on what Bear had told them about his experiment up in the Canadian Rockies. He wanted to try it before anyone could tell him how dumb it was and belittle his thought. Confidence did not come natural to either the young man nor his people. They needed reassurance, not condemnation.

"Then let the rest of us have something to eat, drink, smoke and see if that jars loose more ideas we want to try," Bear got up from where he was sitting and noticed the humans all gathered off to the side out of the circle, talking amongst themselves. Earl seemed to have taken over leadership, with an assist from Sheriff John.

"Hey guys, we're going to break for vittles and a sip if you'd like to join us," he waved them over.

Earl gazed over and shook his head, "We have to get our act together as much as you do. We have to figure out how to contact the right people to pose the right questions to get people thinking, so when this happens, psychically the human race is properly prepared to accept their responsibility," The others nodded, though both John and Brian looked to where food was being brought out of the house with hunger growling in their bellies.

"OK," conceded Earl, "we can talk through lunch, sorry, it has been a characteristic of mine that when I am hip deep in a project or an idea, I don't think about eating or much of anything else. We'll eat while we continue to make our lists. We have to give as much as we are receiving." But he didn't slow down as he made his way to the picnic table filled with fruits, vegetables, and he was quite pleased to note, some meat and bread. Earl couldn't conceive of this insanity having any repercussions on his own situation but if it helped the others, he was all in.

"What are you guys working on?" Bear sat down next to Earl.

"The idea is to find a few, or hopefully more than a few, scientists who would be willing to listen when we present the dystopia looming; what that would look like. Would there be animals, crops, fish in the sea, kind of thing. And convince them through data and observable facts of the real possibility that our vision could happen. Then try to get them to engage and recruit others to the cause, even tangentially, to discuss openly in forums, on television, radio, and newspapers the looming, immediate danger of the road we are on. I know many have tried, already, but if we can present it as impending, not decades in the future, but the possibility this can happen at any time, to concerned citizens, through a concerted effort of most, if not all, scientists, activists, and reporters. Then you all do what you are planning, boom, we get more bang for the buck. If you see what I mean." Earl looked hopefully at Evan praying he would like the idea.

"I love it, maybe we can get some of the regional papers to concentrate on what's happening here with the droughts, floods, and fires and see if we can't get the national people to pick up on it. Yeah, I like it, I like it a lot." Bear waved Alex over and motioned for her to sit, "Didn't you have a bunch of them hippie people, PETA and the Audubon, WWF, all coming to the Bearfest thingy you do every year?"

"Sure, they wanted the same thing we all did. Forests, clean water, clean air, healthy planet, you know, all the crazy shit. Why?" She was all ears and ready to jump into this pond.

"I want you to work with Earl and the others on this. You have much more experience around humans than most of us do. Listen to what they want to do and see if you can't expand on their ideas," he hugged his granddaughter and for the first time in a very long time he felt a shred of confidence invade his soul. "See if Anna Marie can talk to her friends in the scientific community, the ones she hasn't alienated, that is, and Brian seems plugged into the fringe environmental groups, let's see if we can get some real people pressure building on those who pretend to have power.

"How long?" though he hadn't expressed the exact question, Evan knew what Earl wanted to know.

"I don't know yet, hoping within days, weeks at most, but when it happens, we just need it to last long enough to put a little religion into the souls of those in charge, those who can convert more, and into the souls of those who command," Bear shook his head, "Time is a funny thing. Really never thought about it until man came along, then every second seemed a month." He laughed as he walked away.

Earl threw a questioning gaze toward Alex and she shook her head, "When you are immortal you have no concept of time, only what it means to those you watch over. You know when they are born, when they are dying, your job as a Spirit Guide is to ease the process. What is time but a marking invented by man. What we need is something grand that will impress itself on the psyche of billions of humans long enough to demand action and show that that action can mean something for all. We need to expand your plan," she said as she took his arm and motioned to where the other humans had finished eating and awaited them.

Rebecca saw her husband walk away from the farmer and gaze out over the field as if he wanted to join the boys throwing a ball back and forth and just forget all this. She wished she could carry some of his worry and concerns, but knew he wouldn't share, he wanted to protect her, protect Alex, protect them all. He was Bear, the protector of all the people, he couldn't stop being who and what he was.

The boys broke up their game and headed back towards town. A block down the road they disappeared into the tall grass. Sung watched, saw them distort and morph into the landscape. He could chase them down. But preferred to keep this little secret to himself for now. He was the Wolf, if he wanted them later, he would find them.

"I guess the thing I don't understand," began Earl, "and what I relied on was that Earth would repair itself over time. After all, man has been living here a long time, we are like ants scurrying over her, but we should be too small for her to notice. She should be able to shake off any damage we have done like a dog shaking off fleas." Despondency threatened to overcome his normally positive disposition. He couldn't help but wonder over and over what he could've done to slow this down.

"You are only one man, one farmer, one piece of an extremely vast and complex puzzle," Alex reassured. "Have you ever heard of the ant colonies down in South America?"

Earl nodded. He'd seen a movie with Charlton Heston when he was but a child and told her so.

"Excellent," she smiled, damn she was a pretty woman for a Spirit guide, "they were quite small, a bite from one would sting but not cause much damage, but when there were tens of thousands of them, millions, they could destroy a forest, a herd of cattle in minutes, a man in even less time. We are those ants. We used to only be a few million, there were only a couple hundred million at the time of Jesus, we didn't hit a billion until about the beginning of the 1800s, two billion within the next century and now, a mere hundred and change later we are at eight billion. Even someone as great as the Mother can't keep up with that kind of stress on her natural resources."

These were numbers Earl had never considered before, they overwhelmed. "Can't we predict what will happen and won't she adjust?"

"That's the problem with this, change has never come this quickly, this unpredictably. The Mother can adjust when she has the time, time is not our friend and she is very sick."

He looked around the dark wood library where they sat away from all the others. He'd wanted to talk to her without the distractions of all the other discussions going on. He couldn't really put his finger on why he felt guilty, he hadn't caused this, but he had been a part of those who resisted. He wore his guilt like a shroud of shame.

"Guilt serves no master and serves no good, being aware and willing to grow serves all. We make mistakes, hopefully we live to set straight our 'sins'," Earl could tell by the way she said the word she did not believe in the concept. "Right now, we are trying to get the great majority of mankind to see the truth of that."

"I see your point but cannot help feeling I should've jumped on this train much sooner."

"Hindsight is a wonderful thing. The problem remains we cannot see into the future. None of us can," she emphasized, "not humans, animals, immortals, none. Oh, we can tell you what happened ten centuries ago, or my grandfather can, I'm kind of new to the whole immortal thing, but he doesn't know what is going to happen tomorrow. If we could, we would've stepped up much sooner and stopped mankind before it ever got to this point," regret has no loyalty, it latches onto whoever is bold enough to care.

She saw her words did little to alleviate the guilt, the self-recrimination Earl was feeling. "Look, if it means anything, understand you must have meant something to the Mother, she cared for you. She didn't stop giving sustenance to the land so your crops would stop growing, she had given all she had so they would continue. It's not your fault, it's the fault of those who refuse to see or fight those trying to shine the light so others won't see, out of their own greed, lust for power, and immediate gratification. Without a thought of their future or their children's or grandchildren's, they take and the rest be damned. What we have to do now is ignite the fire!" She put her hand on his shoulder and gave him a kind shake, "Get some sleep, we'll talk more in the morning."

His dreams came fast and furious. Sleep had hardly taken over when the first nightmare rode in. He stood in the middle of his land, his dried, cracked, barren land. The plow straps over his shoulders but the horse lay motionless on the ground, he kept whipping it anyway, begging for it to stand, to pull. They had to get the crops in the ground, the rains would soon come and the seeds would germinate but not if they were in the bag, they had to plant them! The horse stared him in the eye, accusing, hatred seeped out of its wounds. The horse glared at his inhumanity; the eyes seemed to cry out their own. He fell to his knees, weeping his self-loathing and impotence. He knew the dead animal was far more empathetic, more humane, more decent than he. He had killed it for his own wants. Just like in the war. He lay prostrate on the ground and waited for punishment.

Next, he stood at the door of a large, opulent mansion, sitting on a low rise, farmland stretched out in every direction before him. The crops lush and healthy, vegetables the size of footballs, corn that reached towards the passing clouds, grain and wheat waving gently in a supple breeze. This was his dream, he was a man of wealth, respect, means, several expensive cars lined the drive and a bevy of farm hands tended the land. He took it all in and smiled, contemplating his perfectly manicured fingernails, his perfectly clean hands, no dirt would dare lodge under those nails. And the horror of that thought, the revulsion he felt for wishing to be pristine and cleansed of the earth he loved almost shocked him out of his sleep. This was as much nightmare as the other scenario.

The third dream was of despondency. He was lost, alone, in a land he did not recognize. He had no sense of direction, no way to find which way would take him to safety. He'd been walking forever, his feet ached, the muscles in his legs cramped and knotted, refusing to move any further, he wanted nothing more than to sit, to lay down, to die. He'd survived the war, for what? There was nothing for hm here, no future, no love, no family, he was as alone as possible in a world filled with billions of others. And he no longer cared. Death be my lover. Hold me close and close my eyes. Take me in your embrace and let me fly among the stars. So, he lay on the hard, hot ground to await the final dance.

The ground was soft now beneath him. The grass like a feather bed, bending to his shape and caressing him. He felt as though he lay with his head on his mother's breast and he was just a babe. He was safe, loved unconditionally, warm, protected. He realized he loved her more than he would ever love any other person and he would give his life to protect her, to reciprocate this eternal love. She was the Mother, not just the Mother of him but of all, and if she required all he was, she would have it. He would shove all want, angst, fear, ego to the bottom of the deepest well and he would serve. He dreamt his reality.

He awoke with an epiphany ringing in his soul. Yes, he would serve the greater good, to do whatever was necessary to save Mother Earth and all those she nurtured. And maybe by doing so he could heal the wound from the war that had never begun to heal. They had done their best not to dishonor themselves or their country, to only do what was necessary to stay alive. But there had come that day, that day that was seared into each and every soul. The intel had been bad, but he couldn't blame their actions totally on that. If they had only taken the time to observe, to really see the village for what it was, but they'd been in battle the day before, the bloodlust was still on them, and they hadn't. They'd gone in killing everything that moved, no matter the size, the sex, the age. It was a massacre. God! It was still so vivid in his mind's eye. He could still smell it, taste it, feel the hatred as it poured from his body just as the ammunition poured from the nozzle of his weapon. He didn't think himself capable.

He hadn't thought of that day with such clarity until this morning. Oh, he'd carried it with him, his sin against mankind, his sin against himself, but it was there, always. A gaping wound in the center of his soul that would carry him to hell. He laughed, would? It had his entire life. The land had helped heal him physically but nothing would ever restore his soul. Until maybe now. But if he was doing this just to heal himself, would it? Didn't he have to do this, give of himself, maybe all of himself, for purely altruistic reasons? Did the purpose mean as much or more than the act?

He couldn't worry about the reason right now, he had to be ready to act. What happened from here might be out of his control, but his actions would not. He would stand with his newfound friends with honor. He took a deep breath as he got out of bed and was shocked by the taste of the air, the scent of flowers, heat, musk, and a pungent aroma of nature. Smells he had never noticed before mixed in with ones he knew intimately, the scent of fresh tilled soil, new growth, but all so intense it knocked him back onto the bed for a moment. The scents refreshed his tired body, mind, and soul, he now stood ready to put their plan into motion. And now he knew how and who would help.

"You look like the cat that got away from the feral dog," chimed Doe as he passed her in the kitchen headed for the fresh air of the backyard. He needed a stretch of the leg and solitude, though when a beautiful woman speaks to you the male has no choice but to stop and respond.

"I slept well, and deep, and had an epiphany just before I woke. So, yes, I feel as if life might be possible." He knew she was just being pleasant; it seemed a characteristic of all the Native Spirits. And yet, there was something about her scent that rang true. Now why would he even think such a thing? Though it was true, standing this close to the woman he could smell everything about her. Where she'd been today. What she'd brushed up against. It was as if his nose was painting an intricate portrait of the woman and her life. Weird. And, yes again, he was buying into the spirit animal theory heart and soul, he had no other choice.

"Care to share?" My god, a pretty woman whose intelligence beamed from her eyes and with a sense of curiosity was as strong an aphrodisiac as had ever been discovered.

"I wouldn't mind at all, but I need to walk. People don't realize how much a farmer moves in a day. You have to till the soil, plant the seeds, fertilize, weed, check on the growth, adjust watering, all kinds of things. This sitting in one place is not doing my mental health much good." He smiled.

"My people like movement as much or more," she grabbed him by the arm and steered him towards the front door.

The day was brightening as the sun crept across the eastern horizon, it was cool but not chilly. They turned left at the end of the walkway heading away from town and into the open fields. There was something different about him, she thought. Not just attitude but something deeper, he scented different, his physical form felt more solid, he was changing, but into what?

"I have been running from a past I tried to forget," he began as they left the cement of civilization and into the natural surroundings of tall grass and open country, "my name is not even Earl. Oh, it's my middle name a gift from a grandfather on someone's side, but I grew up Norman." He said to her blank stare.

"Maybe I should begin at the beginning. I was born Norman Earl Simmons back in Baltimore. We lived in Little Italy, kind of a rough part of town with neighborhoods warring with each other and the area warring with the rest of the city. We were English-Irish and weren't supposed to live there but we were poor and somebody had an Italian aunt or something so we were 'grandfathered' in. Though not happily by either side.

"It was rough but had a lot of joy as well. My Da worked hard to put food on the table and keep a leaky roof over us. Ma picked up odd jobs sewing and such, watching other folk's kids, and raising us. Three boys and two girls, guess I don't have to tell you we were Catholic." He chuckled and she stared. "See, the Catholic church wants all of their parishioners to have lots of kids so the church will grow and become stronger. No worries about whether the poor, dumb bastards can afford a bunch of kids, just their duty to continue to procreate."

"Why would someone want anybody else to have more fawns than they could feed or adequately take care of? Why would you purposefully make those you watch over suffer just for your own power?" Doe thought she had some understanding of humans but this seemed just insane.

"Why does the church do anything?" he shook his head and shrugged, "It doesn't matter, when my number came up, I went to war."

Again, she interrupted his monologue, "Number? What would a number have to do with war?"

This was going to take a month to tell if he had to explain every whackadoodle thing that humans do. "Look, we had what was called a draft, the government gave a number to each birthdate by lottery and if you had a low number you went to Nam. Don't ask me for the reasons, I don't have a clue.

"Things happen in war that you aren't proud of, but you go to war to do things you won't be proud of. Your only job is to stay alive. You're sent to kill someone you never met and don't have anything against because someone who won't go tells you to. No, it's not fair and not right," he stopped her before she could speak the words dancing on her tongue, "Most people who go to war are not proud of what they did but they stayed alive and came home to the families that the people in power told them they went to protect. The whole thing is fucked up and defies rationalization or explanation.

"I was with a pretty good group of guys, we did everything we could not to shame ourselves or live with the horror of doing something terrible. We almost made it." He stopped to watch the sun rise and take in the beauty around him. He wiped his eyes and didn't look at her. "It was a mistake, bad intelligence, I don't know but we, well, we..." He took a very deep breath, then another, "I'm sorry I still can't say what it was, I just can't share that. It's bad enough I have to live with it, have it in my head and on my soul." He took another cleansing breath, shook himself from the reverie, "Anyway when we realized what had happened, we swore we'd never tell another soul but what we would do is live the best lives in service to others we possibly could. Try to get our Karma straight as it were.

"Great idea if you can forget, some could, I couldn't. I tried to kill that guy, Norman, with drugs, alcohol, and finally by getting myself lost in the middle of the country. I buried Norman on that farm and reinvented as Earl, but I never forgot. Kept in contact with most of the guys. They had gone on to greater glory in the name of humanity and here is where the epiphany came. One of them fellas became an environmental scientist trying to save the world for the past fifty years, so nobody likes him already," he snickered at his little funny, she smiled to be nice, "and another one is a marine biologist with some pretty good credentials and Bobby went off to work for the government and has been involved in some measure or other in the past five administrations. I'll bet they could tell me who to contact, whose saddle to put a burr under and which groups give them the most headaches." He beamed.

"Would you like me to help? I don't know what it is but when I speak to men, they pay close attention, they listen," She really had no clue of her own beauty which only increased the cuteness. "Besides I like you no matter what horrors might be in your past, it is your present I like and what you see for your future," she scrubbed at her short brown hair, fringe jacket flapping in time, and smiled, "The past is just that, past, show me a person with no skeletons and I'll show you a person afraid to die."

Bear had that damn itch at the back of his head like someone looking over his shoulder but from half a mile away. He didn't like being watched and hated it when he couldn't tell who was doing the watching. He pushed the irritant to the back of his mind where it could fester while he concentrated on the problem at hand. He knew what needed to be done but didn't know if it could be done on such a grand scale. He stared at the empty sky hoping it held all the answers but all it held was the empty.

His thoughts were interrupted by Glen limping around the corner of the house. He looked like he'd been in a fight and Bear hoped the other guy looked worse. He got up to help Glen over to the table where he could sit and lean before he fell down.

"You want a glass of water? Or maybe something a bit more restorative?" Concern colored each word. He had adopted Glen and now thought of him more as son than friend or boarder.

"Just let me catch my breath," Glen took a deep gulp of air, "and then something to help revive my wits." A half smile was all he could manage.

Evan walked quickly into the house and grabbed the never-ending bottle of bourbon and returned just as Glen's breathing was settling down. He poured three fingers into a small glass and shoved it across the table. Glen sipped, coughed once, and sipped again. His countenance relaxed, his breathing normalized, he leaned back and stretched his legs while hugging himself.

"What happened?" Evan could feel the anger deep in him rising to a dangerous level.

"I tried it," grinned the Dog.

"Tried wha...?" and Even knew. "Start at the beginning and tell me exactly what happened." He knew he should be more concerned with Glen's condition but right now that was overwhelmed by his curiosity to know. What had Glen done? How had he done it? And, most importantly, what were the results?

"You know how you wanted to try your idea before we actually had to make the Move?" Evan nodded, "Well, I knew you'd never have time 'cause you were the big dog, sorry, in this whole thing and everything depended on you. Oh, I know what you told us about the bears up north and all but you wanted to expand the idea. So, I thought since nobody ever really has anything for me to do and I always seem under-foot and all," and at this admission Evan had to blanche. He knew he took Glen for granted, he was his adopted son, you always forget how much they need you more than others. "I thought, this is something I could do.

"I didn't want to try it with people's pets or nothing, but with my kind there's always way too many of us that humans just don't want. Oh, they'll keep breeding us and refusing to spay and neuter, but just toss the ones they don't want out into the wild so they can breed some more. There are, literally, tens of thousands just living on the edge of humanity every moment of the day. No one would miss a hundred or so if they happened to disappear.

"Don't get me wrong, I love my children," and the beatific smile that unabashedly spread across his face gave truth to the words, "I wouldn't hurt them but I knew I could attempt this without anyone the wiser. I thought hard on what you said about children being scattered across large swaths of land and thought, well then, I have to go some-where many of my children are but not all close to each other." He grinned with a pride at his cleverness.

"I took a long time to plan the idea. I knew it wouldn't matter where I was because I can feel where every one of my brood are. You know how it is, not every second of every day but if we concentrate re-ally hard with no distractions, we can feel every single one of them."

At this Evan had to scold himself, he hadn't, for too many dec-ades, not done this exact thing leading to his surprise at the condition of his northern family. He was too wrapped up in the problems of others and then living, once he came back from dead, that he had not been a good steward. Glen was teaching him things he had allowed himself to forgo, but now was not the time for wallowing in regret.

Glen continued, "So, I went out to the high peaks, out past where Sung's people are, and stood on the edge where I could see for-ever. Then I sat with my legs dangling over the edge to be comfortable and tuned into my children. I told them not to be frightened, that I was with them and I was their protector, but we were all going to take a lit-tle journey together." Bear wanted to weep, his pride filling his chest and pushing past his throat, but he held. "I concentrated on them and where I wanted to take them. Really it was easy, I'd been up in that patch of land where the wolves were, I knew it intimately and I thought that might be helpful. And just moved us all across the veil." He said it as if it was the most natural thing anybody could do. "And it worked! It really worked, they all came across with me and we were standing in that pretty meadow. We ran and played, jumped, and got to know each other. I counted them all and checked their condition, like you told how you done with them bears and then I brought them back. More'n three hundred and it didn't feel like nothing. I just thought of all I could find and moved 'em like they was dust hanging in the air. Guess a couple days passed while we was there but time don't mean nothin' to an immortal, does it?" He was so happy with what he'd done Evan wanted to rub his belly and get him a treat. He fought the urge and poured him another dollop of the restorative.

"What happened to you?" He asked pointing at Glen's obviously disheveled appearance.

"Oh, that, when we come back, I was so surprised and proud of myself I jumped up to scream my joy and fell right off that damn cliff edge. Must've fell about few hundred feet but it'll heal in a few," his grin split his face and his eyes lit like Saturn and Venus on a clear cool night.

"Glen, I don't know that I have ever been prouder of anyone in my life. You took a real big chance and you did it all by yourself. Damn, 'bout scared a century or two off me when I seen you coming round that corner." It was true, too, when he'd seen Glen, he had feared something horrible. He wanted to tell him never to do something like that again but he couldn't, Glen was his own man, now. Well, his own Dog.

As everyone came out to see what the commotion was about Bear couldn't help but see how all of them had come together as family, real family. How they cared for each other, one's strengths supported another's weaknesses and vice a versa. They stood strong, complete, no matter what happened to him or any of them, the People would be there to help take care of the needs of all. Mitakuye Oyasin, indeed. We are all truly related!

The Best Laid Plans

After all had settled in with the news of Glen's success they all wanted to try it with their own people, with the admonition from Bear not to fall off any cliffs, and to use what Glen had deduced about knowing exactly where they wanted to take their children. He didn't know if that was absolutely necessary but why mess with a proven strategy.

The temperament of the encampment improved drastically with the news. All three houses and the field behind were beginning to fill up with Cousins from as far away as Africa and China. They came from all over the world as news spread that Bear and his family were going to try and do something to turn back the destruction of man.

The numbers of all the people had fallen drastically over the past few decades. not because they were attacking one another but because of loss of territory, despoiling of habitat, and the wild fluctuations in climate. Many could withstand the excessive heat or cold when it was gradual but now it was like an extreme roller coaster with temperatures fluctuating as much as a hundred degrees within a twenty-four-hour period. The fragile could not handle the stress. People were being extincted by the dozens. They had to look at whatever Bear had in mind as their last stand.

Humans could not be persuaded by gentle means; they needed the sky to fall on their pointy little heads if they were to save the Mother and in so doing save themselves. If the spirit guides of the world could've figured out a way to accomplish this without helping man, they would've. And most surrendered to the fact that many humans were decent and trying to stop the wrack and ruin but didn't have the wherewithal or power. They would have to be engaged as well. They were the ones Earl, Anna Marie and Brian, with some help from Sheriff John, were attempting to rouse into action. It had to be a two-pronged attack. The complete and total disappearance of every animal on the planet along with the protests, work stoppages, and strikes from the concerned. The question was, would it be enough?

The temperature topped one hundred degrees Fahrenheit and it was only eleven in the morning. It was going to be a scorcher. Earl sat in the shade of the back porch, fanning himself with a magazine while attempting to type out an email with one hand. Sweat dripped from his forehead and into his eyes making the typing far more difficult. Tatanka's figure filled the door—seven foot four and wide as the opening—he took a deep breath of the heat before exiting the home and taking a seat in one of the rocking chairs next to the man, the rocker groaning its discontent. Not sweating, not fanning, he seemed quite comfortable though dressed in a heavy flannel shirt, dungarees, and thick shoulder length hair.

"My God," Earl exclaimed, "don't you feel the heat? Doesn't it affect you?"

"My kind do not notice temperature differentials; we are more spirit than temporal. Our children notice it, of course, but we are immune to such concerns. Does it bother you?"

"I spent the majority of the last fifty years plowing, seeding, and living on the land. Hot, cold, rain, snow, you name it but this is just oppressive," Earl wiped his brow.

"Maybe I can assist," he gazed across the open field that lay to the north of Bear's home, concentrating on Earl knew not what, but within a few minutes a gentle breeze came blowing down from the north.

"Did you just do that?" he asked to Tatanka's self-satisfied grin.

"How did you do that?" he continued, astonished.

"We all have our little tricks, I can affect the weather to a slight degree, enough to provide small comfort. My people live out on the prairies, I cannot make the weather change, but I can try to take away some of the harshness." He grinned. "We aren't really supposed to do that, but as long as we don't move the needle too far the Mother does not chastise."

As more came out into the backyard and patio area from the two houses buttressing Evan and Rebecca's home, talk turned to how everyone was coming along with the task of transporting increasing numbers of their children across the veil and back again. Some had suggested maybe a more measured migration would be far less taxing on those who had the largest number of children to move, but Bear had reminded them they needed something grand and immediate. They had to grab the attention of those in charge and the media as well as inflame the passions of those on the front lines. No one was going to believe that a bunch of Native Spirits from all over the world were playing hide and seek with all the animals of the world just to get someone's attention. It had to, at least, appear as though there had been a massive extinction event caused by their negligence.

Earl had contacted his old Army friends from Nam and they had enlisted the aid of every scientist even remotely associated with climate change. All had frantically been writing op/eds, publishing scientific treatise and talking to every gathering that would have them, on the dangers of the path humanity was on. They, of course, were being ignored or lambasted as quacks or charlatans promoting this insanity for their own reward. Though no one could ever actually say what those grand rewards were other than being cyberbullied or doxing.

Anna Marie and Brian contacted everyone they had met in the environmental movement, especially those already prone to protesting and demonstrating. They were working the internet to arouse passions and have people ready to take to the streets in every small, medium, and large town across the globe. All in all, it was a massive undertaking. Exactly what they needed.

Sheriff John was doing everything he could to smooth the path with friendly law enforcement, though many turned out to be less friendly than he supposed. But he worked his phones and gladhanded anyone who would listen. His mood had improved with each passing day as Suzette's condition improved, though she was still weak, she was a fighter. The wacky scientist Anna Marie had mobilized hundreds of concerned citizens along the Pacific coast of Oregon and Washington to help clean up a larger percentage of the garbage, refuse, and chemical spills affecting Suzette's children who lived there. Not that they had cleansed the ocean, but it was a start. The only thing that would bring back all of them to their health and luster was if the numbers of their children increased and were healthy. It was a balancing act and they were fighting for survival.

Suzette was reclining on a lounge soaking up the heat. She had never been affected by heat and cold and though the sensation brought some discomfort she couldn't help but revel in the experience. That was something no one ever took into consideration, when you were an immortal creature of spirit and heart you never changed, never experienced new sensations. The hot, the cold, hunger, thirst, these were for their children not the celestials. They could feel some of what their scions did but never actually know those depredations. She wallowed in the revelation.

Doe sat to one side of her and Willow to the other in case she might need anything, even as simple as pleasant conversation. They were concerned she would not have the strength to move her children. What they were discovering was the larger the group to be moved, the greater the energy needed to move them. Doe had her hands full with the millions she would move, and Willow, well, Willow was attempting to slow the ever increasing of her people's numbers, but rabbits! If Suzette was to accomplish her purpose, she would need help.

They had expressed their distress to Bear who responded with his usual empathy and reassurance. He was of the belief that when the rubber hit the road, she would respond with reserves of strength they were not giving her credit for. Their job, as they saw it, was to allow her to rest and reserve as much of that hidden strength as spiritually possible.

The mood was jovial and there was talk of starting a bonfire until Earl reminded them it was over one hundred in the shade and though they may not feel the heat there were humans here who did! Alex came out of the house with the eternal bottle and Evan's box containing the pipe and tobac. If this was going to have any chance of working, they would need all the help they could get from the ancestors. Pipe passed and bottle now open the pre-celebration was well under way when the four-by-four pickup came crashing around the corner of the house bringing all activity to an abrupt halt.

"Old man," Screamed Frank as he stumbled out of the driver's side door, "you and me is going to have it out right now!"

"What the absolute...?" murmured Evan as he made his way over to where the swaying, braying man stood. "Listen mister, I have no idea what has got under your skin, but I got no quarrel with you. And I ain't gonna start this bullshit up with you again."

Frank seemed confused as if lost in thought, lost in time, lost in space, finally he seemed to find his focus and it was Evan. He was about to put together a few words and see if they could form a sentence when Coyote stepped in the middle of them.

"I know you." He said as he scented the man, though how he could scent anything through the booze and filthy clothes—he'd obviously slept in them for a few days out in the wilderness, his flannel had ground in dirt, his jeans grease covered and drooping—but there was something, a familiar scent that broke through everything else.

"Well, I don't know you and I got no squabble with you, just him," and he pointed an unsteady hand towards Evan.

As he made a step in the direction of Evan, Coyote caught him in the temple with a hard right and he folded into a heap on the lawn.

"Well, that wasn't so hard," remarked Coyote as he shook the sting out of his hand. "Now, let's see if we can discover which wires got crossed over the years."

"You know this guy?" it was John, he had been hot on the tail of Frank and, apparently, had been chasing the truck through town. He'd come racing around the corner, on foot, just moments after Frank had plowed his way into the gathering.

Coyote nodded uncertainly as he considered the lump on the lawn.

"Well, that just might be the dumbest thing I ever seen anybody that dumb do," John shook his head and scratched his chin and he reached for his handcuffs. "Like he didn't see none of you, but Evan. I have seen a man with a burr under his saddle before, but I ain't never seen somebody so fixed on self-destruction."

"Hang on a minute, if you would, Sheriff," calmed Coyote to Evan's surprise, "but there is just something that is way out whack here."

"You got that right," quipped Evan, "surely you remember this big pile o' trouble from the last time."

"I don't think I was ever around this fella back then, but I know his scent from years before," Coyote then gave a brief synopsis of his relationship with Frank from when he was a child until he lost contact with him.

"If you was connected to him, how'd you lose contact?" Bear knew, like they all knew, that if you made that kind of a connection with a human, they was yours for the rest of their natural life. To break that connection something would have had to happen involving another spirit guide.

"Don't know, but I'm bout to find out, though it might take a bit of traipsing around inside his head. I'm up for it," Coyote had never been close to too many and he didn't like losing this one that he'd saved. He wanted to know the why and wherefore.

As the sun hit its zenith, two figures came strolling up through the field from the direction of the river. Sung and Glen were panting slightly, but not sweating, as they, apparently, were completing their morning run. The group was now complete, Oscar filled the two canines in on the excitement so far this morn. Both expressed disgust they had missed the action yet gaining a modicum of respect for Coyote.

Tatanka and Lawrence the Elk had come out onto the yard and now sat opposite Suzette who looked like a child in comparison to the two overly large men sitting before her.

"We have come to reassure you that when the time comes both of us, but mainly me," spoke the giant Tatanka, "Will be there to aid you with your children. We have much respect for you, little woman," grinned the massive Native, "And as my people are nowhere as numerous as when we turned the prairie black with our numbers, my job will be quite easy. I grant you my strength and admiration." He bowed to her from where he sat.

"And I shall help if he is not enough," Lawrence jibed. "Seriously, we know what it will take to move so many of your children quickly and we know you have given so much to the Mother and, therefore, to all of us. It would be an honor to stand by you."

Suzette coughed to hide the sob and looked away so they would not see her tears of gratitude. She bowed back to them, "My dears, you honor more than words can express. I do not deny that the how of moving so many with such little strength was weighing on me more than I could tell anyone. You will have the love of my people and our thanks as long as the grass grows and the sun brings light to all." Now she did let the tears flow as she jumped up from where she reclined to hug both individually, as there was no way she could have gathered them both in her arms.

Coyote came in the house and found Evan sitting on the couch in deep conversation with Alex and Her. He knew She had a name; he didn't think he could utter it, it seemed disrespectful. At a lull in their discussion, he interrupted the momentary silence, "Very strange," he began slowly, "I don't know if I'd ever told you about the kid I saved a while back, but that big lug is definitely him!" He quickly filled in more details of the story of Frank becoming lost in the woods as a child and Coyote, for once, doing a proper and saving the kid without him knowing it. Of course, one repercussion was that from then on Coyote was tied to the guy. Until about a decade or so back.

"When the last confrontation took place," stated Bear.

"Exactly, but I knew nothing about him or you because our bond had been, not quite broken but severely weakened. I wouldn't have recognized him or his essence. One or more of the people has been messing with him."

"How is that possible?" Bear might not know much but he knew once one of the People bonded with a human, the human would stay bonded until its death. What Coyote was saying bordered on impossible. And he only thought bordered, because it seemed to have happened, otherwise, he thought it was impossible. But they were living in the middle of impossible, weren't they?

"I don't know and I can't really tell who done it. I mean, I can tell it was one of the People, it has to be 'cause ain't nobody else could've done this anywho, and the presence is familiar, but not familiar enough that I can put my finger on who!" Coyote's frustration was palpable.

"So, you think him showing up again and what happened years ago is tied somehow?" Bear was trying to put all this into the realm of possibilities.

"Don't see how it can't be," Coyote shrugged.

Alex and Rebecca shared a look before Rebecca turned to Coyote, "You think you can fix him? I mean, can you strengthen the connection between you and him and cut it with whoever done this?" The last thing in this world she wanted was some crazed giant of a man who would show up every so often in Evan's life trying to kill him.

"Man, I just don't know. I'm not sure how they done it or how to undo it without damaging him further. I really don't think this is his fault, just a pawn being played by two different sides, so I'd rather not do more harm. Gonna take some thought and discussion with others, maybe that Oscar guy, he seems pretty astute. I need somebody more clever than I am, but I can make him sleep for a bit, keep him out of our fur for spell, while we try and find someone to fix him final," he could tell Bear wanted to chime in with some kind of funny but thankfully he kept it locked in his jaw. "Bear you got any more of that..."

Evan got up went to the desk in the hallway, opened the bottom drawer, and pulled out his leather gunny sack and handed it with the papers to Coyote. Before he could grab it Bear pulled back, "Maybe we all could use a little mental break away from details and planning. We're pretty much there, just got to pick the date and we're off. Alex..."

"I know," she said as she passed the cabinet and grabbed the bottle and a handful of glasses, her grandmother loading up the rest of the glasses on a tray.

Everyone's spirits were lifted at the sight of the four coming out of the house with the bounty in their arms. All had been intensely concentrating on what was going to be attempted and they all needed a mental vacation. They had practiced with ever increasing number of children and felt confident they could handle the full load when the time came.

Earl, Anna Marie, and Brian had received copies of articles written by Earl's old comrades in arms decrying the wanton destruction of their home as well as posters for planned demonstrations throughout the world. There were copies of books written, treatise spoken in halls of power and pleas from certain religious and spiritual leaders of the end of civilization if mankind didn't take some responsibility. TV video and radio tapes of the call to arms for protests and demonstrations and the reactions from the far-right commentators on how all this was just bullshit and scare tactics by the commies and socialists on the left. It was all quite satisfying. Even the ones screaming it was all just a plot by those hoping to cash in on the coming troubles and supposed solutions brought attention to the problem. Mankind had either lost its mind or finally found its soul, depending on which side of the proverbial fence one sat.

There were those attempting to put legislation into motion for renewable energy and the end of fossil fuels. Replacing plastic with other material that was biodegradable, naturally occurring. Scientists were busy creating genetically altered microbes that could 'eat' and survive on plastics that clogged the oceans. Science was proving to politics that given the time, energy, people, and resources they could find solutions, all that was required was will. Though, many denounced and criticized these innovations as fanciful, most of those with the loudest voices turned out to be supported by giant oil and plastics companies.

None of those assembled in the small ten acres behind the quaint craftsman cottage were supremely confident, but there was satisfaction in the doing. They knew one the great dilemmas was mankind's addiction to immediate gratification; the collective patience of the species was nonexistent. They wanted solutions now and those solutions simple, easy, something that would cause the very slightest discomfort in their lives. And mankind had an extremely short memory. Once things showed the least improvement most of the species would think they had won the war and revert to previous behavior.

The People didn't kid themselves, what they were attempting was to change the course of an extremely large and slow-moving ship, one whose crew was on the verge of mutiny every second of every day. Humans expected that nature would adjust immediately to any and all climate change, but it wouldn't. It would take time. First humans had to stop doing what they were doing to destroy. Then the Mother could begin to heal. If improvement didn't happen quickly humans would move on to other concerns, change the channel to something more entertaining and return to their old ways. Man had the attention span of a gnat, to which the Gnat objected profusely.

Still, it was a time for hope, a time to relax before the coming storm.

Preparations Are Nice, But...

Preparations were now in place; they had done all they could think to do; short of starting a war they would most certainly lose against humanity. This was a dangerous dance, balance, covert acts, peaceful resistance to an overpowering force, taking to the streets, pleading through the news media and hope. Unfortunately, the mainstream media had tired of doomsday predictions as they hadn't happened within the news cycle and showed no sign of immediate climate crises soon. Other than the odd drought continuing, floods, super hurricanes, weather jumping between scorching heat and blizzard, there was nothing out of the ordinary they could blaze across the front page.

Bear chuckled to himself, 'it always came down to hope.' The People had put their hope and trust in him and his plan if it failed a miserable death, he would never be trusted to perform his main reasons for being, to protect the People.

"Ah well, if you're not willing to put everything you love on the line, then what was life? Risking pain, defeat, suffering eternal humiliation all for something you believed in was the definition of life, wasn't it?" he muttered the words, barely audible as if convincing himself.

The plan was, come Earth Day, well, you had like the symbolism, the animals, the birds, reptiles, fish, whales, all the creatures of creation would suddenly and instantly, or so it would seem, disappear. They would be moved on the other side of the veil and bide their time until they saw what the reaction of the human race would be. Anna Marie, Brian, Earl, and the sheriff would remain over here to monitor the situation and let Bear know if he needed to goose any particular part of the world. He, like many of the People, had children and cousins that inhabited every corner of the Mother. He could jump from one hotspot to another if needs be. But he couldn't control humans, not even the ones that worshipped bears or had them as part of their mythology. They had to reinforce the idea that violence was not acceptable and would only crush their chance of success. Mankind had lost their capacity for wonder, their belief in things outside what could be felt, bought, sold, traded or had some form of pecuniary worth. It was sad, but it was truth and he dealt in truth, not wishes. Well, he corrected himself, truth, and hope. He laughed a soft chuckle.

"Something amusing?" asked Rebecca as she walked out the back door and silently joined him where he stood surveying his domain.

"Me, I guess," he shrugged, "Mr. eternal optimist. What I wouldn't give just to have a century where we weren't being threatened with extinction, war, or starvation. Shit, it's always something, isn't it? Maybe we could go away, just the two of us, travel the whole of the Mother for a few decades and get to know each other again." He sighed. Foolish to wish, foolish to dream.

She leaned into him and found his hand, warm, a little course from all the work he did around their home and because he was Bear, and found comfort in the roughness. She snuggled into the crook of his shoulder and just let him hold her. They had never been more complete, never had they loved each other more than when they remembered how much they relied on each other and how much they held each other up. She made him believe and so, he did.

"You know, I never apologized to you for telling the kids not to believe you and those old stories. I should have believed in you. I should have felt the truth of you. I should have given you the benefit of the doubt," she hugged him close.

"Nah, you were right to doubt, a good dose of doubt is healthy, makes people stop for a second to question their own beliefs and truths. And we have Alexandra. So, apology accepted but not necessary. You, when this is all over and, hopefully, the Mother and our children begin to heal, we are going to head to the mountains and rivers where no one can find us and rediscover some lost territory," he let out a low growl and chuckled.

"You are incorrigible!" She whacked him on the arm, but not hard enough to sting.

The great meet had gone well enough, they would do what they could and then it was up to mankind. Anna Marie sighed as she gazed across the small river behind Bear's house. Funny, she thought, that she used that term to refer to Evan. Maybe he really was the Naïve Spirt of Bear, but it didn't matter, the man was strong, commanding and might just do what no one else seemed capable of; saving the planet. Shit, she sure hadn't done much on that order, had she?

Her stunts had been farcical and childish. She was supposed to be a scientist, a woman of letters, educated and responsible, not chaining herself to trees or yelling at oil executives who could've cared less what she thought. They had money to make.

She felt the presence come sit down beside her though she never took her gazed from across the river. She could tell, by the silence, the patience, his scent—weird how she'd never noticed that before—it was Brian. She should be nicer to this guy, he really wanted to help, he cared, and not just about the cause, but he cared about her. Not many people, shit, no one really, had done that ever. Not her folks, her siblings, her supposed friends, no one. She'd been a loner, a whack job they called her. Who cared about things no one else did, stupid things she thought far more important than what clothes others wore, what they thought, did, listened to, what the latest thing might be, you know, superficial things. There had to be more to life than what her boyfriend thought of her new haircut.

"Hey," he finally interrupted her thoughts, "you OK?"

"Yeah, why?" she remained motionless, staring at nothing.

"No reason, I guess." Heartbeats passed, the air came in, the breath came out. "It's just when everybody was discussing the coming events, you were kind of quiet. Then halfway through got up and came out here. Just checking on you."

God, could anybody be any sweeter. She hadn't thought anyone took note of her exit, but, of course, he did. "Just wasn't anything else for me to do or say. I felt like I wasn't needed," she tried to keep the pity out of her tone, but her success rate was low.

"I think you are underestimating what you mean here. These People, or whatever they are, respect you, respect your opinion. Look at the difference you made in Suzette, just by making some suggestions and getting folks on the West coast involved in cleaning up the habitat for the sea otters and moving some to where food was more plentiful. You helped a lot!" He believed in what he was selling and wanted her to buy into it.

"I don't know, they seem to have everything handled," she finally looked at him.

"They have their stuff handled; it is up to us to handle the rest. To handle what you helped put into progress. Damn girl, a lot of what is now taking place in the world is because of you. Your research was used, your contacts went on the television shows and wrote the papers."

"But, see, that's the thing, they are writing the papers! They are appearing on the television news! They are reaping the attention and glory!" She knew she sounded petulant and whiney. She should be thinking of the big picture, all the action now in progress. Shit, they might actually be saving the world. But ego is what ego is, even to those who fight such feelings, you want a little glory to shake down on you. Here she was in some backwater town, completely out of the limelight. She should be leading demonstrations, getting tear gassed and arrested on TV, not sitting, and watching the river flow by her.

"Who cares? We are at the center of what's really happening. We are part of the magic taking place. We are two of only a handful of humans who actually know what is going on, the plan, the awesomeness of helping real spirit animals, out of story and myth, trying to save the Mother and all who live here! And we've put the wheels in motion. People will take to the streets; their voices will be heard. They will come out because of the work, the groundwork, the research, the data collection you did. Be proud. I know Bear is, he told me," he lied, but just a little. He had seen the look on Bear's face when Anna Marie made suggestions and how happy he was with Suzette's progress. "Look we still have a lot of work to do and you're an integral part of that, so let's get our shit together and join the party." He stood and reached for her hand to help her up.

She stood with vigor and fell right into his arms, wrapping him in hers and planting a huge kiss, deep and passionate on his lips. "Thanks, I really do like you." Anna Marie had been mocked by her colleagues for her passionate pursuits of truth in all her scientific endeavors. Derided by family and friend throughout life because she wasn't 'girly' enough. She had been a loner forging her own path for so long she resigned herself to her destiny, tilting at windmills without a Sancho. Anna Marie really didn't need much in life, but someone who believed in her, well, that was a gift from the Goddess.

The demonstrations began as planned two days before Earth Day. April twentieth would go down in history, provided there was to be one, as the day the people around the globe spoke. It was far beyond what Bear and the others could've hoped for. The friends and associates of Anna Marie and Earl had more than done their job. People from all over the globe took to the streets shutting down business, commerce, governments in every major and minor capitol. London, Paris, Mumbai, Moscow, Beijing, Washington, New York, Dublin, Cairo, Jerusalem, every major and minor city brought to complete standstill. Non-violence was the rule of the day, though rules are made to be broken. As usual with humans there had to be violence, looting, cars and buildings set on fire, but fortunately the damage was minimal. Where violence was begun there were thousands who stood in the way of it spreading. They were there to celebrate the Mother and demand industry and political leaders find another course for humanity.

An emergency meeting was held at the United Nations, Secretary General Juan Maria Manuel Santiago Olevares presiding. Pandemonium threatened to disrupt any kind of reasonable discussion but he demanded they act like civilized representatives of mankind. Not by fighting but by talking, finding solutions, and listening to their own people. He had not been a strong Secretary General up until now, but the future of the world was at stake and he found his strength and purpose. They would not watch while Rome burned, not on his watch!

So, they talked, they considered proposals, demands of the proletariat and the millions of children who had closed down their world. It was the voice of the children he found most powerful. Youth had taken a leading role in their demands for a future, a future where they could breathe, drink water from their faucets with confidence, plant crops that would not be destroyed by devasting floods or oppressive heat, and droughts. Where all would have opportunity to live and grow not just the top one percent ruling over all others. The companies throughout the world had to stop polluting and spewing their noxious gases into the air, dumping their refuse into the oceans and lakes, pouring death into the soil. The Mother needed to be rescued before all life on the planet disappeared.

All the People had decided they would meet behind the three houses for a council/celebration on the eve of the transition: April twenty-first. There were at least ten acres for the meet, more than enough for Spirit creatures, with the river for the water creatures, and open land for the rest. Most, if not all, of the representatives of the creatures of Mother would come. Those of the Native America group would bring pipes to share, drums to beat and songs. Those from South America would bring their pipes, their sacred weed, their songs, and dance. The whales and dolphins would bring song, the fish would bring their dance. Each group would bring what was sacred to them, they would share for the first time together since the creation, a gathering for the ages, there was even talk the Mother might come to wish them luck. And though some objected, the humans who had been such a part of this endeavor would be welcomed to stay.

Sheriff John would block off streets to keep the curious away, though most of the town's folk would never be aware of the proceedings. Spirit Guides may not have powerful magic but they could affect a glamour over the proceedings with the little each had. It would last all night. Pipes would be smoked and the smoke sent in gratitude, once again, to the ancestors. Bottles would be passed and passed again, mescaline and high-quality cannabis shared, dance, the steady staccato of drums and the trill of pipes comingling with voices from all languages which when sung together became one. It would be a celebration of hope.

And there was hope, hope like a blanket wrapped all of them. The battle they would fight, they fought for their children, for their dreams, for their tomorrow. Even Bear did the bear dance to the delight of all especially when his mate and granddaughter joined in. They laughed as Willow, Doe, Oscar, Tatanka, Elk and Earl attempted to emulate. Earl laughed the hardest and heartiest at his own ineptness. There was something about that man, Bear considered, he was not who he said or who he might think, he was. Just as the thought strolled through Bear's mind Earl turned and looked deep into his Bear's eyes; and winked. Now, what the hell? But before he could confront Earl he say

Salmon dancing with the others of the ocean and she beckoned him over. He laughed as he hugged her close. Rebecca would need some words.

It was a Tuesday night according to John, humans care about such things, and it had been decided to make the transition on Earth Day which conveniently came mid human week, as that would create the most chaos and media coverage. John had explained to those not conversant with human custom that the weekends were when people went out of their way to ignore any news.

The fires burned high and hot, the smoke bathed the People and ghosts of those long extinct came and danced with them. As the night progressed, the fires burned down to embers and by the glow of those embers, stories were told. Stories from the beginning of time told by those who had lived them, witnessed them, or created them. Anna Marie and Brian sat mouths agape and hypnotized by the drone of Native voices speaking in languages they couldn't understand yet could understand the stories. Oscar told them it had something to do with the magic in the air—something neither of them believed yet could not doubt the affect—and the high quality of mescaline and cannabis. They didn't care. They didn't care if this was all a hallucination, a dream, or reality, they were as woven into the fabric of the evening as any gathered.

Earl wandered off away from the fires to where he could lay in the soft grass and stare at the Milky Way. Doe found him weeping in the grass.

"Are you in pain?" Her concern was almost palpable.

What a good woman, he thought, and just as quickly changed his thought. What a good and honorable being. "This is too much. I cannot believe I am part of such a thing, such a joining of spirit and life; of humanity. It is overwhelming, almost healing." He laughed at the stupidity of his statement. This would not heal what he had done and the tears continued to flow.

"Ah, your war," she reached out to touch his shoulder, to reassure. "I do not understand regret or guilt, but I think they are some of the best qualities of humans." Now she sat down next to him and gazed at the perfect night sky.

"Some of human's best qualities?" that had certainly caught him off guard.

"Yes, I think if you have regret and guilt, it shows you have a good heart, a pure soul or you would feel nothing, otherwise." She took her gaze from the stars to the man, "there are many people who have done awful things and feel nothing but satisfaction. Satisfied with how those horrific acts benefitted themselves, they feel nothing for their fellow humans but disdain. You are a good man, Norman Earl, find it in your heart to forgive yourself, you have earned, at least, a little forgiveness and compassion."

"I'm not so sure," his voice trembled with fifty years of emotion.

Doe heard more in his words, there was something, he was different as if he had become a completely different person. She liked them both. "I am," she leaned over and kissed him as his people do, soft, passionate, with love.

They lay in the grass until the sun came up.

Wednesday morning at sunrise, local time from wherever they had come, all vanished to go complete the task at hand. Wednesday morning all over the world, as the sun peeked over the horizon, it found only...silence. A silence as deafening as any never heard. Not the song of a bird, the bark of a dog, the croak of frog, no cricket, katydid, no chirp of squirrel or purr of cat. Silence as complete as the deepest parts of space.

Police reports began piling up by seven a.m. of missing pets by the tens of thousands, by two in the afternoon there were tens of millions. No deer had been sighted, no ducks, geese, sparrow, or eagle flew the air currents. Llamas, camels, elephants all gone. Fishing nets lay fallow. Crab and lobster pots empty. No cows bellowed in the barn, nor horses snickered in the corral. The plains, mountains, oceans were devoid of life. Man was alone.

Talking heads on television began spewing conspiracy theories before the oatmeal had cooled. It was the hippies and climate changers who had stolen all the animals and had them corralled and hidden away in some godforsaken country. No, it was the end of days and God had come to take his punishment on mankind for his sins of homosexuality, permissiveness, transexuals, and gay marriage. Aliens, aliens were the only ones with the technology to remove every living thing except man from this planet, and they were probably coming back for us! Every off the wall commentator regurgitating every idiotic conspiracy theory, or just making shit up so they could feel relevant, found a spot to spew. It was mankind eating itself from the tail to the empty head.

Anna Marie, Earl, and Brian meticulously chronicled each and every moronic conjecture. They laughed at some, like the one about aliens, but were horrified by others. There were those who were completely convinced that somehow either the Russians, the Chinese, or the deep state had found a way to filch every animal, insect, and fish on the planet for their own use. They would starve out the rest of the world for domination overall. The hue and cry went out to go to war with any nation that might have the capability to steal and hide every single living creature on the planet, just to get their pets back. It was insane, and yet, par for the human course. The three kept hope alive that human would not kill human over what was impossible. No nation had the wherewithal to do what had been done

For weeks theories came and went, people were howling for their governments to intervene. Do something! Humanity appeared haunted, terrified of their own shadows; they were alone with each other for the first time since they evolved out of the primordial mud. Realization of the need for a healthy nature was beginning to dawn on a growing number. They needed animals, therapy animals, sounds, touch, knowing they were not alone. Plants began to die for lack of nutrients provided by animals dying and excreting, people began to go hungry from the lack of farm animals, fish, fowl. Something must be done! If governments thought they had seen demonstrations before Earth Day they soon realized that had only been the tip of the rage!

It was on the third day the opinion piece appeared, first in one small town newspaper before being picked up by larger and larger papers across the land, eventually spreading throughout the kingdom of man. It was a simple plea from an unknown source begging, not demanding, but begging mankind to come together as one to save the Mother, thereby saving the creatures of the Earth, thereby saving themselves. It was a peaceful plea, not threatening war or destruction but instead promising a better, healthier future for all. It was simple, either come together to seriously try to stop the destruction of the Mother and the extinctions of her children or this was their future. The choice was man's no others. And it was simply signed, Ev.

She had shown up at the craftsman home early Wednesday morning. Her train had pulled into Denver three hours late and the rental car office was closed. She'd found a nice lady from the company to 'please come open so she could get her car, it was an emergency and she needed to get to her mother's side'. A lie, but a small one and she would forgive herself. but she wanted to find these people now!

The drive had taken two hours on back roads and forest trails, she was quite certain, before she found the town and then saw the dying smoke from the all-night party and followed it to the house on the outskirts of town. She walked around the back of the home where some activity seemed to be taking place and turned the corner just as a group of people disappeared into thin air with the sound of a momentary hiss and quick pop, like opening a jar of pickles, the scent of dill, and she stood alone in the backyard.

Dizzy, from the train, the car, the stress, the experience of moments ago she sat, pondering the rising sun.

She sat on the dew-covered grass, trying to comprehend what her mind told her was impossible, but what was possible and impossible in this world? It was possible that the world was being devastated by floods, drought, heat, intense storms all brought about by the uncaring hand of man. The fact it seemed very few people in positions of power were willing to do anything to stop that decline seemed impossible, yet here we are. So, what was a few dozen people disappearing into thin air compared to that?

Her head swam, she needed to rest. She hadn't slept well on the train. America's trains were not European trains, running smoothly on well-maintained tracks built for comfort and speed. No, they ran on the same tracks as every freight train loaded down with hundreds of tons of merchandise, coal, and oil that pounded those tracks into submission. She swore the train tracks in America had as many potholes as the roads.

She was alone, there was no life coming from inside any of the three houses standing guard over the empty field, those she had come to talk to either weren't around or maybe evaporated into the next realm. She giggled to herself as there was no one else to hear. She was hungry, thirsty, and tired, and wondered if the back door might be open and if there was food or a bed available. Isn't this how Goldilocks got into trouble?

The kitchen was well-stocked so she sat at the table made herself a vegetarian sandwich and poured a glass of water from the faucet. Hunger sated, she decided to check out the home. From what she had gleaned of the family that owned the place they were do gooders who celebrated bears and wildlife, gave to those in need and helped any who came asking. Well, she was in need of a nap and she'd ask when they showed up. The couch looked comfy enough, she would just lay down and wait there.

The hand shaking her shoulder was insistent and would not be denied. She opened her eyes to find a youngish looking woman with arm outstretched to reach her but standing far enough back in case the prone form was dangerous, she could jump back out of the way. Though Freyja was quite certain if the woman did jump back, she would knock down the young man hiding behind her. It was a comical scene.

"Excuse me!" the woman whispered relentlessly as she continued to shake Freyja's shoulder. "Excuse me! Excuse me!" though she could obviously see that Freyja's eyes were open and she was awake.

"What is it?" Yeah, she was a little grumpy but she'd just laid her head on the pillow and this woman was a bit much to wake up to.

"What are you doing in this house?"

"I'm sorry. I came in to rest, it's hot outside...is this your house?" she asked politely as she sat up.

"No."

"Then I have nothing to say to you," Freyja laid back down, turned over and closed her eyes once again. Grumpy needed sleep.

"Well," she heard the other woman huff.

"She seems pretty tired, maybe we should just let her sleep a little and come back later," reasoned the young man.

"Evan left us in charge and I don't think he wanted us to open a homeless shelter in his absence," the woman's mood was growing ever more pissy by the second at being ignored. "She will wake up and talk to us or I'll drag her out on the street where she obviously belongs!" the woman's voice was becoming more shrill and harder to ignore.

Freyja rolled back over realizing sleep was at a premium and she didn't have the payment, she would have to deal with this shrew. "You are friends with the people who live here?"

"Well, I can't say friends, exactly, but we have been left in charge while they are off on very important business!" Anna Marie was not going to give a millimeter to this squatter.

Freyja took a deep, calming breath, she would get nowhere by antagonizing this slightly power hungry, leftist queen of the three-acre prairie. She had dealt with power since coming to the fore in her hometown of Trondheim in central Norway. She had fought school masters, town mayors, and Prime Ministers who all thought they could control a thirteen-year-old girl on a mission. This woman would have no better luck with the eighteen-year-old woman she had become! She stood, if she was to meet this threat head on, it would be standing not laying down.

She stopped, her words settling back down her throat where they had been born. There was something in the air, a scent she had never known before, a tang on the nostril that tasted sweet on the tongue. As she attempted to identify the oddity of it, she noticed the silence. Not that 'they were out of the town in the country' silence but the absence of any natural sounds. No insects, croak of frog, bird chatter, silence as she had never experienced in her life. Not even when she had crossed the Atlantic by sailboat. The earth is full of life, there is always sound, but here it was absent.

"What has happened?" came the replacement verbiage.

"Whatever do you mean," Anna Marie might be many things and do them well, acting was not one of those.

"What has been done?" Freyja rephrased the obvious, first looking at the woman and then concentrating on the young man who looked guilty and terrified she would focus on him.

Brian might do many things well but lying did not come natural, and he hated trying, so he didn't. "They're gone." He hoped that would satisfy.

Hope is a funny thing, it rarely materializes when needed, "Who's gone?" She pressed.

"Brian..." Anna Marie warned.

But Brian knew Anna Marie, she no longer frightened him. This new girl terrified, though he didn't know why. "All of them," he tried, her glare wasn't buying, "all the animals, birds, fish, everything." The words spilled from his lips like suicidal cliff divers.

"How is this possible?" The sound of awe and wonder filled each whispered word, "and why?" She completed the query.

"They felt it was the only way," said Anna Marie as she glared at Brian promising retribution in the very near future.

Freyja made to sit back on the couch before Brian's furtive glance begged her not to, "Maybe we should retire to the rear of the home."

For the first time Anna Marie and Brian noticed she had a slight accent, as if she had spent a lifetime in effort attempting to rid herself of the fullness of her dialect.

As the three of them walked out back Brian wondered where Earl had got to. The three of them had been charged with monitoring news, opinion, threats, and fear around the world. He should be here to make certain no one spilled the wrong can of beans. He had known Anna Marie for almost two years now and knew when she had her dander up, her tongue was her worst enemy.

"Please to begin at whatever the beginning of pertinence might be," fumbled Freyja as she sat back on one of the many lounge chairs by the dormant firepit.

"Well, I don't know how much we should tell you. We have no idea who you might be or why you're here," snipped Anna Marie.

"I was told that a small group was attempting to find ways to try and stop the world from destroying itself. After much research and begging for any possible help, all roads led here. So, I came and all I find is you both. Do you know more than I or were you just here to help yourselves to an empty house?" a tight smile and nod told the two studying her they would not get much more until they shared some tidbits.

Time is a funny thing, for some it races so fast one can hardly recall all events, for others, in the exact same moment time slows so they can concentrate on every detail. Anna Marie's head swam in the immediacy while Freyja counted her eyelashes. Finally, Anna Marie could not contain her frustration and the implied disrespect another second. She would prove to this child she knew so much more than this child could conceive. Let's see who belonged here and who was the trespasser!

"We were brought here by one of the key members of this group who was impressed by work we were involved in, trying to save a rare tree from extinction," Her grin self-righteous and arrogant, "They brought us here to aid them in attempting to force mankind to cease filling the air with toxins, CO2, methane, and dumping refuse into the oceans, and burning and destroying rainforest, polluting, over grazing, overfishing, destroying the planet!" she ran out of natural gas.

"And you both are experts in this scientific discipline?" Queried the girl.

"We both know something about environmental concerns. I wouldn't say we're experts but I am an environmental scientist, we have been working with these people for some time now," harrumphed a very ruffled environmental warrior.

"Is good," muttered Freyja, "So, who are these others and where are they now?" Her tone curious, not condescending, more respectful.

"They are off working on their own end of saving the world," replied Anna Marie, though the words far less smug than when she formed them.

"So, you don't know?"

That was it, the truth will out. "They are on the other side of the veil with all the living creatures of this planet and the Mother," rattled off Anna Marie with reckless abandoned.

"The veil?"

Brian was about to try to explain when Earl showed up with the sheriff, apparently back from whatever errand had called him away.

"What's happening here?" Asked Sheriff John. "Who's the kid?" She didn't give off the impression of a bad kid but you never knew. Maybe she was skulking around the houses thinking them empty and hoping to find some easy cash, you just never knew who was up to no good.

"She said her name is Freyja from some weird town in Norway," Scoffed the wizened twenty something, "heard we were trying to save the world, so she just showed up," she barked a mocking laugh.

"Is that true?" John was gentle 'til someone pushed.

"Basically." Was all Freyja would give. "I have a foundation that is attempting the same goal."

"Wait a minute. Wait just a minute," Earl got between everybody to calm the situation, "I know who you are. Yeah, you been stirring up good trouble for years trying to get the adults of the world to stop shortchanging the future of your generation and the ones to follow." He beamed, this girl was kind of a celebrity and a genuine conservation warrior and just as quickly his expression changed. He looked abashed, shamed. "I apologize for not believing you. Dumb, but I thought you were just grandstanding, doing what you did for the fame, I'm so sorry." He fell to his knees begging forgiveness. "You would think with everything I've seen in life, war, poverty, how folks treat each other and how I treated myself, I would believe anything. But I just couldn't believe man was strong enough to destroy something so beautiful, so vast, so immense as a whole damn planet. I was wrong, so wrong." He turned to face John, "Sheriff I ain't gonna be wrong again, this girl, pardon me, this woman deserves to know what we are up to here. She could be a great ally. Hell, she might just tip the scales."

Sheriff John rubbed his chin in thought. He'd only known Earl for a few weeks but he seemed a pretty straight forward kind of guy. Not one who flew off the handle for a pretty face.

"OK, this is going to be impossible to believe, maybe you ought to sit down and we'll talk. I don't suppose you drink, do you?"

"Alcohol? Nei!" to which she made a face to halt any further inquiry on the subject.

"I guess I didn't think you would. Ah, well. Look I don't know your thoughts on myths, spirits, fables, folklore and all that kind of stuff and I haven't got a lot of time to explain all of what is going on." He began before she interrupted him.

"Sheriff, I am from Norway. Our myths and fables go back thousands of years, we are born and bred into the belief. It is in our DNA," she smiled and nodded for him to continue.

"See, the folks what live here aren't really your ordinary kind of folks. None of them..." he spent the next hour giving the history of Evan and his 'Family', who they were, what they do. Freyja sat quietly taking it all in. She never appeared shocked, incredulous, or gobsmacked. She listened politely, not interrupting. When he finished all sat watching her, wondering what her reaction to all of this might be.

After a dozen breaths and a head shake as if to pull herself out of this dream she said to him, "Had I not witnessed what I did as I rounded the corner of this house several hours ago, I would think you all quite insane," they all made to talk at once, she shushed them with a glare, "You are right, this is very hard to accept as reality. I will need to think on this for a moment or two."

Earl stepped closer to her and in a hushed, gentle tone, "While you consider the reality, listen to what surrounds you. Believe your senses, if not your logic."

She did. She listened again to the absence of sound. The silence frightened her. She didn't want to believe what they were trying to tell her but truth was truth. If you stopped believing what was right in front of you, then what was the difference between her and those she had been trying to convince of what was right in front of their noses for these past half dozen years. In for a krona...

"What do you need from me? And how will we know how they are making out with their plan," she grinned a mischievous, wicked little grin.

"We are watching the international and national news, checking online for chat groups, seeing if people are taking to the streets. Which they are by the millions. Try to focus on any politicians who might be willing to listen. And most importantly, are everyday citizens being swayed, and what legislation are they demanding, if any, be instituted." Brian swooshed his arm in the direction of the house to their left where all the tech they had been following camped out inviting her to come see for herself.

Inside the house several TV's silently showed politicians screaming, people protesting, children and parents beside themselves wondering where their beloved pets were and talking heads protecting their turf. People demanding that their leaders take the opinion piece into consideration and right-wingers saying they would never give in to a hostage situation. They needed to find this Ev, hunt him down and bring him to justice. They would never accept the demands for renewable, clean technology just to get back a bunch of dirty animals. And so, it went, as it has forever. And continued day after day as they settled in to watch and record.

They were all despondent with the reaction though Freyja told them to take heart in the number of people taking to the streets each day, writing to the papers, leaders, anyone who might listen.

What was the worst that could happen, this Ev group might be wrong and they'd all have to live in clean air and water, and the other life on earth would thrive? Children would grow up respecting the environment and the place they lived? That societies would stop bulldozing natural habitat destroying possible cures for the future just to create unneeded farmland. Would it be so awful if people's health would noticeably improve, asthma patients, heart health, cases of lung cancer dropped precipitously. Someone finally posited, would that be such a horrible thing?

And the right wing answered, "We will not be intimidated! We will not be railroaded! If they don't like the way we live, if they don't want to be good Americans, let them leave! The Globalists will never take over our country, don't like it? Stay in your own country!" Completely ignoring the fact that these events were taking place in every single country around the planet.

The native intelligentsia screamed. "Our children, Our future!"

Anna Marie wanted to throw up, Brian wanted to throw a brick through the screen. The Sheriff shook his head and Earl wanted to cry. Freyja shook her head expecting nothing less.

"How long until these Native Spirits return," asked Freyja with intensity deep in thought.

"We don't know, time is different over there. Why?" Asked Sheriff John.

If You Only Believe

"I need a computer and what's the password here so my cell can get online!" Had Freyja asked for those same things just a mere few months ago the residents of this home and the ones on each side would have stared at her. But change had come to the spirit realm! They were now three days into the absence.

Alex had explained to her grandfather if they wished to keep abreast of all the happenings in the world, they would need computers and access. Suzette nodded knowingly as she had been pushing Bear to enter into the twenty-first century since their last melee. Still Bear had balked. Alex decided if he was going to fight progress, she would do it behind his back. He never knew that this stuff had been brought in.

" I have to contact my group in Trondheim to help organize even more than has been done," she nodded to herself as she counted off on each finger the names of those most important to tie into this insane plan. "And I have an idea about the rest, though I would love to talk to this 'Bear' before we completely implement." She shook herself out of wherever her thoughts had taken her, "but first..." She sat down at the keyboard and began to furiously start pounding out emails.

All had settled in contentedly on the other side of the veil. Food would be no problem for most, as there was an abundance of vegetation here. It would sustain though not nourish but they didn't have to be here forever. There had been no drought on the spirit side so grass grew tall and green across the grand prairie for those who graze, and there were many. Buffalo, elk, deer, horses, cows, yaks, camels. Others could feast on berries and grubs, dig in the ground for root vegetables. And, some could hunt, though it had been decided they could only hunt if, and when, needed. This was a land of peace and tranquility; they wanted nothing to offset the balance. It was good. As long as all remembered they could only shelter here for a limited time. The grass might be greener but it did not contain near the nutritional content their children required for extended life.

Bear scratched at the back of his neck. Something wasn't right, he had missed an important step, though for the life of him he couldn't put his finger on what it was. Maybe it was the Frank thing, he didn't like occurrences which couldn't be explained. The scent of one or more of the People was on the man, but whoever had interfered with Coyote's attachment had disguised their scent so as not to be identified. That meant that whoever it was, was still out here ready to cause mayhem. And he remembered what that had almost done last time. Loose ends made him crazy.

And there was something or someone back at the house, he could feel it. Someone he didn't know and, therefore, didn't know how they fit in. His hope was that Sheriff John, Earl and the two hippie kids could handle whatever was happening. And he grinned and smacked hisself upside the head, Sheriff John could handle damn near anything thrown his way. And that Earl fella seemed capable enough, strong like all farmers, it was a natural strength from work. Farming was hard work, it could beat you down in a hurry if you weren't tough enough. People thought you just went out planted seeds, waited awhile and then picked what grew and made lots of money. Evan laughed to hisself, yeah, right, he had known more than his share of farmers, he knew. And there was just something about this guy, he was part what he claimed but part not, even if he himself didn't realize.

Getting back to the situation at hand, where possible, species that wouldn't cause concern among others could occupy the same pastureland. Where not, they would give space and hold each responsible for the behavior of their people. This would only last a few days over here, though in human time it might be a few weeks

"What's the matter," She knew him better than anyone here. Marriage gave you access to the inner workings of each other's moods and thoughts. She could read him like Cliff's notes.

"Can't fool you, can I?" He chuckled, "There is an itch in the back of my head and between my shoulders that is making me crazy. I've missed something. I don't know what but I feel I haven't thought some important point through completely. Maybe the opinion piece is turning people against us. You know, humans can be peevish when told what to do. They like to think whatever solution presented was all their idea, no matter what the problem, they like to think they are so smart they solved it theyselves. I don't know what it is, I just know I don't like the feeling!"

She rubbed his back hoping to help alleviate the 'itch', though she knew she could never dig down that far. He was a good man, and a better Bear, thorough, if he missed something sooner or later it would come to him. She just hoped it wasn't too late.

"Want I should go back and check on things? Nobody'd be looking for me." She suggested.

"I don't know, if something happened to you, I could never forgive myself. You're still kind of new to this whole immortal thing, it can be quite painful, and knowing it can last forever just adds to the discomfort. Shit," he stared off into the distance as if he could see what was happening on the other side. "you and Alex stay here with our people," he began and shooshed her when she tried to interrupt, "Look, you and I are connected by love, by life, by time, if anything gets sparked over here just think of me, nothing else, just me and I'll know and come right back. But I gotta find out what's happening over there."

Rebecca would've loved to have argued and pointed out why she should go but he was right, he had to see for himself. She kissed him tender on the cheek, his muzzle tickling her own. "Don't forget you promised me a vacation around the Mother, I'm holding you to that." She squeezed his paws and he hugged her.

"I won't be long." A slight hiss and a soft 'pop' told her he was back at their house. She prayed to the Great Spirit that Bear was right and he would feel her thoughts if she needed him.

Evan 'popped' out behind the tall pine on the far end of his property. He didn't want to arrive in the middle of something. Plus, the walk in would allow him to scout any possible problems and to see how the lay of the land was.

Quiet, it was quiet as dawn, the sun peeked over the eastern horizon coloring the sky with hues of red, purple, yellow and streaks of white. That was good, maybe all were still asleep.

As he reached the firepit a loud crash startled him out of his reverie and he bolted towards the sound. Another crash, dishes he thought, and if they were her good dishes someone was going to pay an awful price. He charged through the backdoor almost ripping it off its hinges with a screech and a loud bang, bears not being known known for the silent approach, ready for anything! He thought.

He was greeted by the scene of Big Frank huddled between the hall desk and the part of the wall forming the corner of the doorway Bear now occupied. Across the living room was a petite woman being restrained by Earl, Sheriff John, and Anna Marie. The fact it took all three of them to hold her back intrigued Evan. Where was...Brian hid over in the corner away from the action. His wide grin showed the falsity of his fear.

"What in the hell is going on here?" He did everything he could to appear seriously pissed.

"Well, see, this guy," and Earl let go of the girl to speak, a mistake as she almost broke free from the other two and Earl jumped back into the scrum. Once again under semi-control, Earl turned his attention back to Evan, "This guy came in the house like he owned it, which we knew he didn't, scared the shit out of Freyja," he nodded towards the unknown entity, "And she didn't react well."

"Frank get up, Brian help clean up, and these had better not be something my wife treasures," he pointed at the broken porcelain scattered on the floor, "or there won't be a hole deep enough for any of you to hide in!" His gaze took in all, which he considered guilty until proven otherwise.

"You, young lady, quit trying to bust up my house and settle down!" Bear in control. "Now, tell me who you are. What you are doing busting up my home and why I shouldn't toss you out of here."

Freyja looked as if she was going to say or do something which she would have regretted. Another deep breath in a long series of deep breaths, she closed her eyes and willed herself towards calm. She managed through great restraint to settle herself down, as it would appear the lord of the manor had returned.

"My name is Freyja Pederson, I have come here to see if there is anything I can do to aid in whatever course of action you are taking here," she huffed. "As the three of us were discussing what might be done this 'animal' came barging in and grabbed me!"

"Now wait a minute," Frank tried to slide into the conversation, "I came in and you screamed at me, I tried to calm you down and you screamed some more and started throwing shit at me."

Evan looked to Earl for confirmation or dispute. Earl shrugged and gave a little tilt of his head as if wanting to stay out of this. When he came to the realization that would not be possible, he spoke, "Kind of six of one situation. He came in and startled everyone, we didn't know anyone else was around here, see, guess he was next door or something" he stuttered a bit trying to find equilibrium. Earl wanted to placate everyone but knew the impossibility of that mission, so went back to truth. "Freyja here screamed bloody hell, I'm guessing startling this fella, he tried to calm her down, went to reassure, I believe, touched her to calm her, she took umbrage and began firing whatever she could find at him. I believe it is called a misunderstanding. Bad intel." There was something in the way he said it that told of a greater story than this simple misunderstanding, but Bear thought it would wait until they had time alone.

"Alright, Frank don't touch the girl! Go have a drink outside and we'll talk later. Freyja?" he asked to make certain of her name, she nodded, still fuming, "don't break up my house, my wife has put a lot of love into this place and she would like to keep it intact." He shook the anger and violence out of hisself. "Now, why would you think you could help us do something you know nothing about?"

"All the animals of the world have mysteriously disappeared, someone named Ev wrote an op/ed piece that appeared in every newspaper in the world. I poked around and found out about your granddaughter and her work for conservation. I looked into WWF, The Nature Conservancy, Wildlife Conservation Fund, Sierra Club, every single advocacy group I could find, she has no affiliation with any. She is a lone wolf trying to help others, and her grandfather's name is Evan. You, I am guessing," she glared the accusation, he shrugged it might be true. "So, I come and find crazy occurrences, crazier people and crazy stories. Maybe I come for nothing, but I don't think so." She dared him to contradict her synopsis.

"What do you think is happening here?"

"I am not certain but, though what your sheriff and this other man tell me, it goes against anything I might believe about reality,

Somehow you and the disappearance of all the fauna of the world are connected." Again, she dared him with her look to deny. "I do know that as I arrived several days ago and came walking around the corner of the house, I saw a group of people disappear into thin air. There was a slight hiss and soft popping sound, like someone opening a pickle jar. They were there and then they weren't. And the next thing I know is these folks begin to tell me a wild story before this giant comes in and all hel-lation breaks loose, I believe is the expression."

Evan leaned against the doorframe considering. "Let's go out back and we'll talk." Well, he wasn't denying anything, she thought.

Evan, Freyja, Earl, Anna Marie, Brian, and Sheriff John, sat around the big picnic table, before Frank joined them, though at the other end of the table from Freyja, "Tell me what they told you, let's start there." John made as if to say something glancing over at Big Frank, and Evan silenced him with a quick glare. "I want to know what she knows; what she thinks she knows and what she believes. Bout time this fella found out as well, maybe it'll settle him."

Freyja spent the next half hour presenting a brief synopsis of what she had been told, her people's belief in such tales, what she be-lieved and what she wanted to believe. She was doing her best to sus-pend her disbelief but was struggling with what was before her eyes and what she knew, or thought she knew, to be impossible.

"What do you think of what you have been told?" he asked needing honesty.

"I think it is a bunch of fables, tales, lies and wishes, but mostly wishes. Mine as well," she sheepishly admitted. "I want it to be true be-cause it is so impossible, and I believe impossible is what we need if we are to have any chance of succeeding in convincing those in charge to do something."

"What if I could show you the truth of what you've been told. Do you think you could accept that truth and would you have the capa-bility to never tell another soul?" He gazed deep into her eyes until he could see her thoughts, her truth, her soul.

"Yes. Especially if it will help save the future, besides who would believe me if I told them your truth," she smiled at the reaction she would surely receive if she tried to tell anyone what she had been told. And then started almost coming out of her own skin at the appearance of the giant bear seated next to her. Frank passed out at the abrupt change in scenery.

They left Frank where he lay on the grass, it was warm out and he appeared comfortable. And, really, Evan wanted to see exactly what this young woman brought to the table. If she had any influence, either politically or just friends in high places, well, they could use all the assistance anyone offered.

He was slightly taken aback when she told him about the amount of vitriol his simple plea had unleashed. It certainly had not been his intent. He thought he had worded it so no one could possibly take offense, not feel threatened, or feel as though they had been given an ultimatum. He had tried to gently push on the leaders throughout the world without pissing anybody off more than they had. He, apparently, had failed.

"You say you have some influence over people, what people?" he put the question to her bluntly as he didn't have time for dancing. He slipped smoothly back into Evan.

"The young of the world listen to me, I suppose, and because of that they can apply pressure to those with more power. If you get enough of anybody together, they have influence, if you get enough young people together, they have energy, purity of heart, and don't mind stepping on toes. They like putting pressure on those in power, it makes them feel as though they truly are part of the system. And they can pressure their elders to join them, we have guilt on our side as well." She shrugged, not wishing to overstate her own sway.

"Can you get us in to speak to any who hold power?" Here was the hope.

"I might be able to, but let me ask you this," she was deep in consideration of an idea that popped into her head after seeing this man become bear and then man again. "Are you the only one of your kind that can do what you've just done?" she waggled her hand to indicate the transformations that had taken place.

"No, every one of us can jump between our true form and that of human, why?" He had no idea where this line of questioning was going but he would ride along for a few to see. Curiosity was a congenial companion.

"It's just a thought, but if we can find who has a proclivity and love of certain animals, maybe you could slip a cat or dog, or squirrel, frog, or horse, or whatever into their office to speak to each leader. From what these two," she pointed at Anna Marie and Brian, "have shown me thus far and what I have witnessed on my own, the people of the world are extremely upset by the disappearance of animals, and I mean, most all the people. They rely on the presence of animals for beauty and comfort. People train dogs and such to be therapy animals but, really, all animals are therapy animals. They calm people, reassure humanity that all is well with the world.

"No animals, reptiles, fish, whales or turtles, and people begin to feel lonely, nervous. There are supposed to be animals throughout all creation, now human beings are the only mammals and they are going to lose it soon. The world is too quiet, mankind can hear their own thoughts, there are no doggies and kitties to distract from the horrors we create. I fear the worst, but if certain creatures, one for each leader, showed up and could speak to that leader, convince him or her that this doesn't have to be, maybe, just maybe they might listen. It could even be presented, and I don't know if this is possible, as a dream." She smiled as the ideas kept coming at her. "We are stepping on virgin territory here, I don't know what can or cannot be done, but I believe we should be willing to try anything and everything!"

Evan was impressed with the agility of her mind. This young woman was dancing as fast as she could and her thoughts were flying at her like doves of peace. He would have to consider what she proposed. It would be difficult, and timing would be essential, nighttime did not come at the same time for all, but maybe they didn't have to come at night, maybe it might be possible. Night Stallions had occupied the dreams of human for centuries, he even had some experience running through sleeping minds, probably all the creatures did. And furry little animals as well as the great had appeared in man's stories since the dawn of time. Yes, it just might work. It was time for a meet.

Once again, all the spirit creatures of the Mother joined together in assembly to confer. Evan's backyard and conjoining acreage was crowded with those who roamed the spirit realm. After the sharing of pipe and bottle they settled and Evan explained what Freyja had proffered and then asked if anyone thought it possible.

General murmurings and a few heated discussions proved they were taking the concept seriously, or at least some of them were, but would it come to anything?

"So, you're proposing we enter the dreams of the leaders of mankind and speak to them through those dreams to convince them of the error of their ways?" Fox almost laughed at the ludicrous nature of the idea. It was too simple and most of these leaders couldn't care less about their dreams or what they were supposed to learn from them. To think a talking fox could have any impact on the head of Russia or the United States, China or Brazil was so dumb he did laugh.

But he was one of only a few who thought the idea ludicrous, the rest seemed to be considering it seriously. He stopped laughing. Looking over to where Skunk sat off by himself. He noticed Skunk was not laughing either, rather appearing peeved that everyone continued listening to Bear as a leader.

"How many of you have run the dream road?" Almost every hand went up. All spirit animals enjoyed playing in human dreams. It was easy to slip in, play, influence human minds, teach a lesson or two, plant a seed, and then split. It helped the People understand a little more about the minds and inner workings of people. Which could be educational but also quite terrifying.

"Understand, we will have to all bring the exact same message to every single leader. It has to be succinct, believable. They had to understand the fate of the world, not just a dream but the actual state and future of the world is in their hands. They won't believe the dream at first, so what they would be told has to carry the weight of truth, they have to understand, to the core of their souls, this is valid and they are responsible, no one else."

As soon as the words left his mouth Evan realized how ludicrous, how wrong the idea was. Attempting to force an opinion on someone through fear and intimidation, especially to an unsuspecting mind was not the way of the Mother. It was not the way of the People. No, this would not be their way, there had to be truth spoken to power face to face.

Yes, they would travel the dream roads from time to time but that was because subconsciously they had been invited in. It was the way dreams worked. Humans had a particular problem or fear on their mind usually involving a loved one, job, future, or an upcoming event and they would wish for help or understanding. Many times, they would wish to be castigated for some indiscretion, to be absolved of guilt by torment or pain and suffering. So, they would invite one of the people to come and psychologically exculpate their supposed sin. Night stallions would ride through their subconscious relieving them of a good night's rest and their exhaustion would prove their worthiness. Strange but humans had strange beliefs and poor self-images.

He wanted no part in reinforcing the concept. There had to be a better way to sway the opinion of hundreds of human lords, masters, and rulers to do the right thing by their people and their home. And he was running out of time, they could only keep their children on the other side of the veil for so long before the entire thing would begin to break down. And the Great Spirit only knew what would happen then.

"Fox is right," he bowed his respect and apology to his brother, "I'm sorry, I was grabbing straws in the wind. I am open to listening to any other opinion or suggestion you might have."

Fox stood silent, confused. Was Bear mocking him? Did he suspect it had been he and Skunk all along causing the troubles? He studied Bear and those around him. No, Bear's words appeared to be sincere, he was asking him, Fox, for his ideas! But he had none. Here he was, supposedly one of the craftiest of the People. The one who always found a way to survive and he was as blank as the rest.

"Maybe you could go speak for all of us at their big meet house in the great eastern city," he knew he was digging in a mountain of hay for one little pin but he had to save face.

"You mean have Mr. Beach speak to the United Nations?" Freyja brightened for brief moment then the light went out. "I'm sorry, but I have tried that. They listened politely, then patted me on my head like a parent to a nice child and sent me on my way. Having an old man," she shrugged her concession, he shrugged his truth, "say the same words and make the same demands would be met with the same indifference."

Fox sat back on his heels in defeat.

"Wait a minute," Alex warmed to the idea, "what if all of us showed up to back Grandfather up?"

The others began to murmur questions, to form protestations of the irrationality of the concept. And even if it did how were they to explain their existence to a group of humans who would never accept the reality of that. It would be broadcast all over the world. They were creatures of spirit, not physicality, humans would be driven insane. But maybe a germ of an idea...

"Not if we bar the doors, and short circuit the media." She grinned. "Are we not creatures of energy, of light? Do we not possess some small amount of power which would be magnified by the presence of us all?" She could see others beginning to warm to the idea.

"Yes," Fox was almost jumping with anticipation of the idea and completing the thought, "If Bear could get into the great hall, we all could then join him when the moment was right. Short circuit their television feeds and communications, show ourselves as we truly are, no, wait a minute," he quieted the others as they began to speak over him, "We would appear as human and slowly transform before their eyes. You want shock value? That would be fucking shock value." His evil grin was joyous in celebration.

"I don't know," Bear rubbed his chin and looked to Sheriff John for his thoughts.

"I think it is idiotic and has no chance of doing anything but creating far more problems than we can imagine. There would be screams of coercion, of agreements made under duress, of nations attempting to take over other nations though hypnosis, witchery, and forced Stockholm Syndrome. I love it!" He howled. "It might just be the thing that blows the top off their denial."

"I think it is the birth of a great idea but there has to be a subtle way of bringing the whole thing together that makes it impossible for any leader to deny the truth of the world situation." He sat in deep concentration. There was a plan here if he could just uncover it.

"A way to plant a seed and then fertilize it." Earl had a fingernail in Bear's idea and was trying to pull it along. He seemed to be enthusing without being obvious he was stirring the pot.

"Yes, something out of a Disney movie!" shouted Anna Marie to screams of derision and brays of protest that she was living in a child's fantasy world. She was crushed under the cajoling and shaming.

"No, hang on here," Brian came to her defense, "I think I know what she's getting at. Disney, cartoons, and fantasy, yes," he said as the cacophony began to rise, "Yes, fantasy. Talking animals. Squirrels, otters, deer, moose, elephants, mongoose, chipmunks, it's fucking Jungle Book, only for real!"

Deafening silence stared back at him. "Oh, that's right you've probably never seen Disney movies, but that's what they are all about. Animals, birds, creatures of the sea being anthropomorphized, made human," he said to the blank stares, "people being helped, saved by talking animals." He slumped in his impotence to explain, but he knew in his heart, that was what they needed.

The People began discussing the Nightmare idea once again before Bear shushed all. He was staring at his granddaughter who had this odd, sad, pensive expression. "What is it?"

She took in the massive gathering, "I really like where Brian and Anna Marie, Earl and Fox are headed with this. I know you don't understand but I do, granny you do, don't you?" she locked eyes with her grandmother who nodded slowly, remembering taking Alex to see these movies and the effect they had on them, the other kids and their parents, it was magical.

"Yeah, I do too," Earl looked as if he was about to weep so lost in a particular memory. He wanted them to know, this was the way. "What if you showed up at the residences of these great men and women and spoke to them in your natural forms? Like out of a Disney flick, a talking deer," he touched Doe's shoulder in a tender gesture, she smiled beginning to see where he was headed, "an Orca comes up to some leader on his yacht and speaks to him, tells him of her people's trials and makes contact, then at the prescribed time brings that person to the great meeting hall at the U.N."

Now the People were listening. This made sense, they could tell the leaders whatever needed said, the leaders could tell no one about the meeting with a talking Moose because they would be laughed out of office. Yes, each spirit guide could talk, even if the leader refused to listen, he or she would not be able to deny the truth of their own experience to themselves.

It took the rest of the day and the night with all the animals spirits asking questions about the movies, what they meant to Earl, Anna Marie, Brian, Freyja, even Sheriff John talked about when he took his kids to see these movies of a Saturday afternoon. Alex and Rebecca shared memories, precious, loved memories, of escaping Alex's traumatic childhood. Finally, all agreed, this seemed the best course of action. They congratulated Fox on laying the groundwork, his cleverness. He bathed in the admiration. Skunk skulked away feeling the collapse of her own grand plan.

The Nimbleness of Dance

A cool breeze came out of the north proving winter was not yet ready to give way to spring. The Spirit Animals might not feel it, but the human co-conspirators did. Wrapped in blankets or heavy jackets they sat out back of the craftsman deep in conversation. Each had contributed thought and knowledge to the audacious plan to change the world, but something was being left undone. They couldn't say what, but each could feel it. A nervous twitch in the belly, an anxiety in the back of the head. They'd missed something, something terribly important. But what?

Evan watched from the kitchen window facing the expanse of property leading to the small river out back. He could tell they were concerned, though he couldn't hear what held their attention. Maybe he should, no, he chided hisself, let them work out whatever was chafing. Then, if they needed him, they'd come talk to him. He had to delegate. He was too used to doing everything hisself. He had to realize there were many others just as capable, just as committed as he. He was just so used to being the one in charge, the protector of the People, the one who stood against whatever storm was bearing down on the Mother. Well, now he had Rebecca back, his granddaughter had been transformed or come into her own as an immortal—which had never happened in the history of the Mother, he knew, he'd been there for damn near all of it—and maybe was here to replace him. Could an immortal be replaced just like that? Too many questions, not enough information to find the answers.

Earl was the one who perked up first as the question became the answer. "Shit!" the exclamation, loud, came through the closed window like a breaker coming ashore. The sheer volume caught the others off guard. He slapped his forehead and barked a laugh, almost running outside to where all the humans sat. "You plant the seed, fertilize, weed, water, care, then what?" He looked at the assembled hoping he'd led them to the answer. Nothing.

Sheriff John seemed to come awake from a deep slumber, "Shit, indeed, you reap what you sow!"

Freyja seemed not to understand the quote or what it had to do with what they were missing. "What is the reaping and sowing?"

"From the bible, actually," Earl remembered the quote though not exactly where in the huge book it might be. Bible study was not his forte, farming was, and every farmer lived that quote. "It has to do with getting back what you put out, either as payback or reward. We are putting out a great effort to change the world, what do we get back?"

"The change we seek!" Freyja said simply.

"No, what we get back, if we are lucky, is a lot of promises, a heap of platitudes which they might mean at the moment but politicians are politicians. They'll tell you anything if they think it will satisfy you enough to leave them alone. We have no guarantee they will come through. We need not just to go to them and show them what is happening but also show them we are all serious about a solution. We have to have some skin in the game," John had had plenty of experience when it came to politicians promising and never fulfilling. He was certain this was where Earl was headed.

"Absolutely," Earl grinned and nodded his head, "We have to have our troops in reserve to show them we mean business. We need to mobilize everyone, millions of everyones, set a date to mobilize every person to clean the beaches, fishermen to net as much plastic and garbage from lakes, seas, oceans, stream, and rivers. Clean up the cites, the forests, show these people in charge that it is possible with great will to change the course of a dying planet."

"Then what is their motivation to aid in that change of direction? We are doing it all for them," Freyja wanted more details on this brilliance.

"We target the largest polluters, not the industries themselves, as I don't think we will have the wherewithal but the largest corporations in the worst industries for boycott. I know it seems ridiculous, but what isn't about this whole concept." Earl laughed and slapped his hands together, "You told me you had thousands of young people who follow you," he looked to Freyja for confirmation, "do you think we can get them onboard with the idea of boycotting certain companies?"

Freyja looked thoughtful but still doubtful, "Yes, I can ask, but they are not millions. And we would need the threat of many millions if this is to have a possibility of affecting any corporation that large," she wanted to believe but wasn't buying into this just yet.

"You are forgetting the billions who are missing their pets, their livestock, the song of birds, and the fish for lunch. I believe if we ask, they will respond." Earl's plea was earnest, he was attempting to convince her as well as himself.

She was soon lost in thought, the cool spring air tussling her hair, the sun warming her shoulders

Evan couldn't stand it any longer, he had to know what they were talking about. Rebecca smirked as she held in the laugh attempting to break free as she observed her husband chomping at the bit to get himself involved. He was such a good man/Bear, he couldn't sit on the sidelines while something was taking place. He had to be involved, it was his nature.

"So, what brilliance has hatched in the human sector?" he attempted nonchalance though success would be graded on a severe curve.

"We believe there is a necessity to add more human support to your plan," Sheriff John nodded to include all five humans.

"And how do you propose we gain this support?" Evan grinned to take out any possible insinuation he might be offended they might think his brilliant plan needed more support!

"Well," began Earl, making eye contact with all for his own need of support, "we all agree attempting to nudge the leaders of the world to act for the benefit of all rather than their own interests is a swell idea, but remember you are dealing with politicians. And they can be flexible in their beliefs and promises and have a tendency to care a bit more about their own benefit." Earl shrugged what they all knew.

"So, what are you all scheming to do to avoid their flexibility?" Evan might have been concerned had others brought this possibility to light but he knew these folks, now, and felt confident they had brainstormed good ideas.

"What we are thinking," Freyja looked for permission from the others, nods prompted her to continue, "is to target certain companies, the ones most responsible for dumping their garbage, their shit, into your habitat. The ones that spew toxins into the air, and poison the lakes, rivers, and oceans. We threaten, with the weight of millions on our side, to boycott if they don't clean up their act and put the pressure on da others." The accent she tried so hard to hide would stick its head out from time to time while she spoke.

Evan liked what he heard. Yes, they needed to put pressure not just on politicians but on business, those who would feel the pinch on their dollars. It would move the needle farther, dollars spoke in great volume, with their cash strapped voices also pushing these leaders of the world. A world they controlled through their largess.

Rebecca had remained silent during the discussion. He had forgotten she was there until she spoke. "Let me get this right to make certain I understand the concept, you want to target, say, ten, or fifteen, maybe twenty of the world's worst polluters and boycott their products to put pressure on them so they will put pressure on the leaders of the world?"

"Yes," John said slowly, there was something in the way she asked that he could tell she either did not agree or had another idea. Rebecca remained kind of a blank slate to all of them, remaining in Evan's shadow most of the time. She spoke seldom and usually about the day's activities or the weather, but he always thought there was more to the woman. It was as if she didn't want to push her presence off on others, maybe because she had been dead for so long and now, here she was, immortal as far as anyone could tell, she might have felt a little guilty.

"Why only so few?" She had an idea in mind. If her husband could be outrageous in his thinking she could go along for the ride.

"Well, there are only so many of us and they are so large," Freyja could now feel the same thing John did. She decided to proceed with caution.

"Why not go big? Really big?" The smile that illuminated Rebecca's face could vie with the sun. "How many people, realistically, will be beside themselves because every animal disappears? A million? Two million?"

"Oh, I would guess a hundred times that, easily," chimed in Anna Marie.

"Two hundred million?" gasped Rebecca, though Evan could hear the actor at her peak performance.

"I would think more," Earl said thoughtfully, "Billions possibly. Think of every human who has contact with animals, who, even if they don't own or live with fauna has had some contact with them, watches them on nature shows, zoos, sea world type shows. Yes, I would not think it unreasonable there would be billions." He nodded to the others who shrugged their agreement.

"What if you could convince those billions to go on strike in support of saving the planet? What if you could convince billions of people to stop shopping at major retailers and stores and only shop locally. And even then, only when absolutely necessary? Refuse to drive. Refuse to buy anything wrapped in plastic or Styrofoam. Use only biodegradable products or nothing at all. What if humanity went on strike against burning down their own house? Do you think those in charge might be inclined to listen?"

"So, let me get this straight, you are talking about a worldwide boycott of these companies?" Freyja sat closer to Rebecca wanting to be certain she understood what the woman was proposing.

"No, a strike. Not just boycotting businesses, their products, services, whatever, but refusing to go to work. Unless maybe you work at, say, a small shop, weaver, local. But not multinationals, no oil production, nothing that pollutes or destroys." She counted off on her fingers.

"But how would those people live without work, without pay? They would starve!" Freyja saw the immediate problem and why none would go along with this outrageous plan.

"Not if we take care of them," Rebecca was mentally dancing nimbly, parrying each thrust of doubt.

"How would we do that?" Now Evan was interested.

"Simple, we deliver food and necessities to them."

"To everyone in the world?" Coyote had saddled up to the conversation to make sure the negative side could have its say.

"Ok, here's what we could do, you take your proposal to the United Nations, let them argue it to death, beat it into the ground with negativism and have them vote. We concentrate on the countries who vote death to the Mother, that should narrow it down just a bit." Evan could see the wheels turning, this was what had attracted him to her in the first place, the nimbleness of mind.

"The leaders of those countries will not allow us to bring in food and medical supplies," Freyja seemed to find the one thing that would be the downfall and she felt her hope deflating.

"Really? How do they stop us? With guards and guns? Tanks and planes? How can they stop what they cannot see? Apparently, we can move about the Mother without anyone becoming aware, popping in and out of their reality at will." She could feel the mood shift back towards what she proposed, "We show up in the middle of the night, drop off baskets of needed supplies while the people sleep and disappear. Leave it by their bedsides like fauna fairies. If someone spots us, we are just spirits out of myth taking care of them," she shrugged the simplicity of the concept.

"And how long do you think this will take?" Coyote's withering tone told everyone exactly what he thought of this idea.

"As long as it does," was her simple, honest reply. "How long did it take when the pandemic hit and humans partially closed down their world before the Mother began to heal? How long have you all lived and guided your people? A moment in time compared to the eternity of death. Surely, we can outlast hunger if we bring food. We can outlast loneliness if we show them, they all share the same discomforts. We can outlast the heavy hand of the despot if we bring them hope. How long can evil last once the light of love and truth illuminates the promise of a better tomorrow truly within reach? As far as our own children, we can bounce them back and forth between realms, between empty nutrition and wholesome fodder. We can do whatever is needed to survive, to save the mother, to give a future to the children. That is how long." Rebecca's voice was almost a whisper, a flicker of light in the darkness, carrying far more power than a shout or demand. She waited.

"I think I wish you were my mother, or possibly my grandmother," Freyja wrapped Rebecca in her arms and buried her head in the shoulder of Mama Bear.

In For A Centavo

The incessant tapping on the window annoyed to the point of distraction. There was no way he could get work done at home with this harassment. He had brought work home to his estate to avoid all the distractions of the office, now something or someone was tap, tap, tapping at his window. How they had managed to get on the well-protected grounds was as much distraction as the actual sound. No, it had to be something organic, there was no way a person could've gotten past the guards and the electronic surveillance. He would have to speak to the gardener about whatever limb or branch was ruining his concentration. And he desperately required quiet to concentrate on all that was happening in the world.

Countries were on the verge of war literally all over the globe. It was quickly becoming the worst crisis the planet had ever faced. He and his predecessors had dealt with the usual reasons for mankind to try and destroy himself and his neighbors, drought, famine, religious disputes, territorial quarrels, water rights, or just hate, but this time it was different. The human race had never had to rely only on itself to rein itself back in.

Not now. Not in this day of humans and only humans. People had never realized how therapeutic it was to have animals surrounding them, pets, companions, bird song, the knowledge of fish in the oceans and lakes, cattle, sheep, pigs, and other livestock to feed the hungry. They had all disappeared, gone from the face of the planet. And now, mankind was at each other's throats. The pot was boiling furiously and the whole damn thing was going to explode.

And here he was, the Secretary General of the United Nations desperately trying to find a solution, any solution, that would lower the temperature even one degree. He was frantically searching through files, connections, undercover peacemakers who would put their lives on the line to save humanity, all for naught. There had always been considerations, a line in the sand, mutually assured destruction to halt the madness. And there had been people of peace, reasonable parties willing to compromise and work together to avoid total disaster and destruction. Now, there were no solutions to be found, all had put in their last efforts only to have them spurned, blocked by those who had lost their sense of decency because there wasn't a cat, dog, parakeet, goldfish, llama, or potbellied pig to be found. Without companion animals, humans were truly their own worst enemy.

And now this incessant tapping, this maddening, drip, drip, drip of insane agitation. He wanted to throw a paperweight through the window. Man, without the calming effect of nonhuman companions, was a lost species. He turned to see what could possibly be banging on his window and stopped.

His head swam, he rubbed his eyes with thumb and forefinger to clear his vision, shook his head to put his mind in order. He stared again.

There was a fat chipmunk standing on the sill outside the window intermittently munching on an acorn and using it to tap on the window. Upon seeing it had the Secretary General's attention it seemed to motion with the acorn for him to slide open the window.

What could he do? It was such an outrageous vision, one, because he didn't consider chipmunks to be intelligent enough to communicate with humans, two, the way the creature stood gave off an attitude that demanded obeisance, and three, this was the first animal of any kind he had seen in a month or more. What could he do? He opened the window.

Secretary General Juan Maria Manuel Santiago Olevares stared at the chipmunk. The chipmunk took a nibble of the acorn and stared at Juan Maria giving the man time to readjust to a new reality and allow his brain to kick start his thought process.

Juan Maria tried to wrap his head around the concept of an intelligent chipmunk. And as he gazed deep into the eyes of the little creature hunched down on his windowsill munching an acorn, he realized that was exactly what he had here. The question was why and what was he to do with this singular being.

"I believe the best acorns are the ones allowed to marinate over winter, don't you think?" asked the chipmunk as she attempted to break the tension with small talk.

Juan Maria Manuel Santiago Olevares inched back over to the corner of his large wooden desk and eased himself into a seated position on the corner before he fell over. His eyes remained glued to the small rodent munching nonchalantly on the nut. This vision out of a children's movie who had just spoken to him in perfect English. Juan Maria had been working too hard, too long, and without near enough sleep. Hallucination was part and parcel of exhaustion. He required a stiff drink and sleep.

"Although maybe where you're from not so much," considered the chipmunk, "I must admit I am not completely familiar with the growing seasons throughout the many zones of the Mother. Mayhap yours are just beginning to drop. You are from Brazil, yes?"

This had gone on long enough, thought the Secretary General, someone was fucking with him. Someone had somehow created a robotic chipmunk that appeared real but could talk and they were trying to force him into a nervous breakdown. But he was of much stronger mind than whomever had given him credit for. "Whoever is behind this, it will not work!" He called out into the mostly empty room to whoever might be watching and listening. "I do not know what it is you want from me, but I will not be compelled by distress into making any decisions of anything related to UN business by this trick!" As he spoke, he slowly walked around the room attempting to discover the lens and microphone recording this insanity.

"Excuse me," the chipmunk politely interrupted the performance, "but to whom are you speaking. There would only appear to be the two of us present at the moment." She tossed the rest of the acorn out onto the lawn effortlessly hopping from the sill to the corner of the desk.

Juan Maria fell into the comfortable leather chair laying his arms on the rests before burying his face in his hands. "What do you want of me?" he almost wept.

"Just a few moments of your time, really," the chipmunk shrugged as it examined its claws, "a little conversation and consideration of the future of the Mother."

Juan Maria did not believe he had ever witnessed a chipmunk shrug but in for a centavo in for a real. "Why does my Mother's future concern a small rodent?" And why was conversing with that small rodent becoming more normal to a man of his position.

"Oh, not your mother, though one would wish her good health and many years," smiled the chipmunk, "No, for The Mother. Mother Earth, I believe you would call her. How are humans adjusting to the new reality? Lonely?" Again, she grinned as if tempting the Secretary General to dispute there being a new reality.

"If you had been present for the past few weeks you would know, mankind has not adjusted well at all. As a matter of fact, we seem to be on the verge of a true world war which unless I can find a way to 'pull the plug', as you say in this country, will mean the end of civilization as we know it." The grief that filled his words were enough to break the chipmunk's heart.

"Yes, well, that would be the purpose of my mission. It would appear that mankind is learning a very important lesson, one that we," and here she waved at all his imaginary friends and associates, "would hope he would never forget. You face extinction by your own hand, an extinction you have rained down on many species without a second thought. You have destroyed habitat, fished until the numbers are decimated, hunted until hundreds of species either are, or are close to, being completely annihilated and ruined, never once giving more than a nod of concern. And if you do not change your ways all of the life on our Mother, will die. Including YOU!" He pointed a sharp clawed toe accusingly.

"We," and, again, she spoke not just for herself but for those only she could see, "would like to have a few moments of time with your assembly to address our concerns."

"And who would 'we' be?" When every option has failed and none others present themselves, sometimes insanity and belief is all you have. Juan Maria didn't know why he was falling into belief but he had nothing in either hand to replace it, maybe mass hypnosis and a fictional character would succeed where reality had failed.

"Are you familiar with Boto Cor-de -Rosa, Boitata, Caipora or Curupira?"

"Yes, of course, they are folklore and myths from my country, why?" there was something in the pit of his soul that began to glow with the mention of spirits from his homeland.

"That is who we are. We are the spirit guides, the protectors of the children of Mother Earth." The image of the chipmunk shimmered momentarily, one second a rodent then next a young woman and back to the small rodent again. "Did you know almost every single human culture in this world has some form of myth involving the spirits of animals? Either as protector, provider, or friend? Why do you think that might be? And if you stop for a moment to consider, who has done the most damage to this home of ours throughout history?" The chipmunk stared hard into the Secretary General's eyes, daring once again. "Who hunts only to kill? Not for food, not for clothing, not for the bones to build a home, just to kill?" She pulled another acorn out of some pocket in her fur. "I'm not saying that all humans are bad or we want to dispose of them, just that they could use a little learnin' and understandin' that maybe human cultures don't have to emulate each other in their cruelty.

"This was what we hoped would be exposed by taking a long holiday. You might see that all the other life is disappearing from the Mother. Maybe, just maybe, we can make everyone understand that we all live here together and we will all die together unless someone stops destroying our home." She took a small nibble and sat back on her haunches, "Now, we just want a few moments of time with all the leaders of the world to see if you would like to save yourselves."

"Are you threatening your own war on us?" Juan Maria's radar clicked in. He was not going to bring anyone into the UN who meant violence or trouble.

"No!" Stomped the little foot on the desk, "Why do humans think the only solution to any problem is not understanding, not listening to each other, not working together but war, always war, always death!" The chipmunk took a step back and several deep breaths to calm itself, to regain its equilibrium and lower its voice. "We are going to explain in no uncertain terms what you are doing to all of us, INCLUDING YOURSELVES! We want to give you the chance to reverse the destruction, to save all of us. We believe we can present it in a way all will understand."

"And if some refuse?" He would have his answer before agreeing to anything.

"Then they refuse at their own peril. It is our belief that the great majority will choose life, to them life will return. To those who choose otherwise, then they choose it for themselves and no others." He hopped back to the windowsill before glancing back at the Secretary General. "but I will mention this, I think most humans are getting pissy right now and if you know history you know soon or late, they will turn on those they consider the cause of that consternation."

"I will speak to several others. I will need to present this in a completely different context, but I will convince them. When do you wish to speak?" What was there to lose? His position? That meant nothing when it came to the survival of the world. Let him be a laughingstock, shame means nothing.

"Expect a call from Evan," the chipmunk said enigmatically, she shrugged once again and was gone.

Juan Maria Manuel Santiago Olevares sat back in the fine leather chair and poured himself a tall Cachaca, took a long draught before ringing the bell for his valet

Show Them Hope and They Will Come

Droughts raged across North America, farmland dried out, cracked and blistered. 'Worse than the great depression,' claimed many who had never lived through it. North Africa became dust and death as the Sahara marched south gobbling up every inch of land it could claim. Floods rampaged just south of that inexorable dearth as if washing away whatever life might attempt to stop the onset of desert. Chad, Niger, Mali, and Sudan were dying of thirst in the north while entire cities were being wiped out by water in the south. Siberia's permafrost thawed at an unprecedented rate becoming swampland almost overnight releasing hundreds of billions of metric tons of trapped CO2 into the atmosphere. India, Vietnam, Thailand, southern China were all inundated with constant storms, typhoons and pounding rain and wind, to the point people began to wonder if they would ever see the sun again. Wars began to breakout along borders as countries vied for food, higher ground, or water.

A hurricane formed in the southern Gulf of Mexico, from a low-pressure system of negligible strength that began to gather energy in the super-heated waters as it came north-northeast. Moving in an erratic, wobbly path, it seemed, though intensifying minutely, it would wear itself out before causing extensive damage. That was before it found its path and went from a category one to a category four within hours and slammed into Tampa Bay, the first to do so in decades. It quicky ran across the midsection of Florida—a blessing as it kept the amount of rainfall to less than a foot and a half—before heading eastward into the Atlantic.

It once again tacked on a north-northeast track until a major deviation of the jet stream developed pushing it back to the northwest, directly into the path of massive low coming out of the central Canadian province of Saskatchewan. Whereas they should have collided and either cancelled each other out or possibly bounced off each other, instead they collided and intensified exponentially several hundred miles off the eastern coast of North America, defying the Fujiwhara effect. They continued in a NW direction before smashing into the coast just seven miles south of the Upper Bay and pushing trillions of gallons of water up the Hudson River.

New York City was paralyzed. The northeastern United States was devastated. All businesses were shut down, services ceased, electric power was down from Portland, ME to Washington, D.C and all the way to Chicago. The meeting Secretary General Olevares had worked so hard to bring about would not happen.

He stood in his den/office and watched the torrential rain as the high winds pounded against the triple paned window. He sipped a Cachaca on the rocks. He'd had such hope, such belief this would lead to the world coming together, finally, and attempting to save itself. He knew the futility, he had placed his faith and his career on fantasy and myth, he was a fool. Now this, you'd need a battleship to get through this storm, the amount of water flowing down the streets of NYC had created new rivers, flooding basement apartments, hundreds would drown and thousands displaced. He sighed. He thought of the little chipmunk that had started Juan Maria's feet down this road, the road to his ruin, it would appear. He smiled, it had given him hope, that little hallucination. It'd been worth it. Even as doom closed in around his illustrious career, that hope, that slight possibility, had been worth the gamble.

The knock on the front door startled him. He would have to get it himself as he'd told his valet to remain home with his family in case the storm turned into something worse. Well, something worse this way had come. So, who could be knocking at his door?

He peeked out the small side window and saw the three of them standing on his porch, backs to the door, relaxed, and watching the torrential downpour as if admiring a lovely sunset. They didn't seem to notice the rain and wind, their one capitulation was the small, blue umbrella the young girl held over the older woman and herself. The middle-aged man stood in shirt sleeves and slacks as on a summer's day.

Juan Maria opened the door for them expecting a religious spiel, as only a true believer of some sort could possibly be wandering door-to-door in this driving downpour. He knew he shouldn't, but they looked harmless enough and they were certainly wet enough, maybe he could borrow some karma. Besides, he was bored.

"Can I help you folks?" he asked through his heavy Brazilian accent.

"Secretary Olevares?" asked the man. He was large, thick chested, tall though not overly so, arms like a bear, this fellow could do some damage and he knew who Juan Maria was.

Hmm, he nodded his assent.

"We've come to take you to your meeting at the UN," said the middle-aged woman who held the man's arm, obviously a couple.

Juan Maria looked through the heavy rain but saw no vehicle in the drive. No van, SUV, off-road Humvee, or boat. How in God's name did they think they would transport him? Did they think he would walk through this?

"I'm sorry but the meeting has been cancelled due to the weather," he pointed at the end of the world which they had somehow missed as they made their way here.

"Oh, you won't let a little rain stop us from saving the world, will you?" challenged the pretty twenty something holding the blue umbrella.

"There is no way to get to the United Nations building in this and even if we could, we would be the only ones there," he emphasized pointing at the river running through the streets and lack of a single car, bus, or bicycle on it.

"Oh, we have other means," smiled the large man, "I am Evan, we spoke on the phone a couple weeks back." He held out his hand and Juan Maria took it. His own hand immediately swallowed in the enormity of the hand now grasping it.

He remembered the phone call; the one promised by the chipmunk, it had taken place as planned. It was one of the reasons he forced himself to believe. The man had seemed so reasonable on the phone, not the type to wade through Noah's flood just to say hello. "Nice to make your acquaintance, but as I mentioned there is no way and we would be more comfortable here," he opened the door completely so they could see his well-appointed and comfortable home. "Maybe we could discuss your ideas where it is warm and dry."

"We could never fit all the other representatives in here," announced Evan as he handed Juan Maria his hat and coat, "We'll meet the others in the General Assembly. If you would just hold onto my arm, we'll be there momentarily."

Juan Maria did as asked, not told, but politely asked. He heard the soft hiss and the pop of someone opening a new jar of pickles, the scent of dill filling his nostrils. In the blink of his startled eye, they were standing at the door of the main Assembly room of the United Nations.

The room was filling with representatives from around the world, each accompanied by one or two escorts. Shouts of surprise, shock, anger, displeasure and demands to know who was in charge permeated the hall. Gently each was shown to their rightful seat by their escorts.

"We cannot have a meeting of the general council as we have no interpreters present. No one will know what anyone is saying. This is quite ludicrous," he explained, still attempting reason. Though he did not believe the words as they flew from his lips. He wanted so badly for this man, who sounded so confident, thoughtful, and grounded in reality on the phone, to make this insanity come true. He had believed a hallucination could bring this together, why should he not believe this man, his wife and their, hmm, granddaughter, he supposed, make the rest come true. After all, they were standing in the Assembly Hall, how had that happened?

"Oh, we have ways," Evan spoke seriously though the twinkle in his eyes gave the lie to the seriousness, though not the promise.

Evan and Juan Maria made their way to the front of the hall and the dais that awaited them. As both took their place behind the podium. Murmurs, shouts, arguments, commands, and epithets were rising from the assembled. These fine, honored representatives of the one hundred and ninety-three member states had had their dignity bruised and they were not going to go quietly into listening mode. Evan took the large gavel laying on the podium and banged it hard, once, twice, and on the third, just a tap. It was the tap that focused attention.

"Good evening, honored guests, thank you for coming out in such inclement weather to meet with us." He motioned to those still standing and obviously positioned to stop anyone from leaving.

"What choice did we have?" Shouted a voice from somewhere in the middle of the assembled.

"Honestly?" Evan paused for just a moment, "none." He glared around the room as if he could meet the gazes of each and every one of them. They felt his regard judging each of their souls, "The exact same amount of choice you have given us."

"And who are you?" asked another voice in the crowd.

"Yes, are you terrorists? Are you here to hold us hostage, against the will of the civilized world until someone gives in to your demands?"

"Yes, and what is it that you want? Money, power, to free some murderers or religious cultists?"

"How predictable. With you humans it is always about power, isn't it? Whether financial, religious, political, relationships, it is always about power. Power over each other as countries, as geographic areas, as idealogues, even your spiritual beliefs are about power over each other. Even as lovers, it is seldom shared but a need for power over one and other. How pathetic. You never seem to find it within you to do something honorable or moral, because it might help someone else more than it might help you or hurt them.

"Without the promise of power, you would do nothing. You have no beliefs, no souls, you worship power, you crave it. To have one more dollar, rupee, peso, ruble, pound, dinar, lira, krone whatever you want to call it. You make things up just so you have some form of comparison to show you have more than someone else. Except when it comes to decency.

"You don't have a measurement for that do you? You take, and you take, and you take, never considering the real cost to the world around you. Never taking into consideration how your greed for power affects those without a voice. Well, how are you doing in your world? You have it to yourselves, no more animals, birds, fish in the sea. How are you handling the lonely?

"From what we see you are at each other's throats even more so than usual. Without something to kill for the love of killing you once again turn on each other. If there was a way for us to leave you to your own destruction, believe me, I think we would, but we can't. For you are killing us and the Mother and we will not stand for that." Evan took a deep breath as he felt his temper slipping away from him. He gazed at Her as She stood off to the side, making spiritual contact between them, two people so deeply in love and respect, Her presence comforted him, calmed him, made him feel her love and it filled him. He was here to solve a problem, not create a larger one.

"I apologize," he said to the rising cacophony, "but when survival of one group means nothing to the powerful who control that group's existence, well, I tend to become overly sensitive." He grinned and shook his head. "Maybe it would be best if I explain exactly why we are so concerned about the behavior of those I was condemning."

"We have lived here far longer than your species and have managed to live side by side, surviving by sheer numbers rather than by attempting to horde or go to war because we always believed there was plenty for all. Even when you hunted us, many to extinction, we hoped your lust for blood and glory would be sated and you would leave the rest of us alone. We were stupid and cowardly in that assumption. We are shamed by our actions. We allowed the weakest among our kinds to vanish from the face of the Mother in hopes of saving the rest. It was my fault," his embarrassment radiated like the heat of a desert sun. The humiliation and shame of his poor judgement creeping up from deep within. He'd placated humans rather than fulfill his role as protector of all the people. He was supposed to guide them through the centuries. He wiped a tear of that shame from his cheek and spoke into the now deadly silence. "You see, when you were a very young and nascent species you were closer to us spiritually, physically. You knew our people and you treated them with respect. You only took what you needed, you didn't kill just to kill but for food, shelter, to clothe yourselves. It was the way of the Mother." Emotion, memory filled him.

He gazed out on the quiet, terrified humans seated throughout the hall, though with flight written in large letters on their faces. He realized why, as he observed the hundreds of spirit animals who had reverted to their natural forms. He shook his head as he realized without thinking he had reverted to form and the others had followed suit. Now the assembled human representatives were confused, horrified, shocked, though some sat with huge grins as they were surrounded by the spirits, the spirits their ancestors had worshipped and some still did, the spirits their cultures had been built on. Yes, for centuries they had believed and whispered their prayers to these spirits where only they could hear. Even in the face of the most powerful religious groups, come from foreign faraway lands, come to starve them, beat them, force them into believing in their 'One God'. Still, many had clung to the myths of the past. And now, here they were, real as life. And others, many others sat in awe and joy, they had not seen an animal for months now, they had forgotten, forgotten how much these creatures, great and small, soothed the heart and soul. These were who Bear had to beseech to listen.

"We are here to let you know that we are as real as any of you, any of your beliefs. Your ancestors knew this but you became too civilized, too caught up in the world you wanted to create rather than the one that was already here. A world filled with wonder and a little magic; with an abundance of life most chose to ignore. Or worse yet, to hunt to extinction. We only wish to share the wealth of this garden. Why can't you see that you are destroying the thing you seek?

"You think if you can control the Mother, you can have the ultimate power. Life and Death. Well, you have it, but you are like a child with your deadly possessions; except a child would know when it had harmed another. You don't control, you poison, you shit where you sleep. Yes, you had the power of life and death, why, for once, can't you choose life?"

"So, you would have all of us become vegetarians? And stop technological progress? You would have mankind revert to cavemen?" Came the call from somewhere in the vicinity of the United States representative. Soon followed by laughter and catcalls.

A large bat standing several paces behind snapped her head around to glare at the speaker. Her extremely dark sunglasses showed she was visually impaired, her glare told him she was not blind. Her pointed, short nose wrinkled in concentration as if tasting the air near her for danger or to sense where the sneering jibe had come from.

"No," Evan's voice tired, frustrated. How to explain to beings with the belief they were the epitome of evolution, the top of the food chain that they were no different than those they considered less.

"So, you've only come to preach. To tell us all of our sins and we should repent, yet you have no solutions." The chuckling that had begun with the first outburst intensified. Loud calls for this to cease and demands they be allowed to leave gained in volume.

"What we have come here for is to beg you to consider your course, to see how destructive it is. You ask about technology, why are you so afraid of new technology? Hell, we don't want you to give up your technology but to embrace new, more efficient tech. We don't want you to give up your comforts, your engineering progress, we want you to use them, to create new forms of energy, renewable sources that don't kill. Don't pollute. Don't destroy. Not just us, but yourselves. You are killing the one who gave you life." Evan could feel his blood racing, his vision began to cloud. He knew this feeling, he tried to control it knowing if he did not this would not end well. "Aren't you supposed to be the most reasonable representatives of your species? Come here to find peaceful solutions instead of war? To stop the killing, the senseless deaths brought about by your own hands? Do you really have a death wish?" He wanted to yell, to rail against the utter stupidity, to ask why they couldn't open their hearts, their minds to a better future. He wanted to say, to do so much.

The touch on his arm, the feel of Her presence next to him, Her scent so strong, Her love palpable. She was not here to force him to control but to give him strength to overcome his emotions.

Deep cleansing breaths, eyes closed, concentrating on the mountains and rivers he loved so well. The Mother had sent them to accomplish purpose not create havoc. "All we are asking is for you listen, talk, see there are other ways to accomplish your goals, allow all to live and thereby see that those actions will allow you to survive, to live as well."

"And if we say no?"

"You are free to leave any time you wish. No one here will attempt to stop you. We do not demand anything, we are not in any position to demand, just ask. If you wish to go, then go. All we seek are those who would stand up and say they choose life. They choose the path of clean energy, to stop polluting and dumping your poisons into the life-giving water and land. To cease pumping death into the air. We will speak with those who would choose the future. To the rest, you choose what path you want, but remember there are repercussions, there are always repercussions." He stepped back from the podium. He had not pressured or coerced, he had given them choices and told them there would be price to pay. An almost deafening crack of thunder forced its way through the thick walls punctuating his words.

Silence and tension filled the great hall.

Hiss, pop, dill. Suzette stood before Rebecca, a grand smile splitting her face. She appeared healthier than either Rebecca or Alex could remember her being for a long time. On her right arm was Sheriff John, on her left was Earl. Doe popped in right behind with the two young folks, Anna Marie and Brian, clinging to her like a life raft, terror filled their eyes. All relaxed once they saw where they had been brought and the company they now kept. Oscar took up the rear with an armful of newspapers from around the world.

"Everything alright?" smiled Sheriff John gazing around the hall.

"We thought you might need a few reinforcements," Suzette began.

"Or a few million," laughed Earl. "Don't suppose you might have a TV 'round here, wouldja?"

The uproar throughout the hall began as a murmur once again as the interruption gave them opportunity.

"Who are these people? And how did they get inside this hall like that?" demanded the Russian though his tone also held a certain awe. "Why do they need television, what propaganda do you try to shove down our throats now?" He attempted to sound in control but instead came across a shrill and frightened.

Tatanka strolled over and lowered his head indicating the man might want to sit down, and Lawrence used his antlers to show him where. The Russian might think himself a bear but the size and power of the two massive beasts and the gigantic Bear holding court seemed to cow him.

Evan bowed to Juan Maria, "I respectfully ask if there is screen somewhere to examine what my friends wish us to see."

The Secretary General bowed his respect and smiled. He had no idea what going to happen, or really what was happening at this point in time, but he knew in his heart he was about to witness something no one ever in the history of mankind had. Hell, he already had. He had seen myth come to life, story become real, he didn't care where this was going from there. If this was to be the end of his career let it end in a glorious luminescence of magic.

"I believe there is but no one has ever seen the need to inform me how to make it work." He shrugged; his disappointment evident.

"Hang on," grumbled Sheriff John. He walked to the far back doors, the actual entrance to the hall, exiting into the hallway that connected all things UN to this hall. Within ten minutes he returned through the doors with a late middle-aged black man, janitorial uniform crisply ironed and set of keys hooked on his belt, in tow. "These joints are all the same, nobody knows nothing but the folks who do all the grunt work. This is Augie Bevan, head custodian of this section of the United Nations, here for the past thirty-seven years and the man with the knowhow! I found him doing his job because he needs the paycheck, end of the world or not!"

Augie Bevan sheepishly grinned slight embarrassment at the intro but pulled his keys from his belt to cover. "What is it y'all want me to do?" he looked from John to the Secretary General and then gave a start at seeing all the animals crowded into this hall. He wouldn't say it but he thought to himself, they best not expect me to clean up this mess.

"Very simple," said Juan Maria through his thick accent, "We need you to find a way to turn on the large screen behind the podium and find a way to...what?" He turned to those asking.

"We just want to see if we can find CNN or ABC, NBC any of the big news stations." Earl filled in while Suzette nodded. She was still human. It was reassuring to Augie, he could believe she was on the up and up, he knew he could trust the small, extremely pretty, young black girl.

"Well, that's easily accomplished," he smiled his sheepish grin at her, "see, when nobody's here on Sundays, sometimes me and the fellas come down here to watch the game. Ain't nobody else here and we clean up when we done. So, nobody's the wiser. Just give me a minute!" And he strode through the rear door to another almost hidden door leading to the audio/video booth up a narrow ladder.

Behind the dais a panel slid back exposing a huge blank screen. Within moments it came to life with video of thousands, no, tens of thousands of people, no, Evan took a second to readjust his perception, his mind finally accepting what he was witnessing. There were millions of people marching in the streets of what, appeared, every city in the world. Carrying signs, chanting, singing, drumbeats filling the sky, pipes and voices in every language sang the song of humanity, all demanding the same thing of their leaders, for them to face the reality of climate change. They showed no anger, just demanded life. They laughed, hugged, and danced, a celebration of possibility. They believed they could change the course of humanity by will and numbers.

Apparently, from what all the talking heads could determine, the massive, catastrophic storm was the catalyst, people had had enough. It wasn't just that New York, Boston, Philadelphia, and most of the northeast of the United States was being devastated, the people of the world demanded action to alleviate their own disasters in their own countries. Disasters that had had devastating effects for decades. The people had had enough. Children suffering from malnutrition due to drought in north Africa, flashfloods across Europe, the warming of Siberia and release of CO2, intense cyclones throughout Africa and the Pacific, raging fires across Australia, Europe, and America, flooding throughout southern Asia, there was no spot on the globe that had not been touched by ruin close to annihilation. More were building, more would come. And tens of millions would die, they wanted action, and they wanted it now.

And instead of facing this obvious problem straight on, world leaders were concentrating on how to hoard what little resources they had so their neighbors couldn't. These people, these brave marching singing hordes wanted to save their neighbors, not punish them. They would expect the same in return, feed the hungry, save the children, listen to the Mother, enough death of animals, birds, whales and aquatic life, enough death of man.

The cameras followed the destruction and devastation around the world. The floods left people stranded in their homes, on their rooftops, in trees and clinging to boulders or buildings, anywhere they could get the slightest grip. Thousands were going to die, maybe millions, all because of blind greed. Fires raged burning entire towns to cinders and ash, powerful storms came ashore in SE Asia, Russia, Japan, Mexico. It was like the world was dying in a fit of pain and suffering, and there was no one who could help.

It was the first responders, firefighters, police, National guard, EMTs, doctors, nurses, and people who just couldn't stand by and watch, who came to each disaster. They flew, paddled, rode boats, and modified tactical vehicles, fire engines and military Humvees and transports, helicopters, it was as if the entire world had come to the aid of all good people. Hillbillies with four wheelers and four-wheel drive pickups with air scoops that towered over the hoods so engines would not stall in the deep water. Men and women riding on hoods and roofs attempting to pull, lift, rescue every person they could find from perilous perches. Knowing by putting their own lives at risk some these rescuers would not return, yet they came, their calling demanding they try. They would never be enough, but they would save all they could. These were what true humans looked like, what they did for each other, for those who suffered. They lived their beliefs.

"Those are your people, your fellow citizens demanding you, their representatives, do something and do it now. Can you ignore them? Can you continue to kowtow to the special interests who bring this devastation? Can you watch them die just to line your pockets?" Evan could feel his blood racing, his temper coming to the fore. He did nothing to tamp it down. "Will you deny your people?"

"The people are sheep, they need to be led, shown what they want. They have no idea what is best for them," from the accent and attitude Bear could tell it was one of the secretaries from South America, a dictatorship.

"And only you know what is best for them, is that right?" It was Earl who spoke quietly, almost a whisper, a deadly sound, yet everyone in the hall, spirit animal and human, could hear him clear as if he stood next to them. It was then Evan knew and he grinned. "You disgust me, you come here to promote peace you say, to find ways for each to have better lives. Altruistic bullshit. You come here to cover for your hate, your wars. How many of you are at war right now, small, regional, wars, to take what your neighbors have? How many of you are at war with your own people because they want for food, for decent housing, for life, for freedom? All while they die. They waste away in hunger, disease from bad water, malnutrition, rape, and violence by you. You, who supposedly know what is best for them, so you take everything they don't 'need', like dignity." He spit on their nice clean floor before turning to Augie to apologize, who shrugged, smiled, and gave him a thumbs up.

"You do not deserve to represent these people, these brave, wonderous people, who cling to a branch to save a child, who drown saving an elderly neighbor, who run through fire to save a horse or a dog. You have no souls, no empathy, no right to tell anyone what they need or deserve. The bill will come and you will pay.

"You were given a garden, a beautiful, lush garden with everything you could ever want. You could go forth and multiply to your hearts content and never run out of food, water, sustenance for the soul, you would want for nothing. All you had to do was love each other, love each other as if brothers and siters. To hold each other, care for each other, I gave you everything and you have consistently chosen death, horror, power.

Well, what has that power wrought? Nothing, it does not last, it destroys. It kills children, innocents, it destroys habitat that contain wonders for the future. New medicines, new species, species undiscovered, but you would rather burn it.

"You are being given a chance to save yourselves by saving the Mother," and here she appeared, stunning, solid, in all her perfect glory, "To be what you were created to be, not what you have become. Petty, small, insignificant warts on the ass of something marvelous." Evan understood, the Great spirit did no sleep, did not ignore. "I have lived with you for decades, my good friend Bear taught me, if I am to understand humans, I must know them, live as one of them, fight like them, feel what they feel, think as one of them, I have. I have no desire to continue. See what decency can accomplish."

Anna Marie stood straight, Brian by her side, disgust, anger, and condemnation radiating like two furnaces as they took in the assembled.

The hush and wow of those assembled drew all attention to the giant screen. They witnessed the most marvelous thing anyone had ever seen. From nowhere and everywhere the rivers that had been streets began to fill with dolphins, porpoises, manatees. Every kind of amphibian, fish, sea mammal, swimming towards those holding on by sheer will. Evan glanced around the great hall and noticed all of the spirit guides of water species were leaving, Salmon waved her boa at her and disappeared.

He almost cried. He knew in his heart they couldn't just watch this happening. It was one thing to make a point, to disappear to spotlight a horror, it was another to stand by while harm came to others. His People could not. They had gone back across the veil and collected their own to come to the aid of man.

As he stood silent, his gaze taking in all of his People still here, he watched more vanish. Tatanka and Elk nodded once to him and shrugged as they vanished. What could you do, when you were needed you went. They would head where the worst of the fires were and do their best to stomp down fuel and kick up dirt to help control what man could not. Equine was right behind them, he hadn't noticed she was there, but of course she was. The horse clan might fear fire but they feared loss of pride more, they would come, though many would not live through the night. Skunk and Fox shared a look, a Shrug, not daring to look in Bear's direction before, they too. disappeared.

He saw Doe and Suzette hug before going to lend what aid they might where they would most be needed. All were going to lend support. Oscar bowed to Bear and family before disappearing to fight from the sky. Evan was so proud, the little man who had done all in his power to avoid becoming entangled was now neck deep. He was a good owl.

Bear turned to Juan Maria Manuel Santiago Olevares, bowed to him, gave a kind of Bear salute, "I apologize but I must go. I am considered the protector of all the People, I am needed elsewhere. I wish...I wish," but the words would not come. Juan Marie bowed deeply his respect, admiration, and thanks. If only. Evan wrapped Alexandra and Rebecca in his arms, Anna Marie, Brian, and sheriff John grabbing a tight hold, Earl smiled, he would come, but he would come on his own, and they, too, disappeared leaving only the humans, most of whom would deny, argue, or protest this meeting had never happened. There were no such things as Spirit Animals, Guides, they were myths, fables, stories told around fires late at night to frighten naïve, simple, indigenous, uncivilized, and unevolved. Not those with true religion.

As there was no evidence this meeting had ever happened, no video, no audio recording, according to empirical evidence it had never taken place.

And yet, when the digital video of the thousands of rescues was reviewed reality could not be denied.

The strikes began slowly. People refused to go to work, to shop, to leave their homes. The leaders of the dictatorships, authoritarian re-gimes, despots, and poverty kings didn't have near enough military to force the people to do their bidding. Hell, half of the militaries in all those countries went AWOL, the country's leaders watched as their economies tanked and other nations watched as well. They knew these were the nations who had spit on the chance for cooperation, for com-ing together to invest in clean, renewables, to change the course of the mankind. Yes, they paid attention and saw who felt the retribution of the meeting that never took place.

Meetings took place between people, tribes, neighborhoods towns and those of common interests. They told stories of the old times, when man was innocent and believed in the spirits of trees and animals and the Mother, and the glimmer of hope was born. Just a spark, but if you blow gently every spark can become a raging fire.

Big Frank sat on the steps of his trailer, staring at the mountains. His nightmares had ceased, he had no desire to go to those damn mountains as a matter of fact, he thought, it might be time to move somewhere a little more to his liking. Florida, maybe.

Author's Bio

∞

Mr. Zonneville has spent the last forty-five years as a professional comedian, singer, songwriter and has written five books previous, three novels, American Stories, Carey Come To Me Smiling, and Great Things, A Novel, a biography of his father, Z, and a children's book about one of their rescue dogs, Greta. Harper's is in the works. He has performed throughout the United States, Canada, Ireland, and Holland. He loves his two adult daughters, to travel, write, read, and be married to his most beloved.

CPSIA information can be obtained
at www.ICGtesting.com
Printed in the USA
JSHW012322190123
36483JS00002B/2/J